LITTLE FAITH

ALSO BY NICKOLAS BUTLER

The Hearts of Men
Beneath the Bonfire: Stories
Shotgun Lovesongs

LITTLE FAITH

A NOVEL

NICKOLAS BUTLER

An Imprint of HarperCollinsPublishers

LITTLE FAITH. Copyright © 2019 by Nickolas Butler. All rights reserved. Printed in the United States of America. No part of this book may be used or reproduced in any manner whatsoever without written permission except in the case of brief quotations embodied in critical articles and reviews. For information, address HarperCollins Publishers, 195 Broadway, New York, NY 10007.

HarperCollins books may be purchased for educational, business, or sales promotional use. For information, please email the Special Markets Department at SPsales@harpercollins.com.

FIRST EDITION

Designed by Renata De Oliveira

Images on pages iii, 1, 85, 179, 241, and 289 by patpitchaya/shutterstock.

Library of Congress Cataloging-in-Publication Data

Names: Butler, Nickolas, author.
Title: Little faith : a novel / Nickolas Butler.
Description: First edition. | New York, NY : Ecco/HarperCollins Publishers, [2019]
Identifiers: LCCN 2018022059 (print) | LCCN 2018023322 (ebook) | ISBN 9780062469731 (ebook) | ISBN 9780062469717 | ISBN 9780062469724
Subjects: LCSH: Families—Fiction. | Change (Psychology)—Fiction. | Maturation (Psychology)—Fiction. | Wisconsin—Fiction. | Domestic fiction. | Psychological fiction. | BISAC: FICTION / Literary. | FICTION / Coming of Age. | FICTION / Family Life. | LCGFT: Domestic fiction.
Classification: LCC PS3602.U876 (ebook) | LCC PS3602.U876 L58 2019 (print) | DDC 813/.6—dc23
LC record available at https://lccn.loc.gov/2018022059

ISBN 978-0-06-246971-7

19 20 21 22 23 LSC 10 9 8 7 6 5 4 3 2 1

For Jim & Lynn Gullicksrud
& In Memory of Dave Flam
(1945–2017)

THIS NOVEL WAS INSPIRED IN PART BY
TRUE EVENTS THAT TRANSPIRED IN WESTON,
WISCONSIN, ON MARCH 23, 2008

The earth was plowing the men under,
and the horses under, and the plows. No
generation sees it happen, and the broken
new fields grow up forgetting . . . All the
living were breasting into the crest of the
present together. All men and women
and children ran spread in a long line,
holding aloft a ribbon or banner; they
ran up a field as wide as earth, opening
time like a path in the grass, and he
was borne along with them. No, he said,
peeling the light back, walking in the sky
toward home, no.

—ANNIE DILLARD, *THE LIVING*

SPRING

(1)

THE LITTLE BOY GIGGLED AS HE RAN HIS SMALL SOFT HANDS down the old man's furrowed forehead, over his graying eyebrows, eyelids, and eyelashes, and then settled the blindfold just above his nose and ears before running off into the sunlit cemetery to hide.

"Count to twenty, Grandpa," the boy called out.

"One Mississippi . . . two Mississippi . . . three Mississippi . . . ," said the old man loudly, in no hurry, patient as a dusty cabinet clock in a dining room corner.

The sound of laughter receded. Lyle Hovde continued slowly counting. Pressed against his brow and eyelids, Lyle's red faded cotton handkerchief smelled of his worn Wrangler blue jeans: diesel, gasoline, sawdust, the golden butterscotch candy he favored, and the metallic tang of loose pocket change. Before *six* he heard the boy's breathing, his little footsteps growing fainter, the occasional crunch of a pinecone or fallen white-pine branch under a sneaker, the squeak of long vernal grass in thick shadow, and giggling. By *twelve*, there was just the sound of a crow *caw-caw-caw*ing in the crown of a pine. At *seventeen*, he felt his heartbeat slowing. The April sunlight warming his face felt good, his old barn jacket a comfort, like a tucked-in bed blanket. There was the desire to simply nod off, fall into the soft black sea of sleep. His counting slowed nevertheless, and at *twenty*, he pushed the blindfold up, opened his eyes, and the world was still there in a thousand different shades of fragile budding green and gently faded browns and yellows. There was no traffic on Cemetery Road. Not a single car. No tractors tilling. In the sky, two sandhill cranes descended toward a far-off pond. His back was against his son Peter's headstone. He stood slowly, heard his knees pop in protest. He steadied himself against the granite slab.

"Ready or not," he hollered, "here I come."

It was a small cemetery. No more than a couple of hundred headstones. His shadow tipped away from his boots, long in the fading light. This grandson of his, Isaac, the only grandchild he knew, this five-year-old boy, what energy he enjoyed. All day long, while Lyle's wife, Peg, and their daughter, Shiloh, shopped in Minneapolis, Lyle had been left to entertain Isaac, which was no hardship, no hardship at all. But *my lord*, did the boy run and run and run. . . . It was only late afternoon and already Lyle felt as tired as if he'd been laboring all day long, splitting wood perhaps, or throwing field rocks onto a stone boat.

"When I find you," Lyle called out, "when I find you . . ."

He walked slowly among the headstones. Walked by the graves of old women and men he had known so many years ago, when, about Lyle's own age now, they populated Redford, filling the pews of St. Olaf's Lutheran Church, or standing in the narrow, crowded aisles of Hanson's hardware store, pointing fingers at paint chips, studying cans of insecticide, or slope-shouldering bags of feed. Or there, again, pushing wobbly-wheeled carts through the IGA, the husband navigating while the wife held her long scroll of a list, so much of their life meted out in delicate cursive. Old teachers, farmers, postmen, loggers, milkmen, mechanics, short-order cooks, secretaries, dentists, doctors, firemen, butchers, bank tellers, barkeepers, taxidermists . . .

He almost walked right by Isaac, but the boy chortled, and Lyle spotted him in the shadow of old man Egdahl's gravestone. Part of the fun, Lyle knew, was in being found. So he fell upon the boy, tickling his soft belly, his armpits, and his neck, until Isaac had to catch his little breath. Satisfied, Lyle sat on the ground beside his grandson, and noticing the boy's shoelaces untied, went about knotting them anew.

"You didn't make me take a nap today," Isaac said, licking his chapped lips.

Lyle patted the newly knotted shoes, reached into his pocket, and handed the boy a small yellow pot of Carmex.

"You're five years old. You can't take naps forever."

"Grandma says that a person never outgrows naps. She says everyone should take a nap. Every day. She says that in Spain and Portugal, they shut everything down in the afternoon so people can take their siestas."

"What do you know about Portugal?" Lyle asked.

The boy squinted at Lyle, dabbed a finger in the balm and painted it on his lips.

"You take naps sometimes, Grandpa."

"What's that you say?"

"You take naps. In your chair. Watching TV. You even snore."

"Those aren't naps," Lyle smiled, "they're *breaks*. Your grandpa is just taking a *break*."

"I don't think people are supposed to snore on their breaks, Grandpa."

"I don't snore."

The little boy laughed. "You do, too. Mom even recorded it on her phone. And Grandma told me once that sometimes you even wake yourself up with your own snores."

Lyle mussed up the kid's blond hair.

"C'mon now. Let's clean up your uncle's headstone and then we can go visit Hoot. He's expecting us. Bet he might even have some ice cream waiting for you."

From an old pipe located at the center of the cemetery they filled two aluminum pails with cold well water and Lyle dripped in a few beads of blue Dawn dish soap from a small plastic bottle he'd brought from home and then circulated his hand about the pail, making bubbles blossom in swirling rainbow iridescence. Lyle carried the sloshing pails to the grave of his lost son, Peter, and together, sun on their shoulders, and shining through the thin translucent skin of their ears, he and Isaac washed the gravestone with steel wool bunched between their fingers. The afternoon was cooling with every passing minute. Their hands grew pink and cold.

"Tell me again," said the boy, "how he . . . what happened to him?"

Lyle worked his steel wool against the stone, scouring out bits of lichen and dirt. He looked at his grandson then, felt a surge of love for him, for he was such a kind, sensitive, and curious boy, and more than anything, these were qualities Lyle increasingly valued in the world.

"He just wasn't healthy," he said at last, omitting the tragic specifics. "He wasn't meant to stay, I guess."

"How long was he around? I mean, how old was he when . . ."

"About nine months."

The boy nodded, kept on with his scrubbing, might have thought to himself, *I'm so much older than him*, then, after a few moments, said, "Grandpa, can we go to Hoot's now?"

Rising from his knees, Lyle wiped his brow with the sleeve of his jacket, and emptied the pails of sudsy water in long arcs out and away from the gravestones. "One last thing," he said. "Fill up this bucket here, will you? We'll rinse the stone clean and then we can head on out of here."

He watched the boy race off with the empty bucket. Watched him at the spigot, water sloshing near his tennis shoes. Watched him lean down and open his mouth as if at a bubbler—some drinking fountain—water splashing against his tongue and lips and down his chin. Watched him turn the tap off, and then return, water spilling copiously from the bucket with every labored step.

Lyle took the bucket from his grandson and in three graceful motions sent splashes of water glancing off the face of the stone.

The world, he knew, was divided into two camps of people, as it so often is, or as it is so oftentimes and simply reduced to being: those who find cemeteries places of sadness and eeriness, and those, like him, who felt here a deep and abiding unity and evenness, as if the volume in his life were suddenly dimmed down, the way he imagined it might be, floating in outer space, looking out over everything—the immensity of it all. For Lyle, this was a place to be close to people long gone. A free and quiet place off to the side of things. A place to touch not just his memories, but his future.

"Come on," he said, taking his grandson by the shoulder. "Let's go. Hoot'll be waiting."

"Grandpa, I need to pee."

Lyle glanced around, pointed toward a huge white pine

on the periphery of the cemetery. "Go water that tree over there," he said.

Hustling toward its vast wide trunk, the boy was already tugging his pants and underwear to his ankles. Lyle looked elsewhere: at an untilled field, a nearby dairy farm, the forests that filled the coulees. By and by the boy returned to him.

"You're the only person I know who needs to pee more than me," Lyle said. "But I've got an excuse. I think my bladder has a hole in it."

"A hole?" the boy asked, squinting up at his grandfather.

"Must be a hole. Or a few holes."

"How did you get a hole?"

"Shot. An arrow, it was. Passed clean through me. Left this hole right here." He touched his belly button.

The boy laughed. "Grandpa, that's where your umbilical cord was. The one that connected you to the placenta. I've got one, too. Everyone does."

"Oh," said Lyle. "I forgot about that. Thought that's where I was shot." *And how does he know these things? Placenta? Portugal?*

He guided the boy to his old Ford F-150, opened the passenger door for him, shut it firmly. Then he walked around the back of the truck and, turning, looked at the little boy's head, simply staring forward, waiting for him. He ran his hands along the rust of the tailgate, the scabby flakes of chipped paint. He climbed in, sat heavily behind

the wheel, breathed in the cab's dust and gasoline, its mil-
dewed AAA maps, and . . . *cinnamon*.

He turned to the boy. "You been stealing my gum?"

But the boy only smiled and continued chewing, giggling just a little.

"So that's where all my gum goes. I thought the mice
were taking it."

(2)

THE TRUCK EASED OFF THE KNOB OF A HILL WHERE THE CEME-
tery sat, surrounded by its pickets of white pines and arbor-
vitae, and in every direction, the manifold fields of future
corn or beans, the occasional red barn, patches of forests,
and a half mile off, the proud steeple of St. Olaf's church,
the place of Lyle's baptism, first communion, wedding, and
somewhere down the line, he knew, his funeral. Farther
west ran the Mississippi River, rolling its slow, swirling
way just a bit faster than Lyle's after-supper stroll.

Hoot lived not far from Lyle, in a smallish ranch-style
house on the edge of town. Hoot's home was otherwise
immaculately kept but was dense with the smell of cigarette smoke. Older than Lyle by a few years, and long since
retired, he spent his days perusing the newspaper's grocery
store circulars, scissoring out coupons, and later, strolling

the aisles of the big-city grocers (in La Crosse mostly, or maybe up to Eau Claire) for "deals," or perhaps, more accurately, "savings." His nights were rote—about twenty happy sorties to the refrigerator for a cold can of Old Milwaukee, maybe a T-bone or pork chop to flip in the cast-iron skillet, and burning his way through a pack or two of Camels before retiring to his bed, where he slept fitfully, rising frequently to evacuate all the evening's beer. Aside from Peg, and perhaps Pastor Charlie, Hoot was Lyle's best friend. They were different in any number of ways, but they were both kind, and of course, kindness is a great measure of one's ability to befriend and perhaps love other people.

Lyle parked in Hoot's driveway and, scooching across the bench seat, Isaac followed him out of the truck, racing ahead of his grandfather to poke at the doorbell, a little pale yellow glowing *O*.

"Well, who the hell we got here?" Hoot croaked out in his deep, sticky voice as he opened the door. "Oh, *you* two troublemakers. C'mon, fellas, come on in here."

Lyle shook his hand. "We won't keep you too long," he said. Then, quieter, "Just wanted to swing by and hear about those test results."

"Well, I'm still alive. So I've got that going for me." He rapped a set of knuckles against his skull. "Knock wood."

"Peg wanted me to check in, see if you needed anything."

"Right now, all I need is another cold beer," Hoot said. "You may as well have one, too."

There are many different kinds of alcoholics in the world, and Hoot belonged to that class of drinkers reliant almost exclusively on cheap, domestic, canned beer. He was not a fall-down drunk, never passed out, became belligerent, mean, or even goofy. Hoot just liked to surf the humble tube of a beer buzz, coasting along with just enough magic in his bloodstream to soften the edge of things a little bit. It was many years since he'd divorced, and the cigarettes and beer—the smoke and wet, cheerful bubbles—were his own best company as he sat in the kitchen listening to a baseball, football, or basketball game through the fuzz of his old radio. He was gentle and lonesome, even shy. Lyle could not count the number of nights Peg had invited him over to their house for dinner and how, without fail, Hoot politely refused. *We're having pork chops*, Peg would say. *Are you sure you won't stay? We've got plenty. We even have some of that beer you like in the fridge.*

Lyle nodded, took note of the half dozen or so empty cans neatly lined up beside Hoot's sink, smiled. "That sounds about right," he said. "Thanks, Hoot."

"And how about you, young man? Can I get you a glass of water? Milk? A Coke? I prolly got a can of Coke kickin' around somewhere."

"Grandpa said you had some ice cream," said Isaac.

"He did now, did he?"

"Yes, sir."

"You thirsty, too?"

"The kid's always thirsty," Lyle remarked, and it was true. "Shiloh can't pump enough water and food into him."

Isaac took a seat at the small circular kitchen table, and carefully explored the contours and ridges of the heavy glass ashtray marking its center. Self-conscious about the smell of his house, Hoot repainted the place every single spring, Lyle knew, throwing open the windows to roll thick coats of white over all those yellow-tinged walls and ceilings. He'd once shown Lyle a bathroom in the basement with a crucifix hanging above the toilet. Hoot took the crucifix down off the wall, and there, left in faded white against a backdrop of yellowy-brown, was the foggy image of the cross, left over. Hoot joked that his house was held together as much by nicotine residue as by wood or nails. Lyle wondered about Hoot's beleaguered lungs and a recent trip to the doctor's office, which was about as out of character for Hoot as going for a brisk seven-mile jog, or bragging about a new pink yoga mat.

"Well, he's working hard, aren't you, Isaac?" said Hoot, placing a small glass of water beside the boy's wrist. Now Hoot scratched at his immaculately combed hair, still very dark after all the years. "Ice cream, you say?"

Isaac shrugged. "That's what Grandpa told me."

"Well, you know you can't listen to everything your old grandpa tells you, don't you?"

The boy wriggled on his wooden seat, smiled, unsure how to answer. Lyle took a chair beside him. It is a remarkable thing, watching children develop their own sense of humor, that radar that allows us to laugh at our world, our shortcomings, disappointments, even horrors.

"Huh," Hoot said, "now I'm gonna have to rummage around in this icebox for a second or two. Don't mind me. Ice cream, eh . . ."

"Icebox?" Isaac whispered to Lyle.

"Aha! Here we are. Now we're in business," Hoot said. "Neapolitan. I like it because a person gets three flavors in one. You ever have this stuff? I'm also partial to spumoni. High-end Italian-type ice creams."

Isaac peered at Lyle, any doubt well-eclipsed by curiosity.

"Well, it's a goddamn miracle. Three separate ice creams in one container. Like the holy trinity, I'd say. And better than sherbert, for chrissakes. Just a bunch of frozen fruit juice."

He ran an old scooper under the kitchen tap, then dug out two rough orbs of tri-colored ice cream, and placed them in a dish with a spoon before Isaac. The little boy began eating, nodding his head in approval. Satisfied, Hoot took two Old Milwaukees from the refrigerator and passed one to Lyle. They cracked open their cans, raising them up to each other.

"Mud in your eye," Hoot said.

"Skol," Lyle nodded.

They drank.

"Well now," Hoot said, "you two were out to the cemetery, were you?"

Lyle took a sip of his beer, nodded. "Yep, I had a pretty good helper with me."

They regarded the boy eating his ice cream.

"How's it lookin' out there?"

"Pretty much the same," Lyle said. In his mind's eye he could see the tall trees of today as they had been, thirty years earlier, so much shorter and skinnier. He reckoned many of those trees were about the same age as Peter would have been. In Lyle's youth, much of the land surrounding the cemetery had been uncultivated; old stands of white pine or oak, walnut or hickory, elm or even pockets of wild apple. He remembered days—not so far off it sometimes seemed—when there were fewer headstones, when Cemetery Road was not yet paved, when the tractors in the fields were smaller and certainly slower . . . But that was not what Hoot was asking about.

"Say," Hoot said to the boy. "You want another scoop? I have to ask your grandpa a question out in the garage. You suppose that would be okay, if I borrowed him a sec?"

He was already standing to refill the boy's dish.

"His mother will kill me," Lyle said. "The boy hasn't had supper yet."

"C'mon," Hoot said. "It won't hurt 'im." Isaac grinned, holding out his empty bowl. Lyle threw up his hands.

A few moments later, Lyle followed his friend into the garage, where, beneath separate tarpaulins, not one but *two* Ford Mustangs sat—a 1965 and a 1969—in various states of disrepair. Hoot's smallish pickup truck sat out on the driveway, like a least favored, if most dependable, child.

"You're the only man I know sitting on two vintage Ford Mustangs, neither of them worth a damn," said Lyle.

"Oh, they're worth something all right," said Hoot. "That's why I had to chop 'em up. When Sheila demanded the divorce, I sure as hell wasn't going to let her have one. Only way I could see to stop her was making 'em not run."

"Well, your plan worked," said Lyle. "Worked a little too well, I'd say." Lyle rubbed a hand against his jaw, smiled at the cars. "And you're not a half-bad mechanic either, Hoot. You should've had these running years ago."

"What I should've done is dissect them a little more organized like," Hoot said, shaking his head. "Hell, I just started selling off parts, hiding parts, throwing parts in the garbage. There was no way I was letting that woman drive off in one of my Mustangs."

"You ever hear anything from her?" Lyle asked, though he was fairly confident he already knew the answer.

"Nah, that ship sailed a long time ago. I got no quarrel with her now. If she's happy, I'm happy for her."

"I can't remember now, where'd she end up?"

"Key West. Tends bar down there. Met a nice fella, I guess."

"Huh," Lyle grunted. "I'd always be afraid I was one hurricane away from sinking into the ocean. Like Atlantis."

Hoot surveyed his cars in the light of the single bare

bulb hanging from the garage ceiling. "Mark my words, I'm gonna get around to fixin' one of 'em up though. You'll see. Hell, we could get 'em both fixed up, drive around together. Maybe start a club. Get us some special silk jackets—scarves, those gloves with the ventilation holes. Drive all the way down to New Orleans along the River Road. Drink cold beers, eat fresh jambalaya, look out at the Gulf."

"No club would have us," Lyle said.

"That's why we'd start our own, see," Hoot countered, withdrawing a pack of Camels from his breast pocket and lighting one, scratching at his temple, and blowing out a jet of smoke, "very exclusive."

Lyle flapped up one of the tarps, ran his hand along the Mustang's smooth cherry-red hood. Behind him, Hoot coughed.

"I thought you were going to quit," Lyle said.

"I did, for a little while. It didn't take, I guess. You ever miss it?"

Back in his twenties, Lyle had smoked cigarettes on those nights when he was at a tavern and perhaps already in his cups. He could see that younger version of himself in a smoky barroom mirror: a cigarette bobbing between his lips as he yelled over the barroom din, ordering a beer, or standing at the jukebox, nodding his head to the pounding bass of Johnny Cash's "Folsom Prison Blues." Or there again, on those infrequent nights when he and Hoot would arrive back to work after a long day of delivering and installing appliances, those nights when they'd sit in the break room with a six-pack of beer and a bag of pistachios or pork rinds and bullshit for an hour or two before bidding each other good night and returning to their respective homes. Lyle was always careful on those nights to either hang his clothes out on the line, or quickly throw them in the wash; Peg felt cigarettes were a foolish waste of money and loathed the smell of smoke.

"No," Lyle said easily, "I don't miss it. I guess I don't think much about it." They were silent several moments before Lyle spoke up again. "So, what did the doctors tell you?"

"Just pneumonia. I'm supposed to stop again. This is the last one, I promise. Christ, I was worried, Lyle. Dodged a real bullet."

"*Just* pneumonia," Lyle repeated. "Come on, Hoot. You gotta start taking better care of yourself. I know it's a goddamn terrible habit, I do. But, jeez, buddy . . ."

"I'm seventy-one years old," Hoot said. "You know how many times I've tried to quit? More than I can count. But I'll tell you what: this time I might be scared straight. You know me. You imagine? Me going to the doctor? *Taking myself* to the doctor. Truth was, I couldn't breathe. Couldn't catch my damn breath. Felt like a goddamned fish out of water. I swear—this is it, amigo. Last one. Finito."

From the kitchen, they heard the boy's voice calling out, "Grandpa?"

"Hold on, kiddo," Lyle said absently. Then, "Look, you

need anything—anything at all—you let us know, Hoot. I can buy you that gum, if you want. Nicorette? Or the patches. I'll take you to a hypnotist, or acupuncturist. Whatever you think might help."

Hoot took a final drag from the cigarette, let the smoke pool in his lungs, deep and dark, and then exhaled slowly, letting the butt drop to the garage floor, where he stubbed it out with the toe of his off-brand sneaker.

"No need. I got my marching orders. The doctor even said I could try chewing tobacco if it'd help. But it's time. A new leaf."

"I'm glad," said Lyle, not looking at his friend. "We want you around for the long haul."

"Me too," said Hoot. "I ain't ever had the life of the rich and famous, but it sure beats a long boring dirt nap. Anyway, I'm like those batteries, you know: die hard. Or maybe it was everlast. Naw, I'd rather die hard than be everlasting, I think. Point is, I don't give up."

Lyle could not remember having ever touched Hoot, but he did so now, laying a hand on his old friend's shoulder. "Just, you heard what I said, right? You need anything, you won't be too stubborn to ask, now, all right?"

Hoot stared at the garage floor, a small splotch of oil. "Let's go in and check on that boy," he said.

They found Isaac at the kitchen table, holding his ice cream bowl up so that the melt could run into his open mouth. Both men pulled up chairs and sat beside the boy, simply looking at him.

"You want a cookie for the road?" Hoot asked.

The boy nodded his head.

Backing out of Hoot's driveway, Lyle glanced at Hoot's house and saw his friend standing at the small kitchen window, coughing into the sink, where he was likely washing the ice cream bowl, warm water running over his hands.

(3)

LATER THAT EVENING, PEG AND SHILOH CAME HOME, SHOP-ping bags under their arms, smiles on their faces. They kicked off their shoes and then kissed Lyle on the top of his head, each of them, where he sat in his recliner half-dozing, as he absently watched TV. He was, he realized, relieved by Hoot's news, a weight removed from his shoulders, the dread of losing one of his only friends in the world.

"Well," he said. "How'd you do?"

"So many good deals," Peg replied. "We found some nice pants and shorts for Isaac, and this cute little suit jacket for church. Oh, he's going to look handsome."

The boy went first to his grandmother, and she hugged him against her, and kissed his forehead, and rubbed his ears, and he stood there, absorbing her love and attention the way a cat lies and rolls in the embrace of the sun, resplendent.

"Did he behave himself for you?" Shiloh asked, flopping into a chair and tucking her feet beneath her butt. She motioned for the TV remote, which Lyle underhanded to her.

"Oh, he always behaves himself," Lyle said. "The boy is a prince."

"Well, you spoil him, Dad. That probably plays a role." She eyeballed Lyle with suspicion. "You didn't give him too much junk food, did you?"

"Hoot may have given him a dish of ice cream."

"Italian-type ice cream," Isaac offered helpfully.

"Dad . . . I don't want to be the fun police, but promise me you'll cool it on the crappy foods, okay? Please. You know better."

"Of course, sweetheart. I'll try. But someday you'll see. If it were all up to me, I'd serve the kid ice cream three meals a day. It's what we grandparents do. It's our job. If I wanted the boy to hate me, I'd pump him full of brussels sprouts and kale."

She shook her head at him and the room was relatively quiet: the low murmur of the TV, Peg humming happily in the kitchen, Isaac idly leafing through a year-old *National Geographic*. Lyle sighed, peering out the window into the darkness.

"Are you all right, Dad?" Shiloh asked, sitting up in her chair and shutting off the TV.

He shuffled through some old newspapers on the coffee table beside his recliner. "Just . . . you know. Thinking about Hoot. He's got pneumonia. Said it really gave him a scare. Going into the doctor, and all."

"Pneumonia? That's terrible. But, I mean, how long's he been smoking? Since he was what, sixteen? Eighteen?"

"*Nine,*" Lyle said. "Nine years old if you can imagine. Told me he used to steal cigarettes from an uncle of his and go hide in the hayloft. Accidentally set the barn on fire one time."

"That's . . . Dad, he's been smoking for over *sixty* years."

Peg, who had been washing lettuce in the sink, came into the living room, hands dripping. "What was that?"

"Hoot has pneumonia," Lyle said. "Scared him pretty bad. He's giving up cigarettes, he says."

"Such a sweet man," Peg murmured. "How'd he look? How does he feel? Does he need anything? Can we take something over there for him?"

Lyle shook his head. "He seemed okay. Complained about his breathing, I guess."

"Well, is there anything we can do?" Peg asked.

"We can pray for him," Shiloh said, and without hesitating, drew down to her knees in the dated olive green shag of the living room, reaching for her parents' hands. Then, looking up, her face forceful and serious, she called out, "Isaac, come here and pray with your family." When the little boy moved to her side, both of them dropped their chins to their chests and closed their eyes.

Lyle glanced quickly at Peg.

Shiloh had moved away from home at eighteen to attend college in Milwaukee. She'd never asked for a dime from them, had waited tables, washed dishes, and tended bar to pay for her own clothing, a used car, spring break travels. Somewhere in her midtwenties her faith seemed to have taken on a newfound importance and vitality. She became enthusiastically devout, though it was hard for Lyle to identify her denomination; the churches she attended met in strip malls, failed restaurants, and other defunct retail spaces. She'd grown up in the Lutheran church, yes, but her faith had grown in ferocity since her childhood. She no longer drank even so much as a light beer, a margarita, or a Bartles & Jaymes, and insisted on prayers before every meal. She wore more conservative clothing, quoted scripture frequently, and challenged Lyle and Peg with questions of their own faith.

On those Sundays since she and Isaac had moved back home, she politely attended church with her parents, only to visit another church later, this one in La Crosse, in an old movie theater. And she would spend her entire afternoon and early evening there, in *fellowship*, she would explain. Lyle understood churchly fellowship, but only in the context of two or three mugs of wan coffee and polite chitchat, after which, wasn't it time to head home and mow the lawn? Or rake some leaves? Perhaps clean the gutters or pull weeds?

The truth was, Lyle did not believe in God—or at least, wasn't sure he did. It began after Peter passed away. As if the will to believe, the energy to believe had been sapped from him.

The summer after they buried Peter, there was a family reunion in a park pavilion beside an algae-choked lake. The old people hunkered down at picnic tables, gossiping and recycling stories, trading small-town news, avoiding politics, and drinking scalding coffee from white Styrofoam cups despite the hot afternoon air. Children scampered and scuttled about a nearby playground, sneaking sodas and juice boxes, cookies, ice cream, and dessert bars. Lyle stood listlessly, nursing a beer, lost in the world. He could see Peg, surrounded by a group of wives, no doubt trying to cheer her up, asking if there was anything *they* could do. For months, relatives and friends from St. Olaf's Lutheran Church had been dropping casseroles and lasagnas at the house. Just ringing the doorbell and leaving food on their stoop. So much food it crowded their refrigerator. So much food for just two people, both heartbroken and utterly lacking in appetite.

Setting his last can on the top of the overflowing trash, he grabbed another and strolled down to the lake to stand at the grassy shore. Which was where his cousin found him. This cousin, Roger, was a thin man with ever-unfashionable glasses and a wispy mustache who for the next few decades would be a missionary in Côte d'Ivoire. During that time, his skin never seemed to tan, seemed, in fact, to miraculously grow paler yet, more sallow. Lyle would see Roger every five years or so, when he returned to

St. Olaf's to brief the congregants on his mission in Africa, how their tithes were being used to drill new wells, to buy textbooks or mosquito netting.

So with beer and sadness coursing through him, the sun hot on his face, and feeling angry, alone, and betrayed, Lyle said to Roger after some polite small talk, "Tell me about your relationship with God. Please."

Roger laughed. "Are you serious, Lyle?"

Lyle took a long slug of beer. "Yup. Dead serious, cuz. Lay it on me."

And the missionary, smiling earnestly, looked out over the fetid, stagnant waters, and said, "Okay . . . So, one day, back in college, a friend asked me to visit his church. I didn't much want to. I mean, this was college. There were other things to be doing. You know—Frisbee, girls, partying and staying up all night. But I went . . . And I just remember, sitting there in a pew, singing a hymn, and feeling like God had suddenly filled me up with love. Like I had waited my whole life for that moment to come. Like I was a lantern, and He was the light. It felt like that, like being remade into light. And after that, I began talking to God, and waiting for His direction. That was how I knew I'd been called to go to Africa. To become a missionary."

"He *called* you?" Lyle asked over the aluminum shine of his beer can as he lifted it up to his lips again.

"That's right."

"And, how did he call you, exactly?" Lyle pantomimed

a telephone in his hand, bringing it to his ear. He wanted very much to mockingly sneer, *Hello, Roger? This is God speaking. Do you have a minute, son?*

"It was just something I felt. Like a nudge. Or, I don't know, maybe I felt pulled? It was all those things, I guess, but it was also this all-encompassing impulse. This conviction. I knew I had to do it. And I'd never experienced anything like that before."

"Pulled?"

"That's right. Lyle, are you okay? Are you in pain? Would you like to pray with me?"

Lyle looked at Roger. A man so removed from Lyle's day-to-day life he was almost a stranger. He took another swig of beer, crushed the can, and said, "Sure. Let's pray." For a moment he thought, he even relented, he hoped. *Please, Lord, fill me with light. Please just let this hurt go. Please be with my beautiful baby boy in your heaven.* He felt his body surging with sorrow; felt that he could explode into a fountain of tears.

And so Lyle had stood hand in hand with his cousin in the thick July grass, gnats and mosquitoes and blackflies harassing his ears, the air still, the sound of children at play, the smell of hot dogs and cheeseburgers and bratwurst grilling, the eyes of all their family staring down on them from the packed pavilion, and he listened as Roger prayed for him, prayed for Lyle to allow the Lord access to his heart, prayed for the Lord to lift up Lyle and Peg, out of their sadness and mourning for their lost baby boy, prayed for the Lord to be their compass, and to lead them out of a wilderness of sadness, and then, Lyle was not holding hands with Roger anymore, but instead, their sweaty foreheads were pressed together, and Roger's right hand had found Lyle's chest, and his left hand took a grip of the back of Lyle's sweaty head and he was quiet, save for a low hum, and the gentle squeaky swaying of his Rockports, back and forth. And for a moment, Lyle felt something very powerful—only it was not God, or Jesus, or the Holy Spirit, but rather another human being's fervent, ecstatic belief in the supernatural—and then Lyle remembered his boy, remembered saying good-bye to that little baby at the hospital. Holding his baby with strong, suntanned arms, and touching his little white-pink fingers and toes, and marveling at the length of his eyelashes, his soft fingernails and toenails, and then it was time to pass his body to a nurse, and it was just he and Peg in an afternoon hospital room, and he remembered that so clearly, that anger and defiance, and thinking about God in that moment, and thinking, *Damn you, damn you*. Because what good could come from taking a baby from its mother's arms? What good could come from welcoming an infant into the universe only to steal it away again a few short months later? Why? What kind of a *god* would do such a thing? And the only answers that Lyle could glean were these: either there is no God, or, God is cruel. And he could not bring himself to believe in a God so cruel.

Finally he and Roger separated and Roger said, "God bless you, Lyle. I hope you can make space in your heart for Jesus."

Lyle was silent a moment. "Thank you for praying for me," he said finally.

He supposed he meant it, supposed that, in that moment beside the lake, his family staring down at him, he would have tried anything, *anything* in the world to feel whole again, to be with his boy, to not feel angry. But nothing had changed, in fact; nothing stirred and nothing disappeared. He walked up the incline to the pavilion, where voices were only now rising in volume again as folks pretended like they hadn't just been eavesdropping, spying on him. And what he remembered, years later, was plunging his hand into a very cold cooler to reach for another beer, and holding his arm in that painful ice water for several seconds, and feeling his fingers go numb, and then the cold of an aluminum can in his fist, and someone slapping his shoulder as they guided him over toward the horseshoe pits where a few men were standing, watching him carefully, and then someone handed him two horseshoes, heavy in his hand. That steadied him somehow, the warm iron of the horseshoes in one hand, and the cold aluminum beer can in the other.

Peg moved past Lyle and took hold of Shiloh's hand,

and at this Lyle turned away from the living room and instead walked into his bedroom and closed the door, and shut off the light, and sat down on his side of the bed with his eyes wide open and down the hall he heard his daughter say, "Dad?" and his wife say, "Lyle?" then a brief and heavy silence before the sound of their voices resumed, low and beseeching, "Dear God . . . ," they prayed.

(4)

SHILOH WAS ADOPTED, THREE YEARS AFTER PETER'S PASSING AND after they'd suffered a handful of miscarriages and endured dozens upon dozens of doctors' appointments. Their marriage had taken on a new hue since the baby passed away. A shade of blue that seemed to color every room they inhabited, a cloud that smothered the sun. When they made love, it felt accidental, apologetic. When they kissed, it was with cool, tightly pursed lips. Peg's presence at St. Olaf's, Lyle sensed, was as much in mourning as in observance or celebration. Other parishioners, kind, well-meaning people, would stop her as she and Lyle left the narthex for the parking lot. "Oh, darling," they would say, "we just feel awful for you, for you both. How terrible." And Peg would bravely suffer their sympathy, only to release her sadness in the car as they drove home, bawling into a Kleenex and stomping her feet against the rubber floor mat.

It was during this time that Lyle lost his faith, though he sat in his customary Sunday pew just the same. But oh, how he resented it. And, like water seeping into the crack of a great boulder, he gradually began working on Peg, trying to erode her connection to the church, her faith, as well.

"We don't have to go to church today if you're not up for it," he would say. "In fact, I don't care if we ever go back." Or, "I don't think it is helping. It's just one more reminder of Peter for you. We should go biking, or take a hike. Canoeing. Anything. I think we'd be better off worshipping in the Church of Nature."

But it was at church where they were told of Shiloh by one of Peg's friends, who pulled them aside after the service, telling them of her fifteen-year-old niece who'd just delivered a baby in the women's bathroom of an Indiana McDonald's, and was now staying with relatives about fifty miles away from Redford because her community would not have supported her, would have, in fact, ostracized her—her family, principal, teachers, church, guidance counselor, friends, and fellow students. She'd hidden the pregnancy from everyone beneath ever-baggier clothing. And in the moments after the birth, alone in that loud, dirty bathroom, and later, hiding at a friend's house, the young mother recognized that she couldn't care for the baby and was willing to give it up to adoption. So she lied to her parents, pretended she was going on a Christian youth retreat, and instead bought a Greyhound bus ticket bound for Wisconsin, where her beloved aunt and uncle lived, the only two people in the world she trusted. She showed up on their doorstep with a day-old baby, bedraggled, exhausted, and afraid.

"Where is she?" Peg asked, panicking. "When can we meet her?"

Her friend ran a hand through her hair. "The sooner you can get there, the better. The poor dear is running out of time. She's got to get back home before her parents start asking questions."

So they went. Went straight to their car in the parking lot, Peg darting for the driver's side as she nearly never did. "Get in," she said, without looking at Lyle.

He did what he was told, glancing at his wife out of the corner of his eye. She took the roads quickly. It was early winter, just before Christmas, and the sunlight off the white-blue, frozen fields blinded him. Accustomed to doing the driving, he didn't know what to do with his hands. He opened the glove box and fumbled with a stack of road maps, a tire pressure gauge, a broken pair of sunglasses, a plastic container of orange Tic-Tacs.

"I know you've given up on . . . that you're not sure about God anymore," Peg said. "But here's the thing, Lyle, and you listen to me: I'm not so sure you're right. I'm not saying that you're wrong, or that you're wrong for feeling the way you do. If I could have seen God after Peter died, why . . . there's a good chance I would have killed Him myself. But I have a feeling. About this girl we're going to see. And maybe it was all a very winding path, some kind of elaborate plan leading us here, to this day, to being in this car, and going to find her."

She reached for Lyle's hand. "I need you," she said. "I need you right now more than ever." She looked at him with an intensity he could not recall.

He took her hand. "I'm here," he said, "I'm with you."

The aunt and uncle of the young mother lived in a home that looked very much like so many others in Wisconsin: a three-bedroom 1950s-era ranch on a straight, ash-tree-lined middle-class street. When they were welcomed inside, the smell of sloppy-joe sandwiches and apple pie greeted them. It was meant to be a proper occasion, this meeting. There were dishes of pickles and of sliced vegetables, potato chips, and cheese curds. The aunt and uncle were not much older than Lyle and Peg, but they shook hands all around, and then the mother, Sarah, so young and thin and pale, came out with Shiloh in her arms, all swaddled in a pink blanket, and they could see Sarah was crying, but smiling just the same, and without hesitation the girl stood immediately beside Peg, and in less than a minute's time, the baby was in Peg's arms, and everyone was crying, including Peg, who would not take her bleary eyes off this little baby, who, she knew then, in that instant, was about to become her daughter.

(5)

ALTHOUGH LYLE HAD STOPPED BELIEVING, HE NEVER REALLY
stopped attending church. Indeed, he often suspected he
was not alone in this, that many millions of Christians, Jews,
Muslims, Buddhists, Taoists, and Mormons all around the
world attended their churches, temples, and mosques as
much out of routine or obligation as out of any real fervor
or belief. Or, perhaps, to model a new dress or hat, a new
pair of shoes, or a sharp suit. Guilt, he supposed, must also
have played a role, for certainly not every butt in a pew was
doing the Lord's work 24/7; some might secretly be cheat-
ing on their taxes, sleeping with the neighbor's wife or husband, playing the casino slot machines or roulette tables
with the children's college fund, or who knew what other
litany of shortcomings, from the trivial to the criminal. For
others, it might be boredom or loneliness. But for Lyle, so

much depended on his childhood friend Pastor Charlie, and that lovely old country church in which he had spent so many Sundays as a child, shuffled into that hard-backed pew by his now long-departed parents.

Lyle sometimes heard folks in La Crosse or Eau Claire bemoan urban development, growth, or sprawl as a bad thing, and mostly, he supposed, they were probably right. Who wanted to witness farmland or forests being chewed up by roads and parking lots, studded by hastily constructed and offensive-looking buildings? And for many, he imagined, the quickest emotion was sadness, rage, or some sort of mourning. But his whole life, Lyle had only ever seen his hometown of Redford, its Main Street, its stores and restaurants and bars and churches, steadily empty and then shutter, before finally falling into disrepair, or crumbling back into the earth. And to Lyle, this was more tragic than the advance of commerce, for so much of what he once loved was now gone, and for good.

Attending St. Olaf's was a melancholy weekly reminder of this loss. For over the years, the hair of the parishioners had grown gray, then white, then disappeared altogether, and over time, there were fewer and fewer congregants in the pews, and certainly many fewer children, so that Pastor Charlie's Sunday morning voice felt at once forlorn and defiant in that space, and the pulpit from which he stood more and more flimsy and artificial. Maybe, Lyle had thought, they should just gather in a large circle and talk. And what must Pastor Charlie think? Looking out at that long rectangular space which even two decades ago would have been packed, now populated by a few dozen church-goers . . . The church could no longer support a secretary, people a choir, or facilitate Sunday school classes; there were fewer than a dozen children, sprinkled between the ages of one and eighteen. The service itself had shrunk to a bare forty minutes, of which a full fifteen minutes seemed dedicated to some combination of the welcome, sharing-of-the-peace, whatever announcements (area lutefisk or lefse feeds, funerals, bake sales, weather conditions, and the like), and then finally, the closing dismissal, too soon in coming, at the same time awfully late, hard-won for just about everyone, it seemed.

But Peg and Lyle hung on, and if Lyle had fallen away from his faith, she had long ago seized his wrist, so that, even as they both dangled from this crumbling cliff, she would not let him go; she believed *for* him, and in him, too, somehow.

And so they went, each Sunday, waking early and drinking their coffee, Peg in a nice dress, and Lyle in his threadbare and increasingly tight suit, driving up into the hills where St. Olaf's stood proudly, its tall stained-glass windows, its stately white steeple, its fieldstone and brick, its wide accepting doors, ancient oaken pews, moldering hymnals and Bibles, and the ever-present aroma of burnt Folgers coffee. Every year, the parking lot's cars and pickup trucks dwindled; and every year, Lyle and Peg seemed to park closer to the church's entrance.

Still, Lyle appreciated the routine. Appreciated seeing those old codgers and geezers who came out, every Sunday, in their finest clothing, newly shaved and bathed and perfumed. How deaf many of them had grown! But with their deafness came a new and wonderful intimacy, for Lyle realized that for them to hear him, they had to lean close into his body, and he into theirs, right near their overgrown tufts of ear hair, right up to their big Beltones, and how those fogies might, after shaking his hand, hold on tight, perhaps trembling, and pull him in close or closer still, like they were sharing the most important secret in the universe, or the combination to an ancient vault holding a fortune in forgotten old gold, silver, and precious jewels. Oh, how Lyle loved those moments, of how time slowed for him, how he could see himself, years off and into the future, shrunken perhaps, but clinging to a younger person, as if to a raft or tree root, clinging on as the eddies and rapids of a river tugged at his ankles to pull him downstream and over the waterfalls without so much as a jetsam barrel.

He and Peg had a pew, a particularly favored pew where they had sat for what was now decades. Close to the pulpit, but not too close (four pews from the front, on the left). They shared a single hymnal, Lyle holding it between them, and when the gospel was read, Lyle preferred to find the verse in the Bible and follow along, his finger below the printed words, while Peg needed only to listen. And when Pastor Charlie took to the pulpit, Peg would swing a leg over her knee, brushing her foot against Lyle's shin, while he slung an arm behind her shoulders and there they rested, listening. And if their Saturday-night sleep had been fitful, then yes, they might sometimes close their eyes, hoping that the other would in time gently elbow them awake in the ribs.

Lyle and Charlie had grown up together on neighboring farms, sharing chores, walking to school, playing football, sitting in Sunday school together. It is the most obvious blessing and curse of a small town: your family, friends, neighbors, coworkers, and clergy are forever, it seems, riding in your pocket, staring at you out of their window, intimate enough to intrinsically know when you are happy, sad, distracted, in love, or itching to disappear altogether.

In fact, disappear would have been a fairly apt way of describing Charlie's life after graduating from high school. For several years he worked his way out West, toiling on rail-maintenance crews for Canadian-Pacific until he finally made his way up to Alaska, where, for two decades, he worked backbreaking jobs: crab boats, salmon canneries, logging, bartending, and a stint placer-mining in the bush.

Maybe it was that his body could no longer absorb the abuse those jobs doled out, or maybe it was the long, cold, dark alcoholic winters, or even something else, but in his mid-forties, Charlie drifted back to Wisconsin, entered a seminary, and was more than happy to end up back in Redford at a church the younger seminarians would have had difficulty mustering enthusiasm for (the small salary, the dwindling congregation, the nonexistent office support, and the church structure itself aging and outdated). But none of these things bothered Charlie in the least.

When Charlie reappeared in Redford after so much time away, the two men slipped right back into an easy friendship, the parameters of which had changed over time in relation to their own experiences and responsibilities. For his part, Charlie had become quieter, more reclusive— available on Sundays, to be sure, but otherwise holed up in his home, reading through his shelves of books and listening to his vast collection of vinyl records. This suited Lyle just fine; he had his own family and job, his own life. But when Charlie and Lyle got together for a beer or perhaps to go out deer hunting together, they fell back into a familiar pattern of quiet and curiosity, talking about St. Olaf's, about Redford, their family farms, and, as the years progressed, the inconvenient and sometimes embarrassing ways in which their bodies were beginning to betray them.

Lyle respected his old friend with quiet awe; Charlie had gone and seen the world, worked romantic jobs, called a hundred different women his lover. His life was like a Jack London novel, and Lyle never tired of listening to his adventures. Never married, Charlie lived in the church's parsonage, a small brick bungalow half a mile down from St. Olaf's where he spent most days alone, reading histories of the Civil War, listening to NPR, carving and painting wooden chess pieces, walking the back roads. He was taller and more muscular than Lyle, and had for years kept a beard, the goatee gone yellow around his lips, thanks to his furtive affairs with Old Gold cigarettes and White Owl cigars. His hair was long and floppy, and in hottest summertime he occasionally preached wearing Birkenstocks (Jesus, he liked to joke, would have been the ultimate spokesman for the hippie brand). He carried himself with the detached sort of kindness that seems to inhabit those who have fallen the furthest, suffered the most, and sometimes, frankly, done the most drugs without actually dying.

But he never, *never* lectured Lyle on religion or faith. And so, for years now, hundreds of Sundays, Lyle had sat before his friend, listening to him preach, and what Lyle appreciated most about Charlie's leadership of the church was that he seemed (despite his outsized life, despite his physical size) to be vulnerable. Vulnerable to the elusiveness of faith, certainly, to the difficulty of conviction, to the impossibility of knowing, without a shadow of a doubt, that *this* book, this Bible—interpreted, translated, and copied by so many thousands of hands over so many hundreds of years in so many different countries—could possibly convey the pureness, the essence and undecorated wisdom of God, of the creator of all things. So there were moments at the pulpit when Charlie would lower his head and pause, for five, ten, twenty seconds, and Lyle might lean gently forward, as if he might need to rescue his friend from a lapse of faith, but then, Charlie would look up, stroking or perhaps scratching at his beard, and smile out at the congregation, and simply say, in a voice like early morning loose gravel, "I apologize. Sometimes my record just seems to skip, and I need to move the needle a little, find a new groove."

His congregation adored him because they, too, sensed in him old faults and flaws. They saw in him themselves. There were no sharp corners left on Charlie—only rounded edges, like those smooth river stones a person plucks from the moving waters and keeps in their pocket, or on a bookshelf, rubbing it between their fingers like a talisman or lucky charm.

After church, he would stand at the entrance to the narthex and shake everyone's hands, address everyone by name, and in any season other than winter, the door would be wide open and Charlie's squinted eyes would show his wrinkles, and forty-five minutes later you might find him behind the church, sitting on an old metal folding chair, his legs casually crossed, looking out over the coulee lands, smoking a cigarette, his robes no doubt hanging inside but his white collar still in place.

This Sunday, Shiloh and Isaac came with Lyle and Peg to St. Olaf's and their presence was like that of two long-journeyed astronauts or explorers to the old people who came to them in their pew to hug Shiloh and tousle Isaac's hair. What a joy it was for Lyle to parade these two people he loved so much, and felt such pride in. To sit in church together, as he had with Shiloh so many years ago, when she was just a girl, small enough to fit below his armpit, where she would read a *Boxcar Children* book or perhaps her cherished Laura Ingalls Wilder (whose little-house-in-the-big-woods was not so very far from their own little town).

Shiloh and Charlie delighted in talking to each other, and it was Lyle's friend, more than anyone else, who could coax details from her, bits of her biography she'd never shared with her parents: religious texts she'd studied, theological scholars she'd sought out, service trips to tornado-torn or hurricane-battered communities, ex-boyfriends, jobs . . . This whole life, she only *sometimes* showed her parents, even if generally she was polite, respectful, and reserved.

After church they piled into Peg's trusty Subaru wagon and drove back to Redford, where Shiloh prepared a brunch of fresh fruit, sausage patties, and eggs as Lyle pushed Isaac on the backyard swing, a plank of gray weathered wood suspended by two ropes anchored into a wide, expansive oak branch at the back of their little property. Isaac could swing for hours, and Lyle, for his part, enjoyed the metronomic rhythm of it all: the tree's gentle protestations, the scratchy harmonics of the ropes, and the boy's endless chitter-chatter: everything from an incomplete attempt at a summary of Charlie's sermon, to yesterday morning's cartoons, to questions ranging from the biblical to theoretical physics and the brass tacks of evolution all the way back to favorite colors and pizza toppings.

"Grandpa, if we're descended from gorillas and monkeys, then does that mean Adam and Eve were descended from gorillas and monkeys? Were they, Adam and Eve, more like gorillas? Or more like us? Or, is that just, like, a story? And if Adam and Eve were the first two people, did they start *off* as grown-ups? I mean, were they ever children? Wouldn't that be cool if once, we were all children? Just two children on the whole planet."

And then an immediate segue:

"Grandpa, where *is* heaven? Is it *in* the clouds? Or, like, *past* the clouds? In outer space? And if it's *in* the clouds, what happens on a sunny day? Where does heaven go? And why can't we see the people up in heaven?"

How the boy could ask questions—exhaustively, relentlessly, so sincerely—for hours at a time. Church filled Isaac's little head with glorious puzzles and promises, and afterward, it was often left to Lyle to delicately untangle the knots, always careful not to cut a line that Shiloh had carefully and skillfully secured around herself and Isaac. The world is filled with a near endless array of mysteries, and an even more infinite amount of guesses, grifts, lies, spiels, and here and there, almost hidden, a very few sacred handfuls of answers.

Increasingly, Lyle found that he was most at home in the quiet, near those he loved, not trying to solve any problems or answer any questions, but, rather, just learning how to live more lightly, love more intensely, eat better, and, before his eyes closed at night, to read through the shelves and shelves of books that sadly, he knew, he would likely never live long enough to open, those white-winged birds perched on his chest in the pale light of his bedside lamp, waiting for their thin pages to be flicked lightly by a wet fingertip, and turned, giving over their stories and poems and mythologies. Increasingly, and in direct contrast to his lust for books, Lyle found that he loved nothing more than a good catnap, stealing sleep the way a child steals a quarter off the counter—a small, insignificant but thrilling theft.

(6)

THE SOURDOUGH ORCHARD RODE A SADDLE OF LAND stretching nearly all the way from the Mississippi River sloughs east up to the towering sandstone bluffs where eagles, hawks, and vultures wheeled endlessly, with a county highway to the north of the orchard, a deep coulee to the south, and to the west of course, the river and its namesake road. The morning shadows across this land were extravagantly dark and blue, while the afternoons were drawn in infinite shades of gold and brass as the sun set across the river, over Minnesota. It was an ideal place to be an apple tree.

Lyle rose early most mornings, though not before Peg, who moved about the house in her worn flannel nightgown, now and then checking her cherished laptop, and the family pictures and dispatches she was kept constantly apprised of on Facebook, not so much sharing with Lyle this social media news as talking to herself out loud, saying, "Well now, looks like Maya is pregnant again." Or, "What a shame. Elsa's boy Zachary is getting another divorce." And Lyle, puttering around their kitchen, grinding coffee, washing dishes, wiping down the counters, or spreading butter and marmalade across his toast, murmuring, "You don't say," or something equally banal, for he had in the past, when not *exactly* listening, offered the wrong "That's too bad" at an inopportune time, such as when Peg announced that her cousin Nancy had posted an entire album's worth of photos documenting her travels to Norway: fjords, waterfalls, idyllic harbors, et cetera. He had learned, over decades of marriage, that when he was not actively listening to Peg, it was in fact more dangerous to pretend that he was. Oftentimes, a well-placed humming noise, grunt, or *uh-huh* was best.

His thermos filled, Lyle would say good-bye to Peg—for Shiloh and Isaac would not yet have roused from the two downstairs bedrooms—and drive the old Ford just south of town before angling east toward the small orchard where he was the sole employee, paid cash under the table, every Friday once the owners, Otis and Mabel Haskell, had tabulated his hours from an eighty-nine-cent spiral notebook where such pertinent information was kept stored and safeguarded.

Lyle had spent almost thirty years of his life working

at Redford Appliance & Repair, a small family-owned appliance store on the edge of town that sold everything from toasters and microwaves to snowblowers and lawn mowers and almost anything in between: stoves, washers and dryers, garbage disposals, refrigerators, freezers, dishwashers, vacuums, even furnaces and air conditioners. And what they sold they also fixed and repaired. In this way, even though their market was small, they managed to stay in business, if not exactly thrive, year after year, with a ferociously loyal clientele. Hoot, too, had worked at Redford Appliance, sometimes on the floor, as a salesman, and during the slower winter months, in the back room, performing surgery on busted Hoover vacuum cleaners or old Amana ranges. Lyle had loved his work and his customers, for they were his neighbors, his relatives, his in-laws. When a customer complained about their dishwasher not working properly, he'd known precisely which machine they were referring to and in which room it had been installed. He could imagine that house's circulatory systems of plumbing and electricity. How that house smelled or how it sighed in a strong wind.

"How old's your dish soap?" Lyle might ask.

"Excuse me?" they'd say.

"Your dish soap. Are you using those little crystals?"

"Yeah, the little crystals come out of the green box. Cascade."

"Right," Lyle would say. "Do me a favor. When you

get home, pour about a teaspoon of those soap crystals into your palm and then rub your hands together. Afterward, call me."

And later that afternoon, they would call Redford A & R. "Hey, Lyle, I did what you said and rubbed them soap crystals between my hands. What gives?"

"Did the soap feel hot against your skin?"

"Gee"—they'd pause—"I'd have to think about that." A pause would settle over the telephone line. "No, I never felt anything. No heat anyways. You mean like a burn or something? I don't understand, Lyle."

"Your soap is too old," Lyle would say. "Buy yourself a new box of soap and I bet that dishwasher will work perfectly."

Over thirty years Lyle worked at Redford A & R helping his community in the most basic and measurable ways possible. But by his late fifties and early sixties, as Redford began to slowly depopulate, business trailed off. The day Redford A & R closed was the day Lyle more or less retired, and began accepting Social Security. He was at peace with this even as he wasn't sure what exactly he'd do in retirement to occupy his days, short of becoming a jack-of-all-trades, repairing appliances around Redford until those aging Whirlpools, Frigidaires, KitchenAids, GEs, and the rarefied Viking or Wolf gave up the ghost.

Then, about two years into his retirement, Otis Haskell, who had made it a point to support Redford A & R throughout his life and was considered by many to be the town's resident eccentric-liberal-academic, called him up and offered him a job at the Sourdough Orchard, and that position, such as it was, had become a godsend for Lyle. Not because of the money it paid (which, in truth, was very little), but because the cycles of the orchard gave him something he'd been lacking without even knowing it—meaning. And, too, he rediscovered the glory of working outdoors.

On this spring morning, Lyle parked near the apple house, where the harvest was kept and refrigerated in wooden crates (though by now, it contained nothing but the sweet, leftover fragrance of last year's crop), then knocked on the Haskells' door before entering. They would be sitting at the kitchen table, he knew, waiting for him, reading their morning newspaper, Otis already dressed for the day in his trademark Key denim bibs, a yellow chamois-cloth shirt, a sweat-stained long-brimmed baseball cap with a neck cape, a yellow Dixon Ticonderoga #2 pencil lodged behind his ear, and an ancient pair of white Nikes, grass-stained nearly to kelly green. Mabel still in her nightgown and cheap pink slippers, an overly large bathrobe draped over her slender frame and cinched tightly around her narrow waist.

"Good morning, Lyle," Otis said.

Lyle took a seat at the table. Otis was noshing on an overripe banana, waving a persistent fruit fly away, while Mabel scratched the back of her head with a blunted pencil.

"How's that grandson of yours doing? You ought to start bringing him out here. We can get him all trained up."

"Boundless energy," Lyle replied, smiling. "He keeps us busy."

"And how's my girl Shiloh? She found a job yet?" Otis asked, glancing over the thick and profoundly scratched lenses of his glasses.

Asked to select a single word to describe Otis, Lyle might have chosen *frugal*, or perhaps simply, *cheap*. The man threw nothing away, bought very little, and almost everything he and Mabel owned was in some state of slow, steady disrepair: their pickup truck, their old four-door Volkswagen diesel, their aging house, their clothes, the fences of the orchard . . . Both Otis and Mabel were children of the Great Depression, and their childhoods had been spartan, if not at times desperate. Mabel had grown up outside Tulsa, Oklahoma, and still clutched a distant memory of one of her cousins dying of dust pneumonia. And even though Otis had for decades been a beloved faculty member of the University of Minnesota's Horticultural Science Department, he rarely spent a dime save on the orchard itself; he often joked that this acreage, this assemblage of old buildings, these hundreds of trees, all of it was his own private folly.

"I guess there's a church outside of La Crosse. They might have a secretary job for her," Lyle said. "Isaac could have free day care." In truth, though, he could not quite understand this plan of Shiloh's, ranging so far away from their home on two-lane roads for a job paying nine dollars an hour and without health benefits. And yet, he felt such gratitude for having her and Isaac nearby, he dared not utter even the most benign criticism for fear of chasing her away.

"La Crosse, hey?" Otis said. "That's a little bit of a jaunt, isn't it? Hopefully she's got four-wheel drive. Those river roads get treacherous."

Lyle frowned. "I suppose she could take my truck if she needed to."

Mabel sighed deeply, staring at the puzzle. "A four-letter word for black rock."

"Coal," Lyle offered.

"No," Mabel countered, "ends with an *X* of all things."

Otis rammed the last of the banana into his mouth and said through the mush, "Onyx."

Mabel eyeballed him with equal measures of derision and appreciation. "The old coot's mostly useless, but even a broken clock's right twice a day."

Otis stood from the table and Lyle followed him outside. The morning air was cool, fog collecting in the coulee, and high overhead, a bald eagle was soaring on the day's first thermals.

"I'd like to spray those Macintosh today," Otis said. "Maybe check on the Cortlands, I suppose. We could get some mowing done, too."

They piled tools into the back of Lyle's truck and drove the short distance to the fenced entrance of the orchard, where a ten-foot-high wire enclosure kept the deer from destroying the trees. Otis opened the gate, and Lyle drove right into the orchard. Soon they donned their leather gloves and began the day's work.

Through spring and early summer, the orchard was a place of preparation. Mowing and raking, spraying insecticides, and in places, cutting out dead trees to replace them with new saplings. The fence line always needed repairing, there were piles of dead branches to burn, bandages to be removed from trunks, supports for young trees that needed restaking. More than enough labor for two old men.

Lyle liked working in late spring, before the season's real heat socked in, the air still cool and wet but carrying the warmer promises of summer. Migratory birds were returning up the Mississippi flyway, and there were times he looked up from his work to see some burst of color fly through the sky, or to follow the exotic song of a bird he'd forgotten since fall.

At lunchtime they broke off work and returned to the Haskells' home, the kitchen smelling of Campbell's tomato soup left untended in its pot and beginning to burn. A stack of grilled cheese sandwiches sat on a plate, the orange Kraft slices oozing from between slices of unevenly toasted Wonder Bread. On the counter: a mostly depleted jar of Vlasic pickles, a bowl of stale saltines, and a bag of old Hershey's Kisses chocolates grown chalky with age. Mabel had set out plates and bowls for the men to serve themselves, buffet style, while she sat in the living room, still mumbling over her crossword puzzle, but mostly waiting for her "stories" to begin. Their soap opera was just starting. Otis installed himself in his most favored chair, set a TV tray before himself, worked his feet out of the battered Nikes, and exhaled deeply.

Lyle, still in the kitchen, washed his hands in the sink. The Haskells often bought their groceries at a nearby gas station, whichever store was the cheapest. This gas station also stocked the overripe bananas Otis preferred, on sale for as little as a dime a pound.

"Now, is Hope back with Bo, or is she still fooling around with that other man?" Otis asked as he bit into his sandwich, eyeballing Mabel. "These stories are all the same. I can't keep any of it straight."

"I thought Hope was kidnapped, down by the wharf," Lyle called in from the kitchen. He often dozed during their afternoon "program."

"That's Marlena," Mabel clarified. "Hope was in the hospital, visiting Roman. Now be quiet, please."

Lyle carried his plate into the living room and settled into another easy chair closer to the window where he sat heavily, looking out at the afternoon sky. He wondered what Peg had planned for Isaac, whether or not Shiloh would be working that day, if he might suggest other work for her. Some job that didn't require her to drive so far from home on such narrow roads.

"The police chief of Salem should be ashamed," Otis said at last, crunching a pickle. "So much god-awful crime."

AT ABOUT FIVE O'CLOCK, OR SOMETIMES A BIT BEFORE, THEY quit, locking up the orchard's gate behind them, and drove back to the apple house where they said their good-byes.

"We'll see you tomorrow," Lyle called out as he pulled away.

"I'll be right here," replied Otis, waving a hand, "unless I'm dead."

Lyle shook his head. Otis was eighty-six years old and sharp as a thorn. There were days Lyle wondered if the older man might well outlast him.

———————

SOME DAYS, ISAAC CAME WITH LYLE TO THE ORCHARD. THE Haskells doted on the boy, serving him hot chocolate in the mornings while they all drank weak coffee and watched him in fascination. Mabel withdrew freshly baked pans of cookies and brownies from the oven and Lyle watched as Isaac's eyes grew wide.

Many summer mornings the boy stayed with Mabel, "helping" her clean the dishes, or sitting in her lap as they watched *Sesame Street* or some other PBS program. Once, Lyle and Otis had come back in for lunch and found the two of them eating buttered popcorn, watching *The Sound of Music* on an old VHS tape.

Other times, Isaac sat between Lyle and Otis on the bench seat of the truck as they rode up to the orchard. When Otis opened the truck's passenger door in order to unlock the orchard gate, the boy would follow, closing the door behind them.

Cherished is a strong word, but it is true that Lyle cherished such days. The slant of late-spring light, his hands in the branches, happening upon the delicate nests of unseen songbirds, the sweet smell of cut grass, the earthy rot of wet fallen leaves. The ditch flowers and lilacs, the rare, treasured morel mushrooms, the electricity of bees and their ecstatic drive for pollen, his grandson climbing into the lower limbs of a tree to hide or running through the orchard, a turkey feather in each outstretched hand as if he were flying. Or there again, sitting mostly still in his little blue jacket, pulling grass from the earth . . .

"You know how to make grass into a whistle?" Otis asked once.

The boy laughed.

The old man looked at him with some mock seriousness. "You think I'm teasing you?"

Isaac nodded.

Otis slowly sat down by him in the grass, pulled a single long blade from the ground, and said, "Now, you hold it up here, between your right pointer finger and your thumb. Then you put your two hands together, kind of like you're praying, with this little window between your hands. Then you blow."

And he did, and the sound was like that of a whistle, yes, but also a birdcall of sorts. Isaac smiled.

"Now, just look around—you've got a field of whistles."
He mussed the boy's head. "That oughta keep you busy."

For an afternoon, the orchard was filled with the
sounds of strange whistling, the boy ranging off, down the
ridge, but they never worried about him, that sound carrying, eerie and playful through the rows of trees. And what
better thing than to be a young child, let loose out into the
wide world to explore, without a hint of danger, because it
was adults of course who introduced danger into the world,
always adults.

Other days, Mabel drove up to the gate in the old
Volkswagen and honked the horn, and Isaac would positively race toward her, hardly big or tall enough to open the
gate, but open it he would, laboriously, and Mabel, carefully pulling into the orchard, and Isaac closing the gate
behind her, and then racing to the side of the stout, gray
automobile, where she would hand him a large woven bas-
ket that the child would clumsily carry down toward the
old men, in time Mabel following behind. And then she
would unfurl an old flannel blanket, moth-eaten through
the years, and all four of them would sit and she would dole
out salami, cheese, and mayonnaise sandwiches wrapped
in paper towels. Potato chips, celery sticks, carrots, and
brownies. Perhaps a thermos of apple cider. Once, Lyle
remembered, there was even a bottle of French wine (presented to the Haskells as a gift, of course) and three little
Mason jars, and how decidedly *civilized* he felt, sitting in
that vernal orchard, splitting an entire bottle of Bordeaux,

and then standing to feel the tilt and spin of the planet beneath him, his grandson hugging him about the leg, and then Lyle lifting him up, feeling not sixty-five years old, not at all, but as he'd felt when Shiloh was just a little girl, and he would pick her up and twirl her around and then nuzzle close to her neck. Oh, he loved the boy; and that was all there was to it.

(7)

PEG AND ISAAC SAT AT THE KITCHEN TABLE. THE BOY WORE ONE
of Lyle's old Sunday dress shirts backward, buttoned behind him, red paint splattered over the light blue fabric. The
house was warm and smelled of slow-cooked pork, brown
sugar, and cinnamon. Lyle's mouth watered.

"What are you two birds working on?" Lyle called out,
as he sat down and slowly unknotted his Red Wing boots.

Peg whispered into Isaac's ear and the boy called out,
"None of your beeswax," then giggled before returning to
the construction paper he was painting on.

Lyle stood, reached a hand into the refrigerator, popped
a bottle of beer. He kissed the boy's head and smelled in
the follicles of his hair fresh air and strawberry shampoo.
He picked a twig from the tangles of blond hair, and then
a bit of leaf.

THAT NIGHT, AFTER SHILOH HAD WASHED AND DRIED THE
dishes, after Peg had settled Isaac in his bed and read him
several Berenstain Bears books, the three adults sat in the
living room, absentmindedly watching *Antiques Roadshow,*
with Peg occasionally interjecting, "We had something
like that in our house growing up." Or, "Oh, I remember
that toy." She often narrated the TV shows they watched
together, sometimes offering her own real-time critiques.

Lyle was dozing off when Shiloh cleared her throat and
said, "I have to tell you both something."

He sat up in his chair and clicked the volume down low.

Shiloh studied her fidgeting hands. "Look, it's been
wonderful being home, and I so appreciate your willingness
to let Isaac and I stay here. I promise it won't be forever."

Peg sat forward. "Darling, you're welcome to stay here
as long as you need. As long as you want. We sincerely *love*
having you both live here."

Their daughter moved her long brown hair away from
her face, drew it behind her ears. Her skin was pale, her
dark brown eyes serious and alive. The light in the living
room was soft and dim. The house quiet.

"I just wanted you to know that I'm looking for an
apartment. In La Crosse. We can't be here permanently.
It's important to me to be close to my church and . . . that's
what I wanted to talk to you about. I don't want you to
stand in judgment of what I believe, or how I raise Isaac—"

"Shiloh, we would never dream of—" began Peg.
"You're a wonderful mother."

"It's just that my faith is the most important thing in my life. My faith and Isaac. And you two, of course. And I would love it if we could all *try* to worship together. If you would just visit my church with Isaac and me."

"Of course we could visit your church, Shiloh," Peg said, some measure of desperation in her voice, "we would love that. Wouldn't we, Lyle?"

In such moments, even the briefest of pauses can be interpreted as a reticence, even a refusal, and though Lyle had no interest whatsoever in attending any church other than the one he had been baptized, confirmed, and married in, he was suddenly aware that his daughter held the power to move his grandson away from him, a thought so bleak to Lyle it seemed akin to amputation. So even as particles of time whizzed past him, the conversation fast taking on new intensity and meaning, he forced himself to quickly answer, "Absolutely."

Shiloh smiled, as if in victory. "I'm so happy. It hasn't been easy, raising Isaac alone. And . . . there were many days when the only thing that got me through was my faith."

A sadness overcame Lyle, as if he'd just gulped a very cold glass of water that chilled his veins. There were years in Shiloh's twenties when she had not returned their phone calls. When letters and packages addressed and postmarked to her were returned as undeliverable. Difficult visits scattered over years when they knew little about her, knew not even the color of her hair before she showed up on their stoop at Christmas. It was really Isaac who had brought them back together. Shiloh moving to Minneapolis, and those first telephone calls (mostly conducted between Peg and Shiloh), when for the first time since her early childhood, their daughter asked for help.

And how they had jumped, *leaped* at any chance to assist her. Lyle, moving her belongings into a new apartment, he and Hoot carrying furniture from the bed of the truck up three flights of winding narrow stairs to Shiloh's stuffy studio apartment. Then trips to the hardware store for mousetraps and smoke detectors, a trip to the grocery store to fill her refrigerator, and despite all Shiloh's protestations, Peg had given her five hundred dollars in cash. "Don't be silly," Peg pleaded with her, "think about the money *not* as a gift to you, but as a gift to our grandchild."

Lyle and Peg knew nothing of Isaac's father. Peg had asked only a handful of times with Shiloh waving her hand in dismissal and saying, "He's not even worth thinking about. Trust me." Or, "I don't want to talk about it."

It was Peg who had accompanied Shiloh to the hospital. Peg who waited outside the delivery room. Peg who stayed on with Shiloh in her apartment so that their daughter could adjust to breast-feeding, and sleep deprivation. Peg who fixed meals, laundered clothes, helped change diapers, vacuumed, took out the garbage, bought groceries . . .

"I just . . . can't imagine," Peg had told Lyle over the

phone. "I don't know how she'll do it. All alone." He heard her begin to cry.

It is a helpless feeling when your own child, your *only* child, rejects your love and support, like a flower turning away from the sun. But Lyle understood then, as he did now, that this grown child must be left to make her own decisions, her own mistakes, and what he had always loved about Shiloh, after all, what he had always respected, was her strength, her independence.

"We'll come with you this Sunday," Peg said now, nodding her affirmation. "I can't wait."

"So, then, you don't want to come to church with us? At St. Olaf's?" Lyle asked quietly. "Everyone has been so happy to see you. You must know that. And think of Charlie."

Shiloh shook her head. "I have my own beliefs," she answered carefully, her mood darkening slightly, like a lightbulb flickering in a windowless room.

He did not push the matter, not quite understanding how her beliefs could be so radically different from—*better than?*—those of the church she had grown up attending, but he did as he had done his whole life when visited with confrontation by his daughter: he rose from his chair, kissed Shiloh on the forehead, said good night to Peg, and walked to his bedroom. Lyle had grown up in a family where he could scarcely recall his parents even so much as raising their voices, let alone openly disagreeing with each other, and he had no interest in fighting anyone, least of all his beloved daughter.

———

IN BED THAT NIGHT, HE STARED OUT THE WINDOW. EVERYTHING was where it always was: the boulevard maples and ash and cottonwoods and oaks, the rust-pocked cars of his neighbors, the red fire hydrant, the broken sidewalk bowed up by persistent tree roots . . . *How do you disagree with someone you love so fiercely?* he wondered. He felt something smoldering inside him; he did not like confrontation and yet, if Shiloh's church was the force taking her and Isaac away from them, he was already predisposed to disliking it.

Some time later, he heard Peg enter the bedroom. Heard her take off her clothes, don her nightgown, slip into her side of the bed. Her cold feet found his calves.

"Good lord, your feet are cold, woman," he said, "you're lucky I love you."

"It's your job to warm me up."

They were silent for a while.

"I wish I understood her," he said.

"You don't have to," Peg sighed, "you just have to love her."

"I do."

She patted his shoulder. "So then, grin and bear it."

"Bear what?"

"Holy-Rollers. Bible-thumpers. Fire-and-brimstoners. Whatever awaits us over there."

"Is *that* what she believes?"

"I'm going to sleep."

He turned toward her. "Peg. Is that what she believes?"

He could feel her gaze through the bedroom darkness. A train whistle dopplered toward them, and soon they could *feel* it trembling their bed, a Canadian Pacific maybe, or a Burlington Northern Santa Fe, shaking the small town where it drowsed—shuddering the china cabinets, quaking the curios and knickknacks nestled on dusty shelves, swaying the mirrors and framed photographs hanging from perilous Sheetrock nails, shivering soda cans in the refrigerators of the shotgun bungalows down by the tracks. At the only bar in town, the Railroader, Budweiser and Michelob and Miller High Life and Coors bottles would be vibrating and jitterbugging across the ancient and abused mahogany bar. It was a piercing sound that at once a person wanted to escape even as it was a reassurance, too, like the hand on a cradle, rocking back and forth, the train on its tracks, *ka-ka-ka-ka, ka-ka-ka-ka* . . . the metronomic rhythm of rural America after dark. Everything is going to be all right, the world is still spinning, the trains are still running, the sun will rise tomorrow, and so on.

"I don't care *what* she believes, Lyle. I really don't. I love her, and I love Isaac, and if she wants me to visit her church, I'll do that, happily. No sweat off my brow," she said, kissing him good night.

He turned back toward the window. There was a cat out there, slinking through the darkness, tail raised like a question mark.

(8)

SHILOH'S CHURCH, THE NONDENOMINATIONAL COULEE LANDS Covenant (or CLC), was located in a defunct movie theater outside La Crosse. The concessions stand that once hawked popcorn, soda, and Jujubes now offered free coffee and doughnuts. Congregants milled about the lobby, gathered in easy conversation. Younger children ran up and down the carpeted aisles of the former theater, while older kids hung out in the corners of the building, staring down at their phones. At ten thirty, Lyle heard what sounded like a rock and roll band kick into gear, and Shiloh led them in toward the music.

She wore white flats, a knee-length navy skirt, and a white blouse, a demure lipstick and light mascara on her face. Her hair was subtly curled, her cheeks lightly blushed.

Lyle thought she seemed happier than normal, more engaged with the world somehow.

There were no pews, just row upon row of battered upholstered seats, but the congregants didn't seem to care. Many stood swaying, clapping their hands to the music played by the small band up front. Lyle didn't recognize the song, which seemed to him some sort of ill-conceived rock, all achingly shrill vocals, with plaintive lyrics moving in and out of open worship. Lyle felt, in that moment, that there should be some sort of law against Christian rock music, with the grand exception of Norman Greenbaum's "Spirit in the Sky." Many folks sat in the old theater seats, some now and then glancing at their phones, or sipping coffee from stainless steel travel mugs. Lyle did not know what to do, how to act; he recognized not a soul. At St. Olaf's Lutheran Church, Mrs. Drummond played the organ as she seemed *always* to have done, all through Lyle's childhood and—who knew?—perhaps dating back to the Civil War. And once she began her assault on those keys and pedals, everyone knew to open their hymnals to the appointed page, accepting of their lack of musical ability. Hymns were not so much sung, Lyle thought, but rather *droned*. Only "Thine Is the Glory" had ever stirred something in him to the point that his voice rose much over his normal speaking volume.

But here, at Coulee Lands, the words to songs were projected up on the movie screen and everyone sang *loudly*. He glanced at Peg for moral support but her face was pressed gamely forward. She seemed to be singing along, even clapping her hands, though not necessarily in rhythm. Three songs were sung before the congregation finally sat down, some in attendance already showing a mirthful sheen of perspiration. Lyle checked his watch. About twenty minutes had elapsed. He noticed Isaac drawing on an offering envelope. He wanted to reach out, pull the boy close to him, but they were each in their own seats. So he hunkered down and waited for this to be over. He imagined himself in a foxhole, perhaps playing solitaire.

A young man walked casually to the "front" of the church, just below the movie screen. He wore a longish beard, new blue jeans made to look old, worn work boots, a flannel shirt open at the throat by two buttons, sleeves rolled up, and tattoos marking his forearms. He was tall, taller than Lyle, certainly, who noticed his own posture straightening to what would be its full six feet. The young man looked like the lead singer of a rock band, or maybe a construction worker, out for a beer.

Lyle watched the man intently. Watched him stand looking out at the rows of congregants. His eyes were exceedingly confident, and bright. Lyle peered down the aisle at Shiloh; a smile marked her face in a way he hadn't seen in months, maybe years. She shone back at this man standing before them. With a start, Lyle realized he must be the pastor of this flock.

He thought about that word just then, *flock*. Geese, he knew, flocked. Ducks flocked. Geese and ducks could also positively ruin the lawn of a park with their incessant shitting. He almost made himself chuckle, but steadied himself by studying the congregants. All their necks were stretched long, and slightly forward, toward this scruffy young pastor.

Lyle had never much had the inclination to follow. For decades, he'd gone to church but not reverently, more the way one visited the post office or a gas station, as routine. He cared not for politics; he'd lived long enough to watch every politician he once admired become an abject disappointment, if not a liar. And religion was not much better, in his book—and maybe worse, frankly—his respect and affection for Charlie set aside. So sitting there now, in that catawampus old theater chair, he shook his shoulders, puffed out his chest, and peered down at his shoes. Old gum polka-dotted the floor. He imagined the theater before it had become defunct, the teenagers who must have necked *right here,* the moviegoers chewing their popcorn, falling asleep, weeping, laughing, cringing in horror . . .

"Good morning," said the pastor finally, his voice easy and smooth, with just a hint of a Southern accent, like the last of a bottle of molasses creeping slowly out . . . Lyle felt himself somehow relaxing. He wanted to look up and meet this man's eyes, but kept his stare pointed down.

"Good morning!" the pastor said again, and Lyle could *hear* the smiles on the faces around the church, the smiles curving on the faces of his own family. The church rang with a chorus of *good mornings!*

"Good morning!" the pastor yelled again, and Lyle peeked up momentarily to see that the man was moving around the front of the church, arms raised up in the air like a triumphant coach celebrating a game-winning score.

"Let's begin with a prayer," the pastor said, and now Lyle did look up, for it was his custom since Peter's death *not* to pray, but to instead remain in the world, eyes open, watching others as they prayed. The pastor's thick head of brown hair was bowed down, and ahead of Lyle, rows of believers were leaning forward, hunching their shoulders, folding their hands in their laps, sealing their eyelids.

Lyle didn't listen to the prayer. He was busy people watching, absorbing the old theater. The aged burgundy velvet curtains on either side of the movie screen, water stained in amoebic swirls, accidental paisley. The tiny white lights on the aisle runners, some glowing, others burned out, like a less than reliable airport runway. No pulpit, per se, Lyle noticed—just a flimsy-looking lectern where the pastor's heavy Bible sat. The band's instruments arrayed casually, like teenagers loafing at a party: here an acoustic guitar, there a fiddle, an electric guitar and a bass, a few tambourines, the drums, a trim little Casio keyboard . . . He watched an older woman, out near the front and in the aisle, sitting in her wheelchair, mumbling quietly, and rocking to and fro . . . A young woman, lightly jangling the half dozen earrings looped on one ear . . . A man about Lyle's age, sneezing into a handkerchief with the name *Royal* embroidered on white cloth in blue stitching . . . A

young girl with two blond pigtails, picking her nose . . .
A boy, his face pinched so tight in concentration, his skin
was the color of a beet . . . An irregular dusting of dan-
druff across an old man's shoulder . . . Children with fists
full of crayons, busily coloring . . . Mothers, surreptitiously
scanning cell phones . . . Fidget spinners spinning between
fingers . . . And a few in the flock close to tears, it seemed,
and already, so early in the service . . .

When Lyle finally turned to look at those closest to
him, Peg and Shiloh stood with their eyes closed, relaxed
expressions on their faces. And then there was Isaac, standing on the far side of Shiloh, looking back at him, grinning
impishly, and waving. Lyle waved back, then crossed his
eyes and stuck out his tongue. He didn't think God would
take issue with the benign misbehavior between a grandfather and his grandson.

The service lasted almost three hours. Lyle thought
back to watching *Ben-Hur* in the theater and how there
used to be an intermission during especially long movies.
He knew his weary prostate would have welcomed a half-
time of sorts, because at the final *amen* he rushed to the
men's room and stood at the urinal for what felt like minutes. Then he washed his hands and found his family in
the "narthex" (really, the old lobby of the theater), huddled
together around the pastor. He seemed to be at the finale
of an elaborate magic trick, because as Lyle approached,
Peg and Shiloh applauded while Isaac gave the man an
enthusiastic high five.

"You must be Shiloh's father," the pastor said, extending a hand. "I'm Pastor Steven. Pleased to meet you."

Lyle noticed he wore a chunky white plastic watch, several bracelets of silver, and not a few bands of colorful woven fabric. "That's right," he said, shaking hands, "Lyle Hovde, and this is my wife, Peg."

"Oh, we've already met," Peg said happily. "That was a marvelous sermon, Pastor Steven. Just marvelous. You're an incredible preacher, and for such a young man, too." Lyle could see that she was being sincere.

Shiloh leaned her weight onto the pastor's right shoulder, and he dipped his head to rest on hers.

Lyle frowned.

"You must practice your sermons," Peg continued. "Or maybe you write them down? I didn't see you reading any notes, though . . ."

"I'm going to say hello to some friends, if you'll excuse me," Shiloh said. And then she was off, mingling with a group of people her own age, laughing out loud, pointing at the screens of their phones, scribbling down notes, lifting babies to hips or bouncing babies in crooked arms. *She's got a community here,* Lyle thought. *Not just two old parents and maybe Hoot, Charlie, or Otis and Mabel stopping by.*

"No, ma'am, no practicing whatsoever. It's all in here." He tapped his breastbone. "And up in here." Now he touched his forehead. "I find that a clergyperson who resorts to notes or writes everything down isn't keeping himself or his congregation on their toes. In this church, everything is in God's hands. There's no safety net, here, no air bags. It's all real, it's all really happening. And I'm merely a vessel, if you like, or maybe a conduit."

Isaac had scooted close to Lyle, looped an arm around one of his legs. Lyle glanced down and rubbed the boy's head.

"That's a talented young man, there," Steven said, and smiled at the boy approvingly, giving him a little wink.

"He sure is," said Peg. "We're so proud of him. And his mother, too."

"Talented?" asked Lyle.

Steven looked at Lyle with a focus and intensity Lyle hadn't felt in many, many years, as if this young pastor were looking through him, or past him, scrutinizing every molecule of his being, every second of his life, every pore on his skin.

"Yes," Steven said, "his mother and I believe he's a healer."

"A healer?" Peg repeated. "Isaac?"

"Heal *who*?" Lyle said. "He's just a boy. Five years old."

"I don't believe that much matters to the Lord," Steven said. "Who can say why He dwells in one person and not the other, why He shines a light on this child, and allows other children to malinger, or perish. But I've seen it, haven't I, Isaac?"

The little boy looked up at his grandfather, nodded gingerly, then turned his face to the carpeting below.

"Now, if you'll pardon me, I want to be sure to welcome

some of our other guests this morning," Steven said, shaking their hands once more, before kneeling down beside Isaac and making the sign of the cross on the little boy's forehead, and then touching his blond head, as he straightened up to amble off in the direction of Shiloh and her friends.

Lyle stared at Peg, who was slow to meet his eyes.

"Grandpa?" Isaac asked. "May I have a doughnut?"

Lyle rooted around in his wallet for a dollar bill, and handed it to the boy. "And bring me back the change," he said, with an edge in his voice more forceful than he'd intended. He knew the change would amount to fifty cents or less, more than he cared to donate to this church on this day.

When the boy was out of earshot, Lyle glanced around and said to Peg, "Well, now. Holy-Rollers I was maybe prepared for. But it seems our daughter has joined a cult."

She hit his arm gently with her hand. "I'm sure it's not a cult," she whispered.

"Are you? That man just said your five-year-old grandson is a godda—a *healer*. Whatever that means."

Shiloh moved toward them now, cradling her own elbows, and smiling, her skin glowing.

"Well, dear," Peg began, "your father and I were thinking about heading home. Are you about ready?"

"No," Shiloh said, "but Pastor Steven can give me and Isaac a ride home later today."

"Are you sure? We could take Isaac," Peg offered. Lyle thought he noted a hint of desperation in her tone.

"He's fine here," Shiloh said. "There will be other kids for him to play with."

At the old concessions stand, Isaac was talking to a girl with long curly red hair and pale skin. She wore thick glasses, and peered up at Isaac as if he were a beloved older brother, or a teacher perhaps. He seemed to be offering her a bite of his doughnut, which she gladly accepted.

"It's no trouble," Peg continued. "Honest. We'll feed him lunch and dinner. Something healthy, I promise. Then you can relax here with your friends."

"I *am* relaxed, Mom," Shiloh said. "And he's fine here. In fact, later today we might look at an apartment together."

"Together?" Lyle asked. "You mean, you and Isaac?"

"And Steven," Shiloh said. "Anyway, thanks for coming. It means the world to me. We'll see you tonight."

She kissed them both on the cheek and then turned to find her friends, just as she might have ten, fifteen years before.

Lyle and Peg began slowly moving toward the doors, past the concession stand, their grandson now nowhere in sight, and it felt as if they were exiting the theater after watching a very sad movie on a rainy Sunday afternoon. But it was not raining. Outside, the parking lot was warm and bright, the sun reflecting blindingly off the many dozens of windshields. Lyle found himself reaching for Peg's hand, and they walked to the car this way, the way old people shuffle through a crowded mall or stadium. The future, it seemed, was murkier than they had supposed just three hours before.

Folding slowly into the car, they just sat there a moment, simply staring forward.

"A healer?" Peg said.

"I don't know," Lyle answered. "I mean—well, you know how *I* feel."

"I think you should talk to Charlie. See if he knows anything about this place, this Pastor Steven."

"Ask *our* pastor to spy on *her* pastor?"

"I'm serious, Lyle."

Lyle exhaled. "Me too. I'm not just serious, in fact— I'm . . . I'm a little concerned. Everybody in that church had kind of a glazed-over look to their eyes."

"What do we do?" she asked.

"I don't know," Lyle replied.

He started the car, pointed it south, and they drove on in silence, both of their windows rolled down as the countryside and the Mississippi flowed on.

When they arrived home, Peg hurried into some old clothes and sneakers and was soon in their little backyard garden, vigorously working the soil with a hoe she kept slamming into the earth. Lyle, not knowing quite what to do with himself, just lay down on their bed. Their house so very quiet without Isaac. The boy was almost always talking or singing: while he sat drawing at their kitchen table; building forts all cobbled together from living room furniture and various blankets; riding his bicycle; leafing through the pages of Lyle's *Encyclopedia Britannica* (1985, the year they adopted Shiloh); or whittling a scrap of wood in Lyle's garage workshop space . . . There was always that happy drone in the background, high-pitched but low in volume, as if a playground was just down the street. Lyle would be in the bathroom, shaving, and hear the little boy, chirping on and on to Peg about something he'd seen or overheard in town, some fragment of a song heard on the radio, *So hoist up the John B's sail! See how the main sail sets. Call for the Captain ashore. Let me go home!*

Lyle stood, changed out of his church clothes into blue jeans and an old gray T-shirt, walked slowly out to the garden. Now Peg was pulling weeds, her dirty fists full of dandelions, Queen Anne's lace, ragweed, and quack grass. Little bands of mud streaked her face where the sweat and dirt had commingled. He stood at the diminutive garden fence, nothing more than a three-foot-high section of chicken wire and some two-by-four posts. Enough to thwart the groundhogs and rabbits. Peg was on her knees, and Lyle could see that she was panting, her chest heaving.

"Maybe we need to . . . ," Lyle began. "I don't know. Take it easy on her. Not get too excited."

Peg nodded, until her chin dropped to her chest. She exhaled loudly. "You're right," she said. "But we should keep an eye on her, too. Maybe ask a few questions."

"Do you need a hand?" he asked.

"I love you," she responded.

"I love you, too," he said.

He brought a leg over the fence, then the other, and knelt down beside her, their hands soon in the soil together, and they passed a few hours that way, until it was time to think about dinner. And then they waited in the kitchen for their daughter and grandson to arrive home.

SUMMER

(9)

LYLE AND PEG'S HOUSE HAD NO AIR-CONDITIONING, AND ON the first truly hot day of early summer, Lyle could not sleep. For hours, he rolled back and forth on his side of the bed, like a log spinning in water. He turned his bedside lamp on, and read one of his favorite books, John McPhee's *The Control of Nature*. Then turned the lamp off. Went to the bathroom. Drank a glass of water. Padded back to bed. Counted sheep. Listened hard for any train sounds—none. Turned the lamp back on, and worked a Sudoku puzzle.

Finally, he extinguished the lamp, and walked to the kitchen. Poured himself a glass of milk, drank it thirstily, then poured another and walked onto the small front porch and took a seat on their swinging bench.

The small town moved not at all. No traffic. No trains.

No dog walkers. Too early in the year for much in the way of fireflies or cicadas. Not even any bats twirling and spinning through the night. The leaves on the boulevard trees did not stir or tremble. There was no wind at all.

Was Lyle hungry? Maybe. In the kitchen he cracked the refrigerator and squinted into that white light. Cheese? No, not cheese. Salami? Maybe an apple? Ice cream? Yes, ice cream would do the trick—only, after opening the freezer, he found all of a spoonful's worth of mint chocolate chip, almost worse than no ice cream at all. Peg was infamous for this. Leaving a thimbleful of milk in the carton or a single Oreo in an otherwise abandoned box, a few little puzzle pieces and tiny triangles and some corn dust in a plastic bag once full of tortilla chips . . .

He ate the spoonful of ice cream and threw the carton away then wandered the small kitchen with the cold spoon still in his mouth. That felt nice, the cold metal against his tongue. Opening a cupboard, he grabbed a jar of peanut butter and began slowly eating spoonful after spoonful as he stared out the windows into the dark.

"Grandpa?"

Lyle was so startled he almost dropped the jar. There was Isaac, yawning, in his little-boy underwear.

"Hey, tiger."

"You used the same spoon."

"What?"

"For the ice cream *and* the peanut butter. I saw you."

"Oh. You're right."

Isaac shambled over to Lyle, and hugged him around the waist.

"It's too hot, Grandpa," he complained, drowsily.

"I know."

"Can we watch TV?"

"No, the TV'll just make it harder to fall asleep again. But tell you what, we *could* take a drive."

"To where?"

"I don't know," said Lyle. "A gas station. Maybe get some Eskimo pies. Or McDonald's. Maybe there's a McDonald's open somewhere."

"La Crosse has a McDonald's," the boy put in excitedly.

"All right. Get some clothes on, let's go for a drive."

"Should we tell Mom? Or Grandma?"

"Nah, we don't want to wake them up."

"Maybe we should leave a note."

"*That's* probably a pretty good idea, buddy. You get dressed and I'll write out our note."

"Okay."

"Wait a second, do me a favor and go pee first. It's a little bit of a drive and we don't want any accidents, do we?"

"Okay, Grandpa."

The boy hurried into the bathroom. Lyle leaned on the kitchen counter and, scribbling on a sheet of paper, wrote: *Isaac and I went out for ice cream. Back soon. Love, Lyle.* He dated the note, *After midnight*, which reminded him of the JJ Cale song, a favorite tune from another time in his life altogether.

THEY WOUND THEIR WAY ALONG THE RIVER ROAD, RUNNING the air conditioner on high.

"Mom says we're moving to La Crosse before the school year starts up," Isaac offered from his booster seat in the back.

Lyle exhaled. "Is that right?"

The boy nodded.

"Well," Lyle continued, "how do you feel about that? Are you excited?"

Isaac shrugged. "I like it with you and Grandma. I like it when we're all together. I like the way your house smells."

"And we love having you stay with us, buddy," Lyle said. "Hey, maybe you can show me where you're gonna live."

"All I can remember is that Mom said it was called a duplex, and the neighbors had a bunch of little motorcycles in the driveway."

Lyle looked at the boy in the rearview mirror.

"Little motorcycles?"

Isaac nodded. "Yeah, and they were all dirty and stuff."

The McDonald's was open 24/7, a concept that still unnerved Lyle—a business that may be open for the next hundred years, operating constantly. They pulled into the drive-through and ordered two strawberry milk shakes.

Lyle drove toward the Coulee Lands Covenant and on a hunch asked, "Was your new house somewhere around here?"

"I don't know," Isaac said. "It wasn't dark the last time I saw it. But I think so."

They cruised the night streets slowly, the milk shakes cold in their hands, the air conditioner blasting, the radio's volume low—Van Morrison's "Sweet Thing"—*I shall drive my chariot down your streets and cry . . .* Finally, they turned onto a cul-de-sac of newer duplexes and beige-colored ranches, and Isaac sat up in the backseat. "Wait." He peered out the window, then pointed. "I think it's that one."

Lyle rolled down the window and let the humid night air flow in, thick as swamp water. There were no trees on the boulevards or in the yards, a detail Lyle always connected to poverty. Or disregard. Or impermanence. He stared at the building, its vinyl siding, its unmown lawn, its venetian blinds bent askew in the darkened windows.

"Mom says it's got air-conditioning," Isaac said.

The neighboring driveway held four dirt bikes, caked in mud, and bent beer cans littered the grass. The air held the tang of lighter fluid and charcoal; in a backyard, voices were quietly laughing and when an unseen dog began barking, a voice suddenly boomed, "Shut up." Farther down the street was a pickup truck with oversized tires and a Confederate flag bumper sticker advising, FEAR THIS.

They were quiet for a while, just the radio . . . *And I will never, ever, ever, ever grow so old again . . .* Isaac sucking at the pink milk shake, moonlight catching the broken glass littering the cul-de-sac like a thousand rough diamonds scattered across a dark velveteen gown. Lyle glanced to the other side of the street where someone was smoking a cigarette in the darkness, just a little orange nub of light strobing very slowly on and off. Lyle rolled up the window and they began the journey home.

"Pastor Steven seems like a nice guy," Lyle said, "huh?"

Isaac shrugged his little shoulders.

"He told me and your grandma that you can heal people?"

Isaac looked out the window at passing lights.

"Buddy, what does that mean?"

"I don't know, Grandpa."

Lyle looked at him in the mirror. The boy's eyes were closed.

"Isaac?"

"Good night, Grandpa."

"Isaac. Talk to me. I'm your grandpa. You can tell me anything. I promise."

Lyle pulled the car into the abandoned parking lot of a derelict lumberyard. He turned in his seat. The boy was completely quiet.

"You know how I know you're not sleeping?"

The boy said nothing, his eyes clenched shut.

"'Cause you've got a death grip on that milk shake, for one, and for two, when you actually sleep, your mouth hangs open, just like your mother. Now please talk to me."

The boy opened his eyes and seemed to distractedly suck at the dregs of his milk shake.

"So, why do they think you're a healer?"

"I don't know, Grandpa. Once, there was a cardinal

that hit our kitchen window and we thought it was dead. There were even flies on it. But before Mom could throw it in the garbage can, I touched it, and it flew off."

All right, Lyle thought, *that doesn't necessarily mean anything. The bird could've been stunned.* "What about people though, Isaac? Can you really cure a person?"

With the plastic straw pursed tight between his lips, the boy shrugged. "That's what Mom says."

"And why does she believe that, buddy?"

"Because I guess I've helped some people."

"Which people, Isaac?"

The boy shrugged. "They say something to Pastor Steven. Then Pastor Steven takes me to their house. Normally there's a bunch of people there, and everyone is praying. Then they tell Pastor Steven where it hurts, and he tells me, and I put my hands wherever they told me to, and the people felt better, afterward. It's only happened a few times. Grandpa?"

"Yeah, buddy?"

"I don't want to talk about this."

Lyle stared through the darkness at his grandson, then reached back to rub his little-boy kneecap.

"That's fine," he said. "We should be heading back home, anyway."

"Grandpa?"

"Yes, dear?"

"I have to pee."

"Again?"

"I'm sorry."

"No, it's okay, it's just—" He had no interest in hurting the boy's feelings. "Hold on, I'll get out, too." He realized his own bladder was full. They made their way into a bank of deep shadows and darkness and then there was just the sound of their urine arcing out and dribbling through the tall grass.

The boy fell asleep on the drive back home, and in their driveway Lyle picked him up and held him in his arms, gently shutting the car door before carrying him into the house and down the stairs where he laid the boy in his bed, and brushed hair away from his eyes and leaned down and kissed him on the forehead and then, taking the stairs quietly, he moved through the dark house back into the kitchen, crumpled the note into a paper ball and, finally exhausted, retreated to his bedroom, where he fell promptly asleep.

(10)

IN THE MORNING, THE HOUSE SMELLED OF PANCAKES AND BA-con, coffee and scrambled eggs. Peg and Shiloh were talking, laughing lightly in the kitchen.

"Morning," Lyle said, pouring himself a mug, and kissing his daughter on the cheek. "Where's Isaac?"

"Still sleeping," said Shiloh. "I don't think anyone slept well last night."

From the basement staircase came the sound of little feet and then Isaac burst into the kitchen, leaping directly into Lyle's lap.

"Hungry?" Peg asked.

He nodded.

"How many pancakes can you eat?"

"Maybe three," he said. The boy snuggled against

Lyle, warm as his morning bedsheets, his hair wild and tangled.

Shiloh smiled at them. "Look at you two. Thick as thieves."

The boy nodded. "*We* went out for milk shakes last night. And I showed Grandpa our new house."

Peg set a plate of food and a small glass of orange juice in front of Isaac, glanced quickly at Lyle, and wiped her hands on her apron.

The kitchen was quiet for several moments as the boy tucked into his breakfast.

Shiloh looked at Lyle darkly, cleared her throat. "And whose idea was that?"

"Grandpa's," the boy said around a mouthful of pancakes, butter, and maple syrup.

The kitchen was uncomfortably quiet again. Just the little boy's chewing and the soft sizzle of more pancakes browning on the stove. Far down the tracks a train whistled. Peg jostled some dishes in the sink, but Lyle knew she wasn't washing them, not really. He felt Shiloh staring at him. This was not the way he liked to start a day, with conflict; it was one of his least favorite things, indeed.

"Look, you could stay *right* here," Lyle offered helpfully. "Hell, *I'll* drive you to work if you'd like." He could hear the despair in his own voice, and knew that rationalizing his argument would only make him sound more despondent, drive Shiloh more surely away from him. "The schools are great here. They're smaller. Isaac will get all the attention in the world. And we could help. Drop him off and pick him up. You could save money."

"You've got it all figured out for us, huh, Dad," she said flatly.

"I'm sorry about the air-conditioning, too. I'm going to call Hoot and see if we can fix that right away. Your mom and I should have done it years ago."

"It's not about the air-conditioning, Dad, please! I just . . . I can't believe you were out spying on our new house. It's like . . . all you had to do was ask."

She stood from the table. "Anyway, Steven's going to help me buy a car today. He should be here in about an hour. So . . . I'm going to take a shower."

Lyle touched Isaac's head, rubbed his left earlobe between his fingers. Now Peg really rattled some pots in the sink. Then she shut off the stove and walked toward their bedroom.

"Is Grandma angry?" Isaac asked. "Is Mom angry, too?"

Lyle stood, poured more coffee into the mug. "Of course not, honey." On the griddle, four pancakes sat, their color more black by now than brown.

STEVEN PULLED INTO THEIR DRIVEWAY AT THE WHEEL OF A VIN-tage GMC truck—late '70s or early '80s—all boxy angles and shiny chrome. There wasn't a pinhead of rust on its body anywhere and the paint scheme looked like ribbon candy, shining turquoise and white.

Lyle stood from their front porch and walked out to greet the pastor. "Beautiful truck," he admitted. "What was this, your dad's? An uncle's?"

"No," said Steven. "I bought her used when I was sixteen. Saved all my money from doing chores for a few years. Been plugging away at her ever since. Takes my mind away from work. And I find it's a good way to pull people in, make them feel comfortable. For some folks, it's a dog. Others, I suppose, maybe a book. But people always want to ask questions about old cars and trucks." He paused to smile. "Like you."

Lyle blushed, felt a twinge of embarrassment. His own truck was parked in the garage and not much newer in vintage than Steven's, though fairly well rusted. The cab was like a solarium for moths and flies, all dust, woodchips, and dirt. He'd been raised to take pride in his possessions, to take care of them, and here was this young man, maybe not yet thirty, who had refurbished something old, making it new again . . . Lyle decided to press forward.

"Been in La Crosse long?"

"No, sir. About eight months."

"And before that?"

"Oh, all over the place. Feels like every year, year and a half, I'm being called somewhere new. Recruited to help seed and grow a church. In the past five years I've lived in Oregon, Idaho, Missouri, Minnesota, and now, Wisconsin. You know what they say, 'A rolling stone' . . ."

Lyle wanted to ask what he was doing with his daughter and grandson but instead he studied his old work boots.

"Sir," Steven began, "I just want you to know that Shiloh and I are just going to be roommates. Separate bedrooms. I'm a pastor, sir. I can't be living in sin. This is just to help us, help her to get on her feet in La Crosse. And, as you know, pastors don't get paid much . . . But I am interested in her, sir. And of course, Isaac, too. That boy . . ."

"I'll tell you what, I've only seen it one other time, and never in my own congregation. Out in Oregon, there was an old man who folks'd visit if they felt infirm. I saw him heal people. Saw him destroy a tumor in a girl's belly just by breathing on it. Saw him pray over a stillborn baby boy and revive it; the breath of God went right through him and into that baby's lungs and he began to cry and turned from blue to white to pink just like that." He smiled, big and sincere.

"And you've seen Isaac do that kind of thing?" Lyle asked. "Heal people?"

"Yes, sir, I have. Five times. The first time, well . . . I didn't believe my eyes. I'm ashamed of that now, truth be told. But an old woman had been found out behind the church, all possessed like, and shaking—"

"Wait a minute, *possessed*?"

"That's right. I think a demon had taken possession of her."

"A demon?"

"Or an evil spirit. But I saw it. Saw her writhing there, in the snow, speaking in tongues, her eyes all rolled back in her skull. And Shiloh had gone to her and was trying to comfort her, and by and by Isaac came to them, and I saw him, saw him reach right down and just as simple as that, coax that demon away and bring her back to normal. I remember thinking how, because he's such a sweet little boy, he might have been afraid. Heck, I was afraid. But he was just . . . He was calm. Lyle, he was serene. I've never seen that kind of power in a child before."

"And the other times?"

"Well, sir, if a member of the church reached out to me with a health concern, and if it was a serious enough malady, why yes, Isaac and I would visit their house and pray over them, and Isaac did lay hands on three different congregants, and in each instance, sir, I do believe he healed them. Also, sir, he healed me."

"He did?"

"See, for years now I've been afflicted by these blinding migraines. Like, blinding. So painful that I'd have to hide in a darkened room. So debilitating that there were not a few Sundays I couldn't very well preach, or, if I could struggle through, I certainly couldn't join in fellowship afterward, couldn't pray with folks or shoot basketball with the youth or anything like that. And so, I asked Shiloh one night if she and Isaac could pray for me, if we could hold hands and pray, and sir, I've never felt the presence of God like that before. I could feel it—*feel Him*—just surging, *surging right through me,* up my fingers to my arms and straightaway to my brain, and that migraine just washed away. Haven't had another one since. And that's the truth."

"Huh," Lyle said, looking at his feet.

In a world so often carefully curated on computers and phones and in media, so cultivated and perfected, the sincerity of a man like Steven was stupefying, as if he'd just pinged a stone off Lyle's forehead using a leather sling.

Lyle took a moment more to gather himself and process this revelation. "So, does your church endorse that sort of thing?" Lyle asked. "I'm confused."

"Well, sir, that's a difficult one to answer. My church certainly believes in prayer, the power of prayer. Prayer is how we talk to God, how we change the world, and support other Christians. And yes, we believe the Lord resides in chosen people. That said, we don't advertise this, and we're certainly not going to exploit Isaac or anything like that, no sir. But I'll tell you this: neither will I stand in the way of the Lord's light and make a shadow. No sir." He peered over Lyle's shoulder. "Good morning!"

Shiloh bounded out the front door, past Lyle and Steven, and let herself into the truck.

"Isn't Isaac coming with you?" Lyle asked.

She shrugged. "He's happy here. He and Mom are going to bake together, I think. Anyway, it might be easier without him this time."

Steven reached out to shake Lyle's hand. "Have a blessed day," he said cheerfully.

"Yeah, will do."

The truck pulled away and Shiloh neither looked back nor waved. Lyle stood there a moment before walking back inside.

Isaac stood on a low stool so that his chest was level with the Formica counter, Peg standing protectively just behind him. Flour dusted the floor. And sugar. Isaac turned to smile at Lyle and there was flour in his hair, on his cheeks and clothes. Peg whispered directions into the boy's ear, and he reached here for chocolate chips, or there for a hand blender.

"I thought he wasn't supposed to have cookies," Lyle said.

"These are *organic* cookies," said Peg. "We're calling them magic cookies. Now, tell him, 'Go away, Grandpa.'" Peg had thawed a bit, Lyle noticed, but she still maintained an edge; her smiles were directed at the boy, not at Lyle.

"Go away, Grandpa," the boy cheerfully parroted.

But Lyle did not want to go away. He wanted to stay there, forever, fixed to that point in time and space, that doorway, where he leaned, watching his wife of some forty years, and this miracle of a grandson, standing there in the late-morning light, all the smells of breakfast still there, in this house that he so loved, near those trains that ran through his days, *clickety-clack, clickety-clack*, and the barges, slow-moving up the wide, brown river, and the motorcyclists, barreling down the River Road, and the apples, every day plumping up a little more, steadily bending their boughs, and his friend Hoot puttering idly beneath the hoods of his twin broke-down Mustangs . . .

He did not want to leave this moment in time, not at all, and so he closed his eyes and inhaled the kitchen smells, and touched the door frame, and felt his feet in his boots, right down to his toes, and then exhaled, and had he been a religious man, he might have said just then, *Amen.* But instead, he opened his eyes and there was Peg, turning at the waist to regard him.

"Are you all right?" she asked.

"Yes," he said. He nodded his head. "You bet. Although, maybe we should talk later tonight." He eyed the boy.

———

THEY LAY IN BED, LISTENING TO RAIN RUN DOWN THE ROOF, then stream into the gutters and matriculate downhill toward the river. It was a gentle rain, slow and steady enough that Lyle could hear individual droplets bouncing off the leaves outside. He was happy for it, for the rain; it had broken the heat and there was now a welcome coolness to the air. Still, they would install that air-conditioning next week, for sure, before the oppressive, late-summer warmth really took hold.

"So, what are you saying? Are you saying he can heal people?" Peg said, propping herself on an elbow. "How can that even be, Lyle? He's just a boy. Just a little boy."

The Lord works in mysterious ways, Lyle might have said, but then caught himself. "You want to know what I think?"

They were speaking in whispers, in their own bed-room, the door closed.

"Yes, Lyle, I do. I do want to know what you think."

"I think these Holy-Rollers get something in their head and they convince themselves of it. I don't think Isaac cured this goofball's migraines any more than I could go out there and stop the rain. I think Steven *wants* to believe and so he convinced himself . . . and it probably doesn't hurt that he's taken a shine to our daughter, too."

"Should we be concerned?"

He sighed. "I have no idea."

"*I'm* a little concerned."

"Me too," Lyle said. "Me too."

(11)

THERE WERE MANY VARIETALS OF APPLE IN THE OLD ORCHARD:
Cortlands and Honeycrisp, Gala and Pink Lady, Zestar
and Granny Smith, Golden Delicious and a dozen or more
strange trees, wild varietals, that sometimes produced
fruit, and other years seemed to forget to, or didn't want to.
One theory was that those wild apple trees were naturally
programmed to refuse to yield a crop to keep their insect
enemies guessing. Anyway, it kept Lyle and Otis guessing,
too. The wild apples were imperfect, ephemeral, difficult
to store and transport, challenging to sell, but Lyle and
Otis loved those trees all the more for their individuality.
Some of the wild apples were thin skinned and quick to
bruise. Some were simply not good; they might be aggres-
sively sour, dry and mealy, or about as exciting as chewing
a wad of paper. Some of the apples were mushy fleshed, but

gave good juice for cider. Others provided bizarre tastes or bright, puckering acidity.

The orchard provided both men with rewarding and varied work. This one firm thing they had toward the end of their years. Some mornings Lyle would knock on their front door and enter to find the old couple bickering about a missing TV controller, or an overdue bill buried somewhere beneath a pile of newspapers. And Otis would eventually peck Mabel on her forehead, and the two men would drive together in Lyle's truck out to the orchard, Otis leaving the truck at the gate to open the orchard, and Lyle pulling through the gate and inside the fenced acreage.

Then their day commenced. Yes, there were a final few slugs of coffee as they lingered another minute in the warm cab, listening to the morning news, but then the truck doors were slammed shut, stiff backs stretched and rusty, herky-jerky old-man calisthenics performed, and off they trod into the orchard, their lunch boxes and thermoses left inside the truck and before them, an orchard decorated all in fog and fleeting birds, low-flying moths and butterflies.

Their chores were dictated by the passage of summer. Mowing, raking, the spraying of insecticides. Sometimes they busied themselves with repairs of the fence. And, too, Otis was always creating more work for them, an odd impulse for a man over eighty years old. A few years back he decided that a patch of blueberries would make the orchard more diversified; then came a couple of rows of strawberries, and a half acre of raspberries.

Lyle loved blueberries. Blueberries in his oatmeal, blueberries in his pancakes. Baked in muffins or in breads. Sprinkled on a salad, or cupped in his hand, and eaten by the mouthful. Even on top of a dish of ice cream, perhaps with maple syrup drizzled over the works. He hoarded blueberries in his freezer by the gallon-sized plastic bag. But he did not relish picking blueberries. His fingers were too thick, and in recent years he seemed to have lost some sensitivity in his fingertips. Peg liked to joke that if a person dropped one thin dime on the sidewalk, Lyle might spend a day trying to pick it up. This was a commentary not only on his lack of nimbleness but also on his deep-seated, Scandinavian frugality.

Not to mention the bending. Even protected by knee pads and a thick blanket to boot, Lyle's knees ached, *throbbed*, and his shoulders tensed and bunched. But he had not been raised to complain. So he picked the berries, picked the berries, picked the berries, and ate as he went along, peeking to see whether or not Otis might object to this form of stealing. But for his part, Otis's lips and indeed his chin were stained blue, too.

"How's that grandson of yours?" Otis asked.

"Starting kindergarten this fall."

"That so? Here in town, then?"

"No," Lyle said. "He and Shiloh are moving to La Crosse. They got a little place down there."

Otis stopped his picking and peered at Lyle, the dark skins of several blueberries lodged between his long, crooked teeth. He hooked an arthritic finger into his mouth and began using a fingernail for a toothpick. The sun was behind his head and Lyle could see the errant hairs fuzzing out from his jug ears.

"That right?"

"Shiloh wants to be close to their church," Lyle said, turning his attention back to the blueberries. He had no intention of wading into her relationship with Steven, though he was certainly curious as to what Otis thought about religion, and the finer points of so-called prayer healing. For all their years of working together, this was a subject they had never touched on.

"I never understood organized religion," Otis said at length. "Be a good person. Don't hurt other folks. Don't cheat. Don't be greedy. That seems pretty straightforward to me. I don't need a goddamn guidebook to stay on the straight and narrow. Or a set of stones engraved by lightning. Or some heavenly reward. I don't need a particular day of the week set aside. *All* of our days are important, every last one. You get older, that comes into tighter and tighter focus."

Now Lyle raised up, felt his spine straighten and unbow, felt the sun on his face. "You think there's anything else, Otis, after we've . . . after this."

Otis tossed a few blueberries into his mouth.

"Worm food. That's what comes next. A tasty compost for the grass above, and the trees. Isn't that what old Walt Whitman tells us? That we're both special and not special. No more special than those robins over there, or the damned field mice. We're just another ugly organism, bound to burn ourselves out eventually. Less grandeurous than the dinosaurs, I'd say. I'd like to see what or who is going to follow us, but I'll be long gone."

"No heaven or hell, then?"

"And what about this?" Otis asked, raising his arms to indicate the orchard. "Isn't this heavenly? Look—there's the moon, for cripes' sake. No. No heaven or hell. Just this. Right here. Just these damn blueberries. Thousands of ripe blueberries we have to pick and then figure out how to sell to somebody. Heaven."

Lyle paused, continued unsteadily, "I don't know, Otis. Doesn't seem like such a bad thing, to be reunited with my parents again. My aunts and uncles." He stood quietly. Felt the juice of the berries on his fingers, their sugar. Felt the mud drying on his hands, the morning dew seeping through the leather of his boots and into the warm cotton of his socks. He thought of his son, his lost boy. Suddenly he could not remember what he was doing, there on his knees in the long shadows of midmorning. Lyle did not believe in heaven, but there were times when he desperately wanted to.

"I understand," Otis said. "A day doesn't pass I don't wonder which one of us is going to go first, me or Mabel. I hope like hell it's me. That old bird drives me bonkers, but I can't imagine life without her, either."

"But you don't believe in heaven?"

"No," Otis said, turning back to his picking. "Maybe it's a half century spent in academia. A half century teaching kids horticulture. But I don't believe in things that can't be proven. I don't buy lottery tickets, either. I believe in odds, mathematics, facts, time."

The orchard was very quiet.

"Or," said Otis, "I don't know, Lyle. What do you want me to say? Okay. I believe in heaven. We're all going to heaven. The Big Rock Candy Mountain. Valhalla, Vaikuntha, Elysium . . . I'm a believer, yes sir. Sign me up."

(12)

EARLY ONE EVENING THE TELEPHONE RANG. LYLE ANSWERED, expecting a telemarketer, yet another political survey.

"I need you, buddy," Hoot said, his voice unsteady. "Right now."

Lyle didn't ask any questions, just said, "I'll be right there."

On the drive to the hospital, Hoot writhed on the bench seat of Lyle's truck. Writhed like his clothes were full of fire, full of hot coals, his breath ragged and punctuated by coughs.

"I ain't breathing right," he said. "Can't catch my breath."

Hoot was admitted straightaway to the ER, and Lyle sat in the waiting room, too nervous to read the stale magazines arrayed on the network of coffee tables. Finally he just stood, and paced. Paced and paced. An hour dragged by, then another. The long days of early summer were upon them, sunsets arriving later and later, but now, the sun did set, and the evening was soft and purple against the bright white lights of the hospital.

Eventually, a nurse approached Lyle, and invited him back to the ER, where Hoot lay in a bed, IVs plugged into his skinny arms, and two breathing tubes in his nostrils. He grimaced when Lyle came to his side.

"Remember when they told me not to worry?" Hoot asked. "That it was just pneumonia? Well, they were wrong."

"I don't understand," Lyle said.

"They took X-rays," Hoot said. "I've seen the scans. It's everywhere, they say."

"What is?" Lyle asked, though he already knew the answer.

"Cancer, buddy. The X-rays looked like someone spilled a bag of M&M's in my chest. Only all one shitty color. A bunch of nasty little white tumors everywhere. The doctor even apologized to me. Apologized for calling it pneumonia before. He was pretty broke up about it, I could see that. Just a young guy."

Lyle sat down beside his friend. "Can they treat it?" he asked.

Hoot coughed. "You and I ain't doctors, Lyle, but we both know how that story'll end."

"No, I don't, Hoot. I know you're a goddamned diehard. And I wouldn't bet against you."

"I thought about it, amigo. But the truth is, I'm all that's left. No wife. No kids. The only people who will know I'm gone are you and your family. My sister, sure, but she's got her own life, her own distractions. Maybe my ex-wife will come up for the funeral."

Lyle put his head in his hands. "Well, what about us? We want you around. We want you to fight."

"I ain't sure I see the point of fighting if I'm going to get beat in the end anyway. We're talking chemo. I don't know. I'll probably try a few rounds of it, I guess, see how it makes me feel. But I think I just need to put my life in order. Hey, there's good news, though."

Lyle looked up at his friend. "What's that?"

Hoot smiled darkly. "No need to quit smoking."

———◆———

THEY DROVE FIRST TO THE PHARMACY, WHERE LYLE PICKED UP several new prescriptions for Hoot, then made their way back home. Hoot mostly stared out the window.

"I'll miss the river," he said. "I never wanted to live anywhere else. I can tell you that."

Back home, Peg and Shiloh met Lyle at the door. Both hugged him for what felt like five minutes and Peg wept on his shoulder, a rare occurrence indeed.

"So, is he going to fight it?" Shiloh asked.

Lyle shook his head. "I don't know. The prognosis is bad. He might try a little chemo, just to see how it affects him. I told him I'd take him to the treatments. Honestly, I don't know that I blame him. I don't know how I'd react."

"But you can't beat cancer if you don't try," Peg said.

Lyle shrugged. "He's a grown man. You talk to him."

"Maybe Isaac could help him," Shiloh said.

"What do you mean?" Lyle asked, in a voice that rumbled out lower than he expected.

"He—he heals people," Shiloh continued. "I've seen it. Steven says the spirit is in him. He's got a gift. A God-given gift."

"Darling, he's just a boy," Peg began, "do you really think it's a good idea to promote that sort of thinking in him? He's so young."

"It's not thinking, Mom. It's *God*. It's God moving through Isaac like a channel. Like lightning through water."

"Well, I'm tired," Lyle said. "I'm tired and I'm not going to talk about this right now, if that's all right." He turned his back to them, and began to walk toward the bedroom.

"Dad, Hoot is your best friend! Come on. At least think about it!"

Now Lyle whirled around with as much anger and frustration as he could recall in years and years. "I know, Shiloh!" he snapped. "I damn well know." He slapped his hand against the wall with enough force to rattle the framed photographs hanging there. "And he's going to die."

At that, the three of them noticed Isaac standing in the doorway to the kitchen, his eyes red with tears.

"I wet the bed," he said in a tiny, tremulous voice. "I'm sorry."

Peg was about to rush to him, when Shiloh intercepted the boy and took him up in her arms.

"Why is everyone angry?" the boy asked.

"Oh, sweetie, we're not angry," Peg said soothingly. "No one is angry. Now, let's get you some fresh sheets and you'll be good as new."

"Mom!" Shiloh said sternly. "I've *got* this, okay? Good night." Down the stairs she disappeared, and soon Lyle and Peg heard the sounds of the clothes washer whirling, and the shower running, as Shiloh got the boy cleaned up.

Lyle felt very tired indeed, and more than a little heartsick.

"Let's go to bed," Peg suggested. "Come on. It'll be better in the morning."

And with that, they retreated to the bedroom, where Peg helped him out of his boots, shucked off his socks, and helped pull his shirt off and over his hard, muscled shoulders. Then, trying to shut his eyes, he heard her move back out into the hallway, into the kitchen, and heard the splash of water in the sink, and later, the sound of a teakettle boiling. When she returned, she held two mugs of tea and he smelled honey and lemon.

"Sit up," she said, handing him a mug.

And they sat that way, in bed together, listening to the train music outside, a few passing cars, a whippoorwill.

"Isn't Isaac a little old to be wetting the bed?" Lyle said finally. "He's done that a few times since they came back, hasn't he?"

"I've wondered about that, too," Peg admitted, "but it's been so long since Shiloh was a kid, I have to admit, I don't even remember what's normal anymore. Although, I do know it's different for every kid, and, I mean, it can happen to anyone, of course. Could happen to you or me."

Lyle grunted a small laugh. "I'm not that old, am I?" he asked. "That I have to start worrying about wearing diapers?"

"That's not what I meant," Peg said gently.

"What do you think of this prayer-healing business?" Lyle asked.

Peg sighed. "It's up to Hoot, I suppose. But maybe he should try. What could it hurt?"

"I don't know," Lyle admitted. "Except that it encourages them, doesn't it? Sort of normalizes the whole thing. I mean, we're talking about prayer healing, aren't we? How can our daughter believe in this stuff, in the twenty-first century?"

"Drink your tea and go to sleep, dear," Peg said gently.

So Lyle drank from the warm mug and then tucked himself back in beneath the sheets, listening to the train, and for a long time thought about his friend Hoot, alone in his house, perhaps imagining his own reckoning, his own end-time.

(13)

LYLE FOUND CHARLIE IN THE LATE-MORNING SUN, TUCK-pointing some loose grout between the ground-level fieldstones of St. Olaf's. A folding chair sat vigil beside a wheelbarrow full of wet cement, and a garden hose gushed forth into the green grass. A small, cheap, black boom box was playing classic rock, a genre that Lyle found to be more and more nebulous of late; earlier in the week he'd heard a DJ play Nirvana and then Metallica after Jimi Hendrix and Janis Joplin. "Classic," it seemed, now broadly and murkily meant "not new."

"Lyle," Charlie said gruffly, "come to lend me a hand?"

Lyle sat down in the folding chair, looked out over the country. "What do you know about faith healing?" Lyle asked.

Charlie guffawed. "Well, let's skip right to the heavy stuff, I guess, hey, buddy?"

"I'm serious," Lyle said.

"All right, first, how's my cement looking over there? Maybe give it a splash more water. Not too much."

Charlie finished the seam and washed his hands under the garden hose. "You stole my chair," he said, shaking his head. "You stole my chair and you're here asking me about faith healing. Did you at least bring me a carton of smokes or maybe a bottle of brandy?"

"It's Shiloh," Lyle said.

Charlie nodded, coughed, spit a loogie into the grass. "Of course it is."

"Well?"

"What time is it?" Charlie asked.

Lyle looked toward the sun. "About noon, I guess."

"Listen, help me finish these last few seams and then let's go back to my place and talk."

So they worked together for the next twenty minutes under a morning sun that shone bright and unfiltered, and when the grout was all used up, Charlie washed the face of the fieldstones and then rinsed the wheelbarrow clean, and with the chair and all the tools in tow, the two old men walked back to Charlie's parsonage, where inside, he cut some circles of summer sausage, and some squares of cheddar cheese, and laid these out on a platter beside some pickles and crackers, and then he opened two cold cans of

Leinenkugel's beer and they went out into the backyard and sat on a wooden Leopold bench, and Lyle began to tell Charlie about Isaac and Shiloh, Steven and the Coulee Lands Covenant. The late-morning light felt almost beneficent as a swallowtail wobbled through the air between them. Finally Lyle finished and exhaled, looked at his friend and said, "What do you think?"

"Well," Charlie began. "It ain't good."

"What isn't? Faith healing?"

"That, yes. But it's more than that." He inhaled deeply through his nose. "Look—faith healing or prayer healing happens in a lot of different churches, all across the sociopolitical spectrum. But the stuff you're talking about, the real-deal, Holy-Roller, I'm-gonna-fix-your-hepatitis-by-breathing-on-you . . . that stuff happens in very discrete, very insular churches. It almost never happens out in the open, because if it did, the leaders of those churches know they'd get shut down. Probably arrested." He took a swig of his beer. "Tends to happen at home. A call goes out, you know, like a phone tree, and alerts the congregation that someone is not just sick, but mortally ill. And then folks will come over to that person's house and they'll pray, or do a laying-on of hands. Sometimes, they'll have a healer, but more often than not, it's the congregation doing the healing, maybe the men of the congregation.

"They'll keep it quiet, because if a person ends up dying, it doesn't look good for the church. Specifically, it doesn't look good for the leadership of the church. And it doesn't look good for the family, either, who should've just taken the sick person to a hospital."

Lyle sipped his beer.

"So you're telling me Shiloh believes in prayer healing?" Charlie asked.

"Not just that," Lyle said, exhaling, "Shiloh believes that Isaac is a healer."

"Really?" Charlie sighed. "Why?"

"He's done it a few times, I guess."

"Oh, Lyle. I didn't know she was *that* far out there. Faith healing is beyond fringe. This kind of faith healing, anyway." He finished his beer in one long swallow and sat back in his chair. "I mean, there's nothing wrong with *praying* for someone, praying for a dying person. But the brass tacks of it are that *this* brand of faith healing is criminal. There's no other way to put it. If you know someone is dying, and you pray over them, instead of getting them to a doctor, it's negligent. Or if someone is suffering, and you think God is somehow going to magically cure them, that's out-and-out illegal."

"I feel like I'm losing her, Charlie. She's talking about moving out, which I understand, I do, but . . . What are we supposed to do about Isaac? Just let him get raised up by these, these . . ."

"Have you been to her church?"

Lyle nodded. "One time, yes."

"What's the pastor like?"

Lyle laughed darkly. "That's part of the problem. She likes him. I mean, *really* likes him."

"I don't know what to tell you, Lyle. These types of churches . . . It becomes—everything. It's like a black hole or something. A person gets sucked in, and it's very difficult to crawl back out. People who are critical of the church or break church orthodoxy become ostracized."

"But it must happen. Right? That people leave, I mean."

Charlie shook his head. "From what reading I've done . . . not that much. A person has to have an epiphany of sorts, although it's sort of the opposite of a Christian epiphany. Tends to be a complete fall from grace." He paused. "Like what you had, actually. Sometimes the fall from grace happens because a loved one has died, the prayer healing failed, and they realized the error of their ways."

"How do we help her, help them?" Lyle asked.

"I tell you this, buddy, I wouldn't do a thing to push her away. And I'd keep that kid as close to your side as you can. If you want, I can try to talk to her, but I'm afraid she's too smart; she'll see what's happening. No. For now, just do what you can to be there to support her. The thing about a church like that, what you're describing, is that if you're not careful, that church will swallow her up, and . . ."

Charlie chewed at a fingernail.

"What?"

"You might not see her again. It becomes them against the world. That's what they believe. That everyone is trying to get them. Their faith becomes stronger for it."

Lyle finished his beer and the two friends sat quietly a moment or two. Lyle wanted to say, *I'm scared*, but he didn't, didn't dare vocalize what he felt for fear that it might just make it more real.

"Lyle," Charlie said. "Stay as close as you can—you hear me, buddy? Close as you can."

(14)

FROM THE LAST OF AUTUMN'S FRENETICALLY COLORED AND doomed leaves, until Memorial Day weekend, the River Road and the communities along it lay largely forgotten. Why drive 55 mph north on that winding road through no-nothing, podunk towns when a motorist could blast straight up or down the gut of America at 70, 75, 80, 85 mph on Interstate 35, or there again, those great asphalt veins 90 and 94. And so the stores along the River Road routinely closed around Christmas only in order to reopen again in mid-May, just in time to crank the windows and doors open and sweep the old cobwebs from every corner and shelf. For most of the residents, winter was a blissful time. The roads were free of tourists, free of motorcyclists, free of drunk drivers. All quiet, save for the barreling freight trains.

But then there was all the energy that swooped up the river with summer. And it was everywhere, in everything. The colossal cottonwoods lining the riverbanks burst out bouquets of green leaves, and later, threw their soft fuzzy seeds down with such mirth and abandon that along curbs, in doorways and entryways, the white fluff formed gentle banks of not-snow. And the flowers, first hyacinths, then daffodils, and then, the profusion of lilacs. Lilacs! In princely purples and showy whites, so perfumed as to saturate the air, any room . . . Then the frogs, the tree toads, the peepers, crickets, and cicadas; the entire insect universe throbbing to life and exploding in a cacophonous exultation. Enough so that some human neighbors might slam shut their nighttime windows. If not to mute the invertebrates then to pump down the volume on treetop- and telephone-pole-sitting owls, hooting all hours like a bunch of drunks hollering down the bar to be heard.

And then, last of all, the tourists, of course. In their new Volvos and Volkswagens, Subaru wagons, Jeeps, and minivans, too. Flip-flopping their way alongside the River Road, peering into pottery shops, bouncing into and out of boutiques, and finally ducking into cafés, bakeries, and bars to recharge on croissants and scones, white wine or cold-pressed coffee, free samples of cheese, or waffle cones of ice cream.

Lyle didn't mind, as long as they left their money behind, like wet footprints destined to evaporate. But that summer, he didn't have much patience for the tourists and their lollygagging smiles. His daughter and grandson were moving out, and his best friend was dying. The world, it seemed, was darkening.

———◆———

HOOT HAD NEVER CARRIED ANY EXTRA POUNDS, BUT NOW HE was reduced to little more than skin and bones, fragile as a scarecrow. On the days when Hoot had a doctor's appointment scheduled, Lyle would chauffeur him to the doctor's office in La Crosse or Eau Claire, where the two men would sit in cool waiting rooms, leafing through battered magazines.

"I want you to know," Hoot began, "that I'm leaving everything to my sister out in Oakland. Everything except the cars. Those I want you to have."

"Hoot . . . there's no need. Let's just focus on what the doctor has to say. There's no need to be plan—"

"Lyle," Hoot interrupted, "you're my friend, and I love you, but you're being an idiot. I'm dying. And I'm trying to get my ducks in a row here. I'd tell my sister straight up, but it's better this way. If she found out I was dying, she'd want to move in and then I'd have her nagging me to take chemo all the time and you know, stop smoking. She'd have me eating goddamn tofu and drinking kombucha or some shit. So, it's just . . . it's better this way. I've already written her a note."

Lyle was quiet a long while. Then he said, "I wish there was something I could do. Something to help you."

Hoot coughed. "There is something."

Lyle sat up.

"Peg is always trying to get me to come over for dinner—"

"Hoot, she'd *love* for you to come over sometime, she's been—"

"Shut up, Lyle. I'm trying to tell you my last goddamn wish."

"Okay," Lyle agreed, folding his hands in his lap.

"I'd like to come over for dinner. I'd like for Shiloh and Isaac to be there. Even Shiloh's goofy pastor boyfriend. And maybe Otis and Mabel. Invite Charlie, too, if you'd like. I want us all to be dressed up. Like it was Thanksgiving. Or Christmas. Even Isaac. I'll buy him a coat and tie if he doesn't have 'em. I don't much care what we eat. The truth is, I don't have an appetite anymore. But I was thinking about the holidays and the . . . look . . . I don't know if I'll have enough steam to make it to November, so I'd . . . I'd really appreciate this."

His voice broke. Lyle had never heard his friend express sadness. Not in over twenty years of knowing the man. Never.

"I always loved Thanksgiving," Hoot continued. "Loved it as a kid. Our house all full of people, all my cousins and aunts and uncles. The smell of food, and the adults a little kinder than usual, probably because they were half in the bag. The pie and ice cream. So . . . that's what I want, that feeling. You understand me, amigo?"

Just then a nurse called out his name. "Horton Shaw."

Lyle rarely heard his friend called by his full name.

"You okay?" Lyle asked softly. "You ready to roll?"

"I don't know, buddy. Right now, as the late, great Joe Cocker would say, I'm not feelin' so good myself . . ."

"Let me help you up," Lyle said, standing to help Hoot gain his own balance, grabbing his friend by his bicep, up near the armpit. The arm he held was thin as a broomstick, fragile as an October cornstalk.

"Who names their goddamn kid Horton?" Hoot asked. "It was like my parents wanted me to be bullied."

Hoot stood and the two old men shuffled toward the nurse, who smiled gamely.

"What's this appointment for?" Lyle asked. He passed Hoot to the nurse, who touched the man's back.

Hoot continued scuffling forward. Without turning back to Lyle he said loudly, "Oh, just to remind me that I'm dying."

Hoot passed through a doorway and Lyle called after him, "I'll be right here."

———◆———

AN HOUR LATER, HOOT EMERGED, LOOKING HAGGARD AND frail. Two nurses helped him into the waiting room. Lyle stood up quickly, rushed to his friend.

"All right, buddy. Jesus, don't make a scene. Just get me home. I'm beat."

"Okay," Lyle said, "let's do it."

"First, one stop. Gotta git me a tank of air. Guess I'm one of those old bastards now, lugging around my own atmosphere. Anyway, I'm sure pure oxygen isn't dangerous or anything, right? Probably perfectly safe to keep on smoking my cigarettes. No worse than those morons you see at a gas station, puffing away while they're pumping ninety-one octane. Dumbasses."

BACK AT HOOT'S HOUSE, LYLE HELPED HIS FRIEND IN THE door, but then Hoot waved him off. "You're a good friend, Lyle. But git on home. Tell Peg I say hello."

"I can hang around, if you'd like . . ."

"Lyle, get outta here. What do I have to do? Lie? All right, I'm going to take a shit now. You want to hold my hand while I'm on the commode?"

"Fair enough," Lyle said. "Just . . . call me if you need anything."

LYLE WAS A BLOCK AWAY FROM HOME WHEN HE TURNED ON A side road and drove off, into the countryside, the setting sun burning like an acetylene torch bright in the rearview mirror. He drove out to an old abandoned quarry, a deep, deep cup of sandstone high on the bluffs where the water below was as clear and turquoise as the Caribbean. He sat there, needing badly to cry, only no tears came and in his frustration and sadness he finally just slammed the door of the truck, looked for the largest stone he could find and, hefting it over his head, threw it down into the serene waters where it made an impressively loud *kerplunk*, with a violent splash that sent ripples out across the water. Then he dragged himself back to the truck, glanced at himself in the mirror, and drove on home to Peg.

(15)

IN HIS ENTIRE LIFE, SIXTY-FIVE YEARS OF IT, LYLE HAD NEVER had to *walk on eggshells* around another person. He'd never even had to think about it. He'd grown up in a family of stoic, Norwegian-American farmers where no one said what they felt, or at least very rarely, and the result was that feelings were like spot fires, meant to be quickly extinguished, and in private. Peg, who had been raised in a similar middle-western family, had become a third-generation high school mathematics teacher, which is to say, an impossibly patient paragon of logic and fact. Of course, Lyle and Peg were never callous or cruel. It simply meant that in their own lives, hard work and the ability to endure were valued above all else. No one, they had thought, deserved to see themselves as particularly special. If they'd had a motto or a credo it might have been: *Keep your head down,* *do your job right the first time, and clean up at the end of the day—and above all, don't make a mess of things.*

From the beginning, though, Shiloh had steadily agitated this worldview, and Lyle and Peg were more than happy to accommodate her, spoiling her, with new clothing, new shoes, ballerina regalia and dance lessons in La Crosse—anything she wanted, really. Because to them, so long-suffering, so expectant, she was a miracle. And that somber, stalwart community Redford, already trending older back then, how those geezers doted on her, everywhere she went like some parade princess who needed no float, no tiara. Free lollipops and cookies everywhere she set foot, and from passing cars and curbs, everyone calling out her name and honking their horns in salutation. Because, and this is still true, there are small towns all around the world so intimate and connected that one citizen's pain or exuberance is felt just as acutely by her neighbor. And that was how the small town of Redford helped Lyle and Peg heal and move on—with sincere welcome and joy. In this way, Lyle and Peg detached from their old worldview—it sloughed off and fell away and soon enough they forgot it entirely; this is what love did, can do.

Shiloh, they knew, *was special.* And she could make any mess she liked. They would clean up afterward.

But now, around Shiloh, Lyle treaded very lightly, so much so that he felt he was tiptoeing through his own life, and when she left a room, or jumped into Steven's truck and retreated down the driveway, Lyle let out an audible sigh of relief.

Nowhere was Lyle tenser than inside her church, where he sat, ramrod straight, his muscles so strained he seemed better prepared for a fistfight to erupt than the process of taking communion. For no longer could he and Peg enjoy the relative anonymity of attending a service in the back of the old theater. Now, with Shiloh and Steven openly "dating" (Lyle did not particularly understand the twenty-first-century definition of this term), they sat in the front row, so close that Lyle could hear the charms and bangles clattering on Steven's wrists like tambourines. Unwittingly, he and Peg had reluctantly become something akin to church elders.

There was no doubting it. Steven was a natural-born speaker. And more than just being a talented speaker, he was very clearly well-versed in scripture. Lyle had now listened to several of Steven's sermons, scrutinized them all scrupulously, and though he was absolutely sure he did not agree with Steven's analysis of the gospel, he could hear many others in the sanctuary offering their amens, and not a few folks standing from their seats and waving their hands in front of them like trembling leaves.

Steven prowled the sanctuary like a panther, speaking directly to his congregation; there was the sense that he knew each person intimately, but more than that, he knew each person's greatest weaknesses, fears, and past crimes. Not only supremely confident, this young man was supremely righteous, and he wore that righteousness, that sanctimony, like a proud purple cloak, exuding an impossible mixture of youthful fashionability and the sort of gravitas normally found in people ten, twenty, even thirty years older.

On this Sunday, his sermon seemed to loosely swirl around the morality of abortion, a topic Lyle had never heard mention of at St. Olaf's, where politics were held at arm's length or more. Lyle was not surprised to hear Steven condemn abortion, in the abstract, but he *was* surprised when Steven stopped pacing the old movie theater directly in front of Peg and him, as he began to talk to the congregation about their own lives.

". . . there is a woman amongst you, friends. A woman whose birth mother was just a fifteen-year-old girl when she was delivered into the world not in a hospital or even the warm, safe confines of her family's home, but rather the filthy bathroom of a fast-food restaurant. Now, this story might have gone a different way, even a hundred different, tragic ways. What *if*, friends, that little baby, now a woman amongst you, had been murdered before she'd ever been allowed to draw a breath of air? What if, friends, that woman's mother had used a contraceptive, like the all-too-popular and so-called next day pill? What if that baby, who is now a beloved member of this congregation, had been abandoned, thrown away, left behind, as so many innocent children are every year, every month, every day, every hour, *every instant* in this country. Left in a trash can or perhaps beneath a blanket of paper towels and garbage in an alleyway Dumpster. What then, friends? What of our world? Our own lives? This church . . ."

Here, Steven's voice trailed off. Lyle stared at him and he could feel the blood rushing to his face and ears, could feel his heart rate surging.

"But I have good news, friends. The Lord did not abandon that baby. The Lord spoke into the ear of that young mother, and he consoled her, and through prayer and neighborly goodwill, the Lord's will worked its way through a network of believers until His bidding, His vision for that child was delivered unto her true parents."

The church was so very quiet now that Lyle could almost *hear* the blood coursing through his ears, could certainly hear an unseen parent outside the sanctuary talking to her small child outside the bathroom, helping him zipper his pants . . . It had been many years since Lyle had considered that day when they first met Shiloh. But think about it he did now, and the trouble with Steven's narrative was that, to Lyle's way of thinking, it very conveniently left out all the characters—all the Christians—who *had* abandoned her; who had judged her; who, in effect, had forced that fifteen-year-old onto a Greyhound bus in search of some safe passage, some safe harbor.

"Friends, those true parents had never met this child, or her mother. They had never even seen so much as a photograph. They just got into their car, and drove toward her.

Like those three magi following a star . . . Some of you have asked me, 'Pastor Steven, how will I know if God has called me?'"

Now the young pastor smiled out at his flock and they returned his smile with laughter and mild, muted applause, for his question, they knew, was obviously a rhetorical one. Lyle began to fidget in his chair. He could not control his hands, began kneading them; his feet tap-tap-tapped at the floor. He aimed his eyes at the ground. He was furious. This was *his* story. That day, those feelings and memories, they were *his*, and Peg's. But this young man was narrating Lyle's life like it was a red roadside billboard, some garish banner to be dragged above the beach behind a loud little airplane.

"Friends, those parents, those brave parents, who I am happy to say are sitting here today, living testimonies of God's grace and goodwill, they heard that call, and without a doubt in their hearts, they journeyed out trusting in Him."

Steven placed his right hand on Peg's shoulder now, and she began crying. Lyle looked over at his wife, more than a little surprised because she was a person who displayed little emotion typically, and was not prone to crying at all, especially in public. Lyle was all the more surprised when Steven's left hand landed on his own shoulder, and gave his sixty-five years' worth of corded muscles, cartilage, and bone a strong squeeze. Then he moved away from them, preaching again to a congregation that by now had been whipped into a steadily rising frenzy. Peg dabbed at her cheeks with a Kleenex.

"You don't think God is *still* performing miracles?" Steven boomed. "You don't think God is *still* walking amongst us? You think it's all history, all just words in a dusty, boring book?"

Every person in the movie theater was on their feet now, except Lyle and Peg—every person clapping their hands and shouting words of encouragement at their pastor. The room was loud, and suddenly stiflingly warm. Members of the church band, Redeemed, now took to their instruments behind Steven and began first playing softly, but then gaining volume, as if punctuating his every point.

"*Each* of you is a miracle, and God sees you, just as you see me and I see you. We are *all* miracles! Every child is a miracle, and that is why you all must be brave and go out into this wicked world and hold a torch up against that darkness, and if you're at work, or if you're at a barbecue or a baseball game, let those moments be opportunities to share your faith, and to pass along your fire. You need look no further than members of your own church. Brothers and sisters here, inside this room. You can save each other. You can save lives for Jesus."

Lyle realized that in the entire theater, he was the only one still sitting down, and that even as Peg's back was turned to him as she embraced Shiloh, his daughter stared down at him, while the young pastor, whose arms were raised, basking in the sunlight of applause, was looking at him as well, a grin on his bearded face, sweat running down his forehead, and collecting in his dark, upraised eyebrows.

"I want to end today's service with a special performance," Steven said, just as a group of children surrounded him on all sides. Lyle looked up. Steven wrapped his arms around the two kids closest to him. "We all agree children are gifts, children are miracles. So what could be better than settling back in our chairs, just for a few minutes, and listening to these miracles sing."

Lyle instantly recognized the song the children's choir sang, then found Isaac among all the little faces, saw the boy singing proudly, his mouth stretched into a little *o*, and beside him, the girl Sadie, who every time she seemed to forget the words would glance at Isaac and then regain her place. Lyle noticed that they held hands, held hands as their choir director, a very, very short woman, not even close to five feet tall, drew the music out of the children, her thick, short arms moving to the music as she pointed to this child and that one. And despite himself, despite his frustration, Lyle relaxed into his seat and enjoyed his grandson's singing, the spectacle of these children, joined together in "You Are My Sunshine."

AFTER STEVEN LED THE CONGREGATION IN THAT SUNDAY'S final prayer, the theater vibrated with the palpable glee of a small group of people united: dozens of faces shining with perspiration, hugs and handshakes, voices loud in jubilation and greeting. Lyle fumbled with the pale yellow bulletin in his hands, pretending at one point to have dropped it beneath his seat so that he wouldn't have to rise and gladhand. Exhausted, angry, and feeling increasingly trapped, he realized that perhaps Shiloh was lost, that there was no undoing her path to this place. But Isaac . . .

Lyle did not know how to keep the boy close, how best to protect him, and what, if anything, there might be to fear.

Peg was standing beside a group of women, laughing freely. He looked around for Isaac, for his grandson, but the boy was nowhere to be found. He felt very alone, so he retreated to the bathroom, where he closed himself into a stall, sat down, and ran his hands through his hair. He waited in there for a while until the lobby seemed to grow a little more quiet, then he flushed the toilet, and stood at the sink, splashing water on his brow, then staring into the mirror. He looked back at the worry in his own face.

(16)

SHILOH WAS HAPPY WHEN SHE WAS NEAR STEVEN, AND THESE
were the times when Lyle or Peg might casually volunteer to babysit, saying, "Aw, you two kids go out to dinner.
Drive up to Red Wing. Or even Stillwater. Heck, take a
couple days. Go on up to the Boundary Waters. Has Steven been up there? Pretty soon it'll be too cold. Go on.
Your mom and I will be fine with Isaac. *You'd* be doing us
a favor."

Lyle tried to play it cool, tried not to push too hard.
It was a tactic that had allowed him the space to escort
Isaac to choir practice, where Lyle quietly delighted in sitting toward the back of the theater, listening to that collection of small voices rehearse, giggle, and generally fidget
as their director tried desperately to corral them, organize
them, harness their impossibly erratic focus. And yet, if

he could have, Lyle might've suggested, ever so subtly, that Shiloh and Steven take a trip to the Gobi Desert, or far up the Amazon River, perhaps a leisurely camel ride from one extent of the Sahara to the other . . .

"Dad, are you sure? I don't want to inconvenience you . . ." Lyle, Shiloh, and Steven stood on the driveway, all three of them shifting their weight from foot to foot, kicking at little stones, tracing cracks in the cement with the toes of their shoes.

He shook his head. "Shiloh, he's our only grandchild. Go on. Have fun."

Steven had proposed to her a few weeks earlier, and though they were not yet openly sleeping together, the so-called impropriety of a weekend spent in the same motel seemed somehow lessened. Certainly, Lyle asked no questions in regard to their sleeping arrangements. The fact was, he didn't care to think about his daughter's sex life; still, he found their charade as phony as a three-dollar bill.

"The Boundary Waters might be fun . . . ," Shiloh said. "We could rent a canoe, do a little camping. Might be a fun, cheap trip . . ."

"There you go," Lyle said. "Though, if you hear any fiddle music, promise me you'll turn back."

Shiloh looked confused.

"Sorry," Lyle said. "That was just a little *Deliverance* joke."

"That's okay, Dad," Shiloh said, shaking her head, "you're fine."

THEY LEFT ON A MONDAY IN EARLY AUGUST, THE BED OF STEVEN'S pickup truck brimming with camping accoutrements, both of them looking as tickled as two teenagers in love. Steven honked the horn as they pulled out of the driveway, but Isaac was already running into the house, Peg hot on his heels, the plan for the evening that they'd make pizza from scratch, watch movies, and drink root beer. Lyle waved lazily at the lovebirds, then walked into the house.

———

THEY HAD A FANTASTIC FEW DAYS, DRIVING UP TO MINNEAPOLIS to sit in the new Minnesota Twins baseball stadium, Isaac marveling at the city's humble handful of skyscrapers. They spent a night at the St. Paul Hotel and in the morning, walked to the farmers' market, the children's museum, and the science museum, where Isaac marveled at the few dinosaur skeletons on display. Before leaving the Twin Cities, they stopped at Mojo Monkey's, a funky little doughnut shop, and they sat near the front window, Lyle savoring his coffee as Isaac gawked at the steady line of loyal customers banging into and out of the bakery.

But that night, the night they came home from St. Paul, something was wrong with Isaac. He was tired. Lyle and Peg chalked it up to all the driving, and the excitement of the trip. The boy asked, actually *requested*, to crawl into bed at five that evening, and the next morning, he didn't wake up until after ten, and then only when

Peg sat beside him, to mop the sweat off his boiling brow.

"He's got a fever," Peg said worriedly. "I don't know. Should we call Shiloh? Or just take him to a doctor?"

"For a fever? I don't think we need to bother her if it's just a fever, Peg. Let's see how today goes."

The boy spent all of the afternoon on the couch in their living room, and this despite the beautiful weather outside.

"We could go visit Charlie," Lyle tried. "Or head out to the orchard? I bet Mabel would make you a caramel apple. We could go fishing. Wouldn't you like that? Go down to the river and watch the barges?" He rubbed at the boy's shoulders. "What do you say, kiddo?"

Isaac's eyes were dull, his face sallow.

"Sweetheart?" Lyle said, looking more closely at his grandson. "How do you feel? Are you okay? Can you talk to Grandpa?"

The boy's lips were chapped and so Lyle dabbed his finger in his pot of Carmex and spread it over Isaac's lips. Made the boy sit up and offered him a cold glass of water.

"I'm just really tired, Grandpa. Is it okay to just keep watching TV?"

Lyle sat beside him on the couch and they watched one of the Harry Potter movies before Lyle realized the boy was asleep. Lyle picked him up off the couch and carried him downstairs to his bed and sat beside him, the worry mounting.

THE NEXT MORNING THEY DISCOVERED THAT ISAAC HAD WET the bed; the sheets were soaked with pungent urine, but even this hadn't woken Isaac up; he lay there, so groggy he couldn't speak to them.

"We're taking him to the hospital," Peg said now.

"What about Shiloh?" Lyle asked.

"There's no time for that," she insisted. "This isn't right."

Lyle knew the route to the ER all too well from chauffeuring Hoot, but he took the roads faster this time, and when they pulled below the vestibule of the hospital, he carried the boy to the admitting desk and some nurses came out and took him away, with Peg following right behind, and Lyle was left to complete the paperwork.

After about an hour, Peg emerged from the ER, holding her elbows and looking exhausted.

"How is he?" Lyle asked.

"Dehydrated," she said. "Lyle, he's got diabetes."

"Diabetes? I don't understand."

"They've got him on an IV drip and they're going to pump him full of liquids but . . . that's what it was. Poor guy." She collapsed into Lyle's chest. "It's why he's always so thirsty. It's why he wets the bed all the time. Diabetes."

"But . . . I mean, did Shiloh know about this?"

"I don't know, Lyle. Does it matter? We know now, and we're going to have to talk to her about it. I'm going to call her cell phone right now and let her know what's happened."

TEN HOURS LATER SHILOH STORMED INTO ISAAC'S ROOM where Lyle and Peg were sleeping in reclining chairs; it was well before dawn. Steven was just behind her.

"Who told you to bring my child to the hospital?" she roared. "Did you even think to call me? Or is this just some kind of power play? Get me to leave town so that you can steal my son?"

Two nurses hustled into the room just as Peg was rising from her chair, her eyes wide with confusion and horror, Lyle still utterly groggy, and Isaac asleep in the bed somehow, though suddenly tossing and turning.

"Shiloh!" Peg said, rushing to her. "We didn't have a choice!"

"I'm going to need you all to calm down," a nurse said forcefully, insinuating herself between Shiloh and Peg. "All right? Everyone hear me? I'm going to need you to calm down *right now* or I'll call the police."

"Call the police," Steven said evenly. "And ask them how this child came to become so sick."

Lyle rose out of the chair slowly, though now he was well awake. "Excuse me?" he said.

"Who are the parents of this boy?" the nurse asked.

"I am," Shiloh said. She took Steven's hand. "We are."

The nurse held her hands out, palms down—*stay cool.* "All right then," she began. "Ma'am. Sir." She looked from Peg to Lyle. "I'm going to have to ask you to leave, please."

"I don't understand . . . ," Peg began. "We didn't

mean to . . . Can't we just . . . can I at least kiss him good-bye?"

"Ma'am, please come with me," the nurse said.

And with that, Lyle and Peg were led out of the ER, toward the hospital's entrance.

"Wait a minute," Lyle said, stopping in the hallway. "We didn't do anything wrong. That boy is our grandson. Our only grandson. He was sick. We didn't even know he was diabetic. How could we have known? No one told us that. Did our daughter even know he was diabetic? What's going on here? How do we know he's going to be safe?"

The nurse sighed deeply. The hallway in which they stood was quiet—not a doctor or nurse or janitor in sight—the cheap terrazzo floors bright and shining with a fluorescent glare from the ceiling lights. Far off, the drone of a floor polisher could be heard.

"Look," she said, "our hands are tied. I can see that you're good people. I can. You did everything right. But there's nothing I can do. We have to follow protocol. We have to follow the law. My advice? Go home, get a good night's sleep. Give your grandson's mom time to cool down, and then regroup. This happens with a lot of parents. Especially younger ones. They're just wound too tight." She looked around the hallways again, and then gave Peg a quick hug. "Look, you didn't do anything wrong. Go home. Your grandson is going to need you again, I'm sure of it."

IT WAS THREE DAYS BEFORE THEY SAW ISAAC AGAIN. SHILOH wouldn't answer her telephone, wouldn't respond to texts or e-mails. Lyle hadn't been working at the orchard, preferring to stay home in case Shiloh suddenly stopped by, unannounced.

Lyle was at the kitchen table when he heard the front door ease open. "Hello?" he called. By the time he turned in his chair and was about to stand up, Shiloh was walking toward him in the narrow hallway.

"Sweetheart," he said quietly. "We've been trying to call you."

She nodded wordlessly.

"How is Isaac? Is he okay?"

"He's fine," she said, her voice weak, her eyes aimed at the ground.

"What's the matter, sweetheart?" Lyle asked. "How can I help?"

"You don't believe, do you?" she asked. "You don't believe in God."

Lyle sat down again, and sighed deeply. He felt very heavy, sitting on that small kitchen chair, the wicker and wood groaning beneath him. He peered out the window and saw Peg in the backyard, pinning laundry to the line.

"I don't know," Lyle allowed. Then, "No, I suppose not."

"Well, Dad, I hate to say it, but you're the reason Isaac was sick. Can't you see that?"

"No," Lyle said, utterly dumbfounded. "I don't understand. How could you think that? Or say that?"

"It's easy enough to parse out, though, isn't it?" Shiloh continued. "You're the sickness, the weakness. It's through you that Satan found Isaac. It was in this house where he fell sick. I shouldn't even be surprised. You're so focused on the air-conditioning when you should be worried about you. Your soul."

Lyle knew not what to say so he looked at the kitchen floor, the old linoleum. He was barefoot, and so he stared at his toes. Stared at his toenails, now yellowed with time, thick and gnarly as a broken wooden shim. He thought of Peter just then, that little boy, and could almost feel the child's minuscule weight in his arms, feel his soft new skin, so smooth, and the little gurgling sounds he made.

"I love you so much," he said. "You and Isaac both. More than you'll ever know."

"Well, I'm going to collect the last of our things. Isaac starts school in a couple of weeks."

"How's he doing?" Lyle asked.

"Dad, I really don't want to hang out and talk right now. But he's back to usual, okay? It wasn't long after we came back he started to feel like normal. And that's the power of prayer, isn't it? Satan can't take hold when Steven and I are right there. Especially a man as strong in his faith as Steven."

Lyle nodded his head. "Of course."

"We haven't given up on you yet, Dad," Shiloh said. "Steven's sure that if you pray with him, he can bring you back. He even talked to me about baptizing you again."

The room fell silent and then Lyle said, "Please don't forget about that dinner for Hoot. Next weekend."

"We'll be there," Shiloh said, and then disappeared into the basement, where Lyle could hear her rummaging through drawers and then, in a closet, freeing the last few garments from their hangers. Then the rhythm of her feet on the steps as she moved back upstairs, and the detached, resigned sound of her voice saying, "Bye, Dad. Oh, and one other thing."

"Yes, darling?"

"I don't think I want you anywhere near Isaac, Dad. Not until you've really changed. Not until you've come back to God."

(17)

THEIR BACKYARD WAS SMALL BUT OVER THE YEARS THEY'D shaped the space into a kind of courtyard: brick pavers, a modest fountain, and through the seasons a steady parade of gentle blooming: hyacinths, ferns, hostas, irises, and lilies. In the deep shadows close to the house, Lyle liked the thick, cool green moss that grew on the rocks he collected from various road trips and brought home, one of his only hobbies, really, geology. At either property line grew a row of mature lilac bushes that draped out over the lawn and, in spring, exploded in extravagant purple perfume. To the north, where the backyard ended, an old limestone wall rose up the hillside, and here, in the only part of their backyard that drew much sunlight, Peg planted patches of herbs and succulents, sprays of coneflowers and daisies.

Peg had seen photographs in a design magazine, or

maybe it was a movie, and had a grand vision for Hoot's "last meal," which was what they were secretly calling it, though certainly no one hoped that would be true. And so for a week Lyle stood clumsily at the top of a ladder, stringing white Christmas lights in crisscrossing patterns above the lawn, from lilac to lilac, with Peg advising down below, pointing here and there, a hoe in her hands as she helped guide the lights just so.

When he wasn't hanging up lights, Lyle had been at work in his garage, ever since Hoot had mentioned the idea of the dinner, really, building a long rectangular table from barn boards he'd scavenged from area farms. The table, four feet wide and twelve feet long, had taken him dozens of nights' worth of work out in the garage, listening to the Milwaukee Brewers or Minnesota Twins on the radio, swatting away the moths and june bugs that came curiously toward the hanging fluorescent lights of the garage. He'd spent many days planing all the boards, and then sanding them smooth before applying two coats of clear veneer made from a mixture of pine tar and linseed oil.

Peg would come out to the garage before she went to bed, and Lyle would remember those moments for all the remainder of his days. His wife, this woman he'd known forever, it seemed, standing on the driveway in her bare feet, or perhaps her old beaded moccasins, gripping her elbows, as she stared at him from the darkness, and then smiling at his table, and coming to him, and wrapping her arms around his belly and pressing her face into his shoulder blades, and once she said, "I'm so sorry, Lyle, I'm so sorry you're losing your best friend."

He set his paintbrush down then and touched her hands, and they stood that way a long time, swaying to some unknowable music until finally he said, "You're my best friend."

"It's different though, isn't it?" Peg said. "I think a person can have a few best friends. I mean, I really don't care to drink beer with you the way Hoot does. Or watch Packers games, or talk about old cars. I'm happy you've got a friend for those things. Just like I'm sure you don't want to go shopping with me, or play Scrabble."

They were quiet a moment.

"Time feels like . . . like it's moving too quickly," Lyle said. "I can't seem to hold on to things. Can't seem to slow anything down."

"I'll hold on to you," Peg said.

They kept swaying there, in the summer night, the cement beneath their feet warm and damp, and in the corners of the garage, mice moved furtively, and frogs creaked and croaked in the unseen tree branches, and down near the river, a train was blasting north through the night, and they could feel it, could feel the ground trembling, see the light in the garage flicker and quaver, and Lyle wanted to say *I'll miss him* but he was afraid that if he even spoke those words out loud, he would begin to cry; so he kept them, behind his lips, where they swelled and expanded, and his skull felt heavy, and his heart felt fragile, and so he closed his eyes and felt his wife's arms wrapped around him, the way a child might embrace a tree, and he squeezed her tighter still.

"Your table is beautiful," she said at last.

"You think so?" he asked.

"I do," she said, walking to the table and running her hand across its smooth surface. "The wood is beautiful."

"That wood's probably a hundred years old. It's not all from the same barn, but I tried to make sure to pick only hickory."

"Did you have a plan or something? A schematic?"

Lyle shook his head. "We had one like this when I was a boy." He shrugged. "They're called harvest tables and at the end of the season, when the crops had been harvested, my dad and his brothers used to haul a table like this out in the field and we'd have a big dinner."

"You never told me that before," Peg said, moving a strand of hair off her forehead and behind an ear.

"One of my best memories was of my dad, after baling the last of the year's hay." Lyle sat down in an old chair beside his crowded tool bench. "It was very hot. Late August, I think. Maybe even early September. It was dusty, and we were all out in the fields, throwing bales into the wagon. It was too hot to wear a shirt, and I remember that, all of us out there beneath the sun, sunburned, and we were working together, and my mother kept bringing us ice water with slices of lemon, and how wonderful that water tasted, and looking out over the field and there were my uncles and cousins, and they were singing, and when we finished, it was late afternoon, and my father said, 'Let's go for a swim, boys.' And then he took off all his clothes except his underwear, and I'd never seen him like that before, you know? Never seen his stomach, for example, or really, his knees, even, and then he ran toward the creek, and I remember him diving in, and we were all just so stunned, so surprised, because we'd never seen him like that, so happy. And we all followed him into the creek and we were splashing each other and our mother was watching us from the bank and she was laughing, too.

"I can see him now," Lyle continued, "at the harvest table after we'd gone swimming. One of my uncles had brought out a cooler of cold beer and the adults were drinking, even my mom, and then we had a picnic out there, in the field. Nothing special: corn on the cob and bratwurst and potato salad and pickles. I suppose we were poor, but I don't remember it like that. I was just happy."

He offered a little laugh and rubbed at his jawline. "That's my favorite memory of my dad. Swimming with him in the creek. Seeing him smile. Feeling like I helped him do some hard work, that I'd contributed something."

"I love you," Peg said. "You know that?"

Lyle sighed. "I love you, too."

"Coming to bed?"

"Are we in pretty good shape for Hoot's meal? Should I keep working?"

"Nothing left but the cooking," Peg replied. "But

Shiloh and I can handle that. The day of his meal, all you have to do is help set the table."

"All right, then," Lyle said. "Sure, I'm beat. Let's go to bed."

Lyle took one last look at his table. The train was gone now, the night void of its immense noise. He turned off the garage light, brought the rickety paneled door down. Peg held out her hand and he took it, and they walked into the house together, down the hallway they walked so many times to the bed that accepted them, just as they were, and where they lay on their backs and stared at the ceiling, and both worried about their grandson, that wondrous boy they so feared for, and his mother, whom they loved so much their hearts ached with the recognition that she was no doubt slipping farther and farther away from them, their house, their tiny little town, like a dingy floating away from their foggy shore.

(18)

ALMOST THE ONLY TIME LYLE WAS ABLE TO SEE ISAAC WAS SUN- day, though even then Shiloh insisted on placing herself and Peg between grandfather and grandson, but there was nothing she could do to prevent Isaac from running into his arms when the boy first saw him enter the church.

"Grandpa," the boy said, "I *miss* you."

It was almost enough to demolish Lyle, to disintegrate his heart right there as he held Isaac tightly and rubbed at the boy's head.

"I missed you, too, tiger. Can't wait to hear you sing today, though."

"Guess which song we're singing?"

"I don't know, buddy, which one?"

"'Jesus Loves Me.'"

"One of my favorites," Lyle said. Then smiling bravely at Shiloh, "Good morning, sweetheart."

"Good morning, Dad," she replied coolly.

———————

ATTENDANCE AT COULEE LANDS, IT SEEMED, WAS SOMEWHAT IN decline, Lyle thought, as they took their seats. The band, Redeemed, had lost at least one member—the drummer loudly absent—and every sound, every cough or sneeze, every child's whisper, every creak of those old chairs took on a new and alarming stridency. When the children's choir finally took to the two rows of risers behind the battered lectern in front of the movie screen, their number was certainly shrunken, though Lyle could not say by precisely how many.

The choir director assumed her usual place in front of her pupils, standing on an old apple crate, and then swung her arms to kick the performance under way.

It could not be said that Isaac was a naturally gifted singer. In fact, Lyle derived great pleasure not in the quality of Isaac's voice so much as its volume. The kid just *belted* out those old Christian classics, unselfconscious and proud, and from his place in the choir he would smile and wave at Lyle and Peg until they smiled and waved in return, as all around him, his choirmates wobbled through the performance in something aspiring to synchronicity.

Lyle remembered with some guilt the final years of Shiloh's schooling: the arguments, the slammed doors, the dinner-table disagreements . . . When she finally left for college, there was a sense of relief in dropping her off at the dorm. He and Peg had done their job. They'd seen her through and hopefully raised a strong, independent young woman. Those first several months as empty nesters hadn't been surreal at all, let alone sad; rather, a serene quiet enveloped their house and Lyle found the peace conducive to long hours of reading and woodwork. When Shiloh returned for weekend visits or a holiday, he was happy to see her, of course; he always would be. She was his daughter and he loved her more than anything. But he always welcomed the peace that resumed when the visit was over.

When Isaac had been born, Lyle did not expect to be as excited, as profoundly touched as he was, holding that infant in his arms. But he was. This baby boy who reminded him of Peter, yes, but also the miracle of Shiloh's entrance into their lives. Isaac represented another chance for them, for Peg and him, another chance to marvel at the beautiful fragility of new life, only with the added benefit that this child wasn't theirs—not every dirty diaper was theirs to change, not every late-night crying jag theirs to soothe.

And now, this five-year-old boy, this wonder.

Finally the singers took a humble bow and the congregation offered a round of sincere applause. Isaac scurried back to where Lyle, Peg, and Shiloh were sitting, but only instead of choosing his seat, he darted toward Lyle and sat in his grandfather's lap.

"Well done," Lyle said, kissing the boy's head. "*Well done.*"

(19)

THE DAY OF HOOT'S LAST MEAL WAS THAT RARE LATE-AUGUST
occurrence, a bluebird day—mild and beautiful, a northern wind having brought cool air down from Canada, and
down by the River Road, no freight trains barreling, no
Harley-Davidsons growling, and no motorboats on the
river, buzzing north and south. Redford was quiet. Shiloh,
Steven, and Isaac drove up in Steven's old pickup truck
and when they bounced into the driveway, packed tightly
across the truck's bench seat, Lyle allowed himself to admit they looked very much like a family.

Shiloh did not so much as peck Lyle on the cheek and
Steven followed straight behind her, lugging several plastic
grocery bags laden with food. Watching Steven struggle
toward the house, Lyle suddenly realized that his arms
were crossed tightly against his chest; it hadn't dawned on

him to help this man, potentially his own son-in-law. Lyle was grateful for the fact Steven had abstained from calling him Dad; he preserved some hope that Shiloh might yet lose interest in the whole thing and move back home. But the engagement ring on her finger, the bounce in her step, and the flush in her cheeks suggested otherwise.

"What time's dinner?" Steven asked, juggling the bags as Lyle opened the door for him.

"Six," Lyle said. "After you deliver those groceries, maybe you can gimme a hand moving this table out to the backyard."

"Yes, sir," Steven said. "Ready to serve."

Lyle found Steven's persistent politeness utterly annoying. Had it been possible to pause time just for a moment, Lyle would have loved to punch the young man in the nose right then—only to resume time and watch the sap tumble to the ground, stunned and stupefied. He did, however, derive some pleasure in the simple act of that juvenile fantasy.

With Shiloh and Peg prepping the meal in the kitchen, and Isaac in the family room watching a movie, Lyle and Steven carried the harvest table out into the backyard and began setting it for dinner. First with an Amish tablecloth (white cotton and white lace accented here and there in navy blue) and then with the old china Peg's grandmother had given her and the silverware they reserved only for Thanksgiving and Easter. Lyle set five bottles of Bordeaux on the table (all bought during their trip to Minneapolis, from the venerable Surdyk's).

"Oh, I'm sure we won't need all that wine," Steven said, laughing. "Shiloh and I don't drink."

"That's perfect," Lyle said, brightening, "more for the rest of us." Then, "You do know Jesus drank wine, don't you? I don't think it's against the rules."

"For one thing, I don't want my judgment clouded," Steven said. "I prefer to remain pure of mind."

"I see," Lyle said. "Yes, I'm sure it's much safer that way."

"And two, I wouldn't want to be tempted into embracing any . . . so-called carnal desires." Steven seemed to be both frowning and blushing.

Lyle smiled. "I'm no theologian—"

"We know *that*," Steven replied, smirking.

"What I was going to say is that, while I'm no theologian, I find it very hard to believe that any God, any Supreme Being, is out there monitoring your alcohol content and then expressing disappointment when perhaps you feel compelled to kiss or hug the person you love. That just seems, I don't know, petty."

"Well, I am a theologian," Steven replied, "and I don't need wine to kiss or hug the people I love."

"Of course you don't, Steven," Lyle said.

The young man exhausted him with his certainty of the world, the afterlife—everything. He glanced at his old Timex. Two o' clock. Hours until dinner. The kitchen was too small to accommodate many helpers and Lyle's one responsibility—the grilling—would be done only in the final minutes before the meal. He was tempted to open one of those so-called unnecessary bottles right now, if only to ease the suffering of his time with Steven.

"Maybe I'll head over to Hoot's," Lyle said, "see if he wants to come over early, or if he, you know, needs any help around the house."

"I'll come, too," Steven offered cheerfully enough.

The young man was inexhaustible, it seemed.

"Oh, you don't have to," Lyle said. "Maybe Shiloh wants you here."

"I bet she'd just as soon get rid of us," Steven said, giving Lyle's shoulder a light, jocular punch. "I'm ready when you are. I can drive."

Realizing that Steven's truck was blocking the driveway anyway, Lyle nodded his agreement and they drove over to Hoot's. The truck was outfitted with such a fine sound system, it seemed a waste to not crank some Creedence Clearwater Revival, but the stereo remained off, and soon enough they were parked in Hoot's driveway and then making their way to his door, which he answered in a billowy sweat suit, trailing his tank of oxygen, a cigarette pursed between his lips.

"Christ," he said, "you're early. I know I'm dying, but I'm sure I can make it until tonight, at least—maybe even tomorrow morning."

Hoot retreated inside his house, leaving Lyle and Steven to wipe their feet on the welcome mat and follow him. Lyle could see Steven put on a brave face as they moved inside and almost immediately Hoot placed a cold can of beer in the bewildered young man's astonished hand. Before he could refuse, Hoot had touched the younger man's can with his own in a toast, raised the can to his lips and took a long, long swallow.

"What are you supposed to be?" Hoot asked Steven now. "A Mormon hipster? Do they have those?"

"No sir, I'm a preacher."

"Really," Hoot said, eyeballing the young man. "Huh."

"How are you feeling?" Lyle asked.

Lyle sat down at the table next to Hoot and glanced over at Steven, who stood in the doorway, unsure what to do with himself or his hands. He held the can of beer as if it were a live grenade.

"I don't know, Lyle. Not too good, I suppose. I'm tired all the time, and sore, my hair's falling out. Bought myself a red watch cap to cover my head. Makes me look a little like Jacques Cousteau."

Hoot regarded Steven.

"You haven't touched your beer, hipster."

"Steven doesn't drink," Lyle explained. "He's afraid he'll give in to carnal desires."

"I see three men in this kitchen," Hoot said. "Two of them old as shit. What do you think, preacher? Can you keep those carnal desires corralled?"

"He also likes to ignore the fact that Jesus drank wine," Lyle put in.

"There's no proof that what Christ and his disciples were drinking was actually fermented," Steven said defensively.

"I'm sure you're right, guy," Hoot laughed. "I'm sure Jesus made it very clear he only drank unfermented grape juice. I'm sure that was always readily on hand back then, what, two thousand years ago in Palestine."

Lyle took another sip of beer. He liked this, watching Hoot harass Steven.

"Come on, Padre," Hoot said, "sit down and talk to us. Lyle tells me you're a real Bible-thumper."

Steven moved cautiously toward the table and slipped into a chair. "I'm a pastor, sir. So yes, I suppose that makes me a Bible-thumper, though I prefer other terms like devout, or—"

"Then tell me something, Pastor. My doctor says I got less than a year to live. I think he's being generous. Given the amount of weight I've lost and the kind of cancer that's eating me up, it feels to me like I'd be lucky to make it to Christmas, maybe Easter. So my question is this: What are my odds of meeting Saint Peter?"

"Sir?"

"The pearly gates, man. They gonna wave me in or not?"

Steven fidgeted in his chair, examined his hands nervously. Lyle had never seen the young man so off-balance.

"Have you accepted Jesus Christ as your Lord and savior?"

"I don't know. I guess."

"You guess?"

"Yeah, I guess. I mean, I was baptized and confirmed and all that happy horseshit. What else is there?"

Steven sat back in his chair and almost, *almost*, took a sip of his beer.

"Have you repented your sins?" Steven pressed.

"What sins?" Hoot asked, and then burst out into a deep, rattling laugh, all phlegm and cigarette tar, from the bottom of those two old, tired, tattered blackened lungs. The laughter soon enough graduated into violent coughing, and Lyle took the can of beer from Hoot, setting it on the table, and placed a hand on the man's back until he seemed settled.

Steven shot Lyle a look of concern.

"I've seen that truck of yours," Hoot said, "a real dandy."

Steven nodded humbly. "My first love."

Hoot rose wobbly from the table and with two thin fingers signaled for the men to follow him. "Then I think you'll appreciate what I've got in my garage. Course, Lyle's seen it all before."

Out in the garage, Steven was speechless, at first, standing in the doorway near an old avocado-colored refrigerator that, in healthier times, was always chock-full of cold beer. "My Lord," he said, "will you *look* at that."

"You know anything about cars?" Hoot quizzed.

Steven moved slowly and reverently toward the cars. "Well, to me, it looks like we have two late-sixties Ford Mustangs on our hands. Slightly different vintages . . . The bodies seem to be in about perfect condition . . ." He ran his hands along the hood, over the driver's-side mirror, the top of the driver's-side door. "Can I look under the hoods?"

"Be my guest," Hoot said, sitting down in an old folding lawn chair.

Steven popped the hoods and peered into the guts of the two machines. He made a popping sound with his tongue and bounced his head around from side to side, like he was unraveling a riddle. "Looks like you chopped 'em up a bit."

"Had to," Hoot explained, lighting a cigarette, "my ex was gonna sell 'em, take the proceeds with her and abscond for Florida."

"All the parts still here?"

"No, sad to say. Some are still kicking around though, I think, right here in this garage, or else down in the basement. Might've sold a few along the way, just to make things interesting. At the time, I just started pulling stuff apart, you know, making it hard on her."

"And you've never tried to put them back together?"

Hoot shrugged. "I just retired a few years back. Most days, I came home from work, cracked a beer, made myself dinner, put my feet up, and before I knew it, it was already the next day and time to start all over again. I haven't been much for putzing around here in quite a few years."

"Well," Steven began, looking at his watch, "would you mind if I had a crack at it?"

Hoot drew deeply on his Camel, and regarded the young man. "You want to play doctor on my Mustangs?"

"I can't get them both fixed up, but between the two, I can get one started today, I can guarantee you that. And you give me a month or so, I bet I could have both of them up and running."

"*Bullshit*," Hoot growled. "We got less than three, four hours before my dinner tonight."

"What do you want to bet?" Steven grinned.

"Okay," Hoot said, "what have I got to lose? I'm gonna be dead inside a year anyways."

"If I can get one of these cars started today, before dinner, you have to come to my church, every Sunday until Christmas."

Hoot barked out a laugh. "All right. And if you can't fix up that car . . ." He drew deeply on his cigarette and coughed. "I say you gotta drink five shots of Jägermeister tonight at dinner."

Now it was Lyle's turn to laugh and clap his hands.

Steven walked over to Hoot, held his hand open, spit into it, and presented it to Hoot. "We got a deal?"

Hoot spit into his hand and Lyle stood up to watch the two men shake.

Steven immediately reached into his pocket, and with his cell phone balanced against a shoulder, began calling a number of people, all while his hands groped around beneath the hood, touching hoses, fiddling with wires.

"I'm going to need some better light in here, though," Steven said.

"I ain't helping you there, Padre," Hoot said. "You've got a hotline to Jesus, a working cell phone, and enough ego for all three of us. You figure it out. I plan on sitting right here, drinking a few beers, and then watching you get loopy on Jäger-bombs. It's gonna be great."

———

BUT IN LESS THAN THIRTY MINUTES, NOT A FEW SOUPED-UP late-model cars, hot rods, and jacked-up trucks were parked out in front of Hoot's house, and their drivers, some of them from Coulee Lands Covenant, came lumbering up the driveway carrying parts in their hands, or heavy duffel bags on their shoulders. One man pushed a cart laden with three different car batteries. All of them were polite, and quick to shake Hoot's hand, and always listening and laughing to his stories and jokes. By and by, almost a dozen men were collected inside the garage: many gathered in pockets of easy conversation, some leaning under the hood, others passing around tools or holding a trouble light over the engine, some occasionally sitting behind the wheel to fruitlessly turn the key, or perhaps, just to pretend to drive the old automobile.

Just after five o'clock, Steven handed the key to Hoot and said, "Why don't you give it a shot."

Hoot looked up at him, his eyes wide with amazement, disbelief. "You're shitting me."

The pastor shrugged. "Give it a try."

The men in the garage, many of them now sipping cold cans of beer, or twirling cigarettes between their fingers, moved to the margins of the garage, looking at Hoot with wide smiles on their faces.

Hoot stood uncertainly then, withdrawing the breathing tubes from his nose, took a drag from his cigarette, dropped the butt to the garage floor, and moved slowly toward the car. Steven eased the driver's-side door open for him, and guided Hoot into the seat, where he sat looking ever so frail, that old Mustang by now almost too muscular for its owner. Looking around at the crowd inside his garage, Hoot paused a moment, then turned the key.

The engine hesitated and coughed twice. Hoot tried again.

This time the car roared to life, rumbling low and loud and kicking up a dark blue-black cloud of smoke. Everyone cheered and clapped, twelve or so men, some big and beer-bellied, others with giant beards or all covered in tattoos, men you'd never have thought to see display much emotion of any kind, were now recklessly smiling and chanting, "Hoot! Hoot! Hoot!" And Hoot, behind the wheel, joyous and flabbergasted, shifted the car into reverse and was easing back down the driveway like he might just drive off into the sunset when Steven ran up beside the driver's side and said, "Now hold on there, Dale Earnhardt. We might need to get some air into those tires. How long's that car been sitting there?"

Hoot placed a hand on Steven's forearm. The air around the car vibrated with V8 power. "I don't know . . . ," Hoot began. "I don't know what to say."

"Well, a *thank-you* would suffice."

Hoot nodded. "Thank you . . . I just never thought— never imagined I'd ever drive her again."

"Probably feels pretty good, doesn't it?" Steven said, smiling.

"Hell yeah it does," Hoot said. "Feels like I'm twenty years old again."

"Don't forget," Lyle said, leaning on the Mustang, "we need to get you into some nice clothes for your big dinner."

"I'll be damned," Hoot said, shaking his head in disbelief. "Sonuvagun fixed it. I just can't believe it."

———————

IT WAS A SMALL PARADE OF SLOW-CRAWLING ANTIQUE CARS, glossy muscle cars, and big-wheeled pickups that followed Hoot in his Mustang to a nearby gas station so that his aged Firestone whitewalls could be pumped up properly, and then the parade rumbled down the River Road toward downtown, going about twenty miles per hour, holding up the summer traffic but pleasing the sidewalk tourists, who offered waves and whistles, and when Hoot finally turned off into Lyle's driveway, all those trailing vehicles honked their horns and hollered out their congratulations as they drove on, Hoot standing there, leaning proudly against the old car, pumping a thin arm in the air triumphantly.

Lyle and Steven each took an elbow and escorted Hoot into the backyard where the harvest table was immaculately set, candles glowing and the Christmas lights above glistening against the dusky sky. Peg and Shiloh stood waiting in high heels and beautiful dresses with light shawls pulled over their shoulders, and there was Isaac, in little-boy seersucker and his battered Chuck Taylors. Charlie was there as well, in a too-tight wool suit coat with elbow patches and a plain black necktie. And Otis and Mabel had come in their best outdated duds. Everyone hugged Hoot and he kissed the women and the top of Isaac's head, and when Peg offered him a glass of wine, he paused and said, "You wouldn't happen to have any of the beer I like kicking around, would you, dear?"

At which Isaac ran into the house, reemerging a moment later with a cold can of Old Milwaukee that Peg poured right into a champagne flute. He looked at her with good humor and said, "You probably could have saved the glass."

"Tonight," Peg said, "we use every glass in the house, every bit of china, we drink every drop of wine, we eat until we can't eat any more, we listen to good music, and we celebrate your . . ." Here, she faltered for just a moment, glancing down, before looking up again, and saying, "And we celebrate you, our friend. So let's have a toast."

Lyle quickly poured two glasses of wine and passed one to Peg; for their parts, Steven and Shiloh had bought a bottle of nonalcoholic wine and they, too, raised their glasses in the air.

"To Hoot, who leaves no can of beer untouched," Peg said gamely, braving back the tears Lyle knew she dearly needed to shed, yet could not.

They all touched glasses and the night commenced.

———•———

A RECORD PLAYER WAS SET ON A SIDE TABLE AND ISAAC WAS kept busy shuffling between LPs but mostly returning to the Beatles, which seemed to suit Hoot just fine where he sat, sometimes singing along quietly with "Hey Jude," which also happened to be a favorite of Isaac's. Each time the boy would slide right into Hoot's lap and they'd gently sway to that ecstatic lullaby of a song, *Na na na, na na na, na na na, Hey Jude . . .*

"We played this song at my wedding," Hoot said quietly. "Can you imagine? All these years later? All the ways the world has changed. And this song here sounds like it was recorded yesterday, like it could be recorded ten years from now."

They began with cheese and sausage, apples and berries, sliced bread and fresh butter. Then pork chops and grilled peaches drizzled with twenty-year-old balsamic vinegar, then a kale salad, green beans, and, for dessert, a cheesecake all adorned with strawberries, a cherry pie, and homemade vanilla bean ice cream to accompany them. By the time coffee was brewed, the darkened heavens stretched out over their heads like a starry chautauqua, a grand circus tent all perforated with light.

Hoot did not eat much, but sat happily enough, one leg crossed over the other, bobbing his head to the music, occasionally requesting a song and little Isaac sorting through the records until he found what had been described to him, Bob Dylan's "Nashville Skyline" or Neil Young's "Harvest," and then dropping the needle into another well-worn groove. In this way, the hours passed, until they all noticed that Hoot seemed to be drifting off, his head no longer bobbing, but rather sagging onto his left shoulder, or his chin resting on his chest.

Lyle leaned over to his friend and placed a hand on his shoulder, rather startling Hoot, who said quietly, ". . . such a beautiful night . . ."

"You about ready to head home, Hoot?"

"Tell me that Mustang won't turn back into a pumpkin," Hoot said quietly.

"No," Lyle said, "this isn't that kind of a fairy tale."

Hoot glanced around the table, at the nearly guttered candles, the gentle sway of the Christmas lights overhead, the empty wine bottles, the half-full cups of coffee, the forks covered in drying cherries or cheesecake, the faces of his friends, then to the stars and the ever-patient moon.

"Oh, I don't know about that," Hoot murmured.

Isaac had fallen asleep a few hours before, but everyone else walked Hoot to his newly resurrected Mustang, ensconcing him in the passenger seat, from which he waved a weak good-bye, like an exhausted grand marshal, and then Lyle eased the car down the driveway, with Steven following behind in his truck.

At Hoot's house, Lyle escorted him inside while Steven guided the Mustang back in the garage. For perhaps the first time in their friendship, Lyle entered Hoot's bedroom, and sat his friend down on the bed, pulling off his navy blue suit jacket, and his white button-down shirt, and then his old dress shoes, socks, and pants, leaving Hoot in just a white T-shirt and his underwear.

Then Hoot said, "I'm sorry, amigo, but could you reach into my closet and hand me that Packers sweatshirt there? I get a little cold sometimes."

And Lyle helped his friend into the sweatshirt and helped him to lie down in his bed and then he pulled his sheets up over his shoulder and said, "Good night, old buddy."

But Hoot was already asleep, snoring softly.

Lyle stood there and looked around at the stark bedroom, nothing more than a queen-size bed, two bedside tables, two lamps, and a chest of drawers on which three framed photographs sat. Curious, Lyle padded softly across the room and peered at the images. There was an old photo of Hoot with his parents and sister, probably dating back to the late fifties, and a shot of Hoot with his wife, just after their wedding, the two smiling broadly, her veil blown back off her face. It had been taken from behind the car, with empty cans of beer dragging off the rear bumper, white rice on the black pavement and in Hoot's dark,

Brylcreemed hair. The third photo caused Lyle to reach out and pick it up off the dresser. It was a moment Lyle hadn't thought of in years and years.

Shiloh's high school graduation party. Peg must've been the photographer, because she was not in the picture. It was just Hoot and Lyle, with an eighteen-year-old Shiloh squeezed between them in her graduation gown and mortarboard. They were all smiling, and every detail was true to life: Hoot had a cigarette in his left hand, almost cut out of the photo, but not quite, smoke drifting up; Lyle looked so much stronger and broader, his hair much thicker and more blond; and Shiloh, her smile just a bit more guarded than theirs, a bit less wide, and her eyes, not quite focused on the camera, but somewhere else, just off to the side, some friend, perhaps, laughter, another conversation . . .

Lyle set the frame back down on the dresser, closed Hoot's door, and walked out of the house, taking care to lock the front door before climbing up into Steven's truck.

"Thank you," Lyle said, "for fixing his car. I hope you saw how happy that made him."

"It was nothing," Steven said. "My old man was a mechanic. My whole childhood was handing him tools or sitting behind the wheel, turning the keys on cars that wouldn't start while he stood over one engine or another, scratching his head. It's kind of second nature to me."

"Still, it was a good thing you did. A real decent thing to do."

"Cars are a lot easier than people, Lyle," Steven said

dryly. "A car tells you when it's broken, tells you how to fix it. A car even comes with a manual. There were, what, a couple hundred thousand Mustangs made around 1969? Maybe a little more than that . . . Even if they're not all perfectly alike, they're close enough. I don't need to tell you that humans aren't quite as easy to diagnose."

Steven pulled to the foot of Lyle's driveway and extended his hand. "I'll be praying for your friend."

Lyle shook hands with Steven and said, "Good night."

Now he walked up the driveway, feeling very tired indeed, and there were Peg and Shiloh on the front stoop, barefoot. Shiloh stood and hugged her mother, then came down the driveway toward Lyle and without pausing to hug or kiss him, briefly touched his hand in passing, grimacing slightly as she did so, as if merely touching him were painful. He could not remember a time when they were further away from each other, when even the idea of embracing her father seemed somehow sinful.

"Good night, sweetheart," he said sadly.

"Good night, Dad," she replied matter-of-factly, shutting the passenger door.

FALL

(20)

LATE ONE MONDAY AFTERNOON IN MID-SEPTEMBER, LYLE AND
Peg drove the River Road to La Crosse, where they picked
up Isaac after school and then drove back to Redford and
the Sourdough Orchard, which was closed on Mondays,
but otherwise in full swing, with apples decorating the
branches of the trees, the apple house full of wooden crates
of fruit. Any other day of the week tourists would have
been jamming the humble parking lot and tumbling out to
spend their money on apple butter, caramel apples, freshly
fried apple fritters, hot apple cider, or bags of freshly
picked apples. These days, after months of hard work in the
orchard, brought clear delight to Otis and Mabel, one of
whom worked the old cash register while the other guided
customers around to the apple slingshot, the apple trebu-
chet, or the playground of sun-faded plastic toys that was

hauled out of storage just for the all-important month of September. But today, while everyone caught their breath after a busy weekend, the orchard was quiet.

They found Mabel yelling directions to Otis, who stood in the refrigerated apple house stacking crates on a red Radio Flyer wagon.

"He's going to spill those apples," Mabel said to Peg. "I tell him things, and he just ignores me, like I'm not even here. But you watch, he'll spill those beautiful apples everywhere and we won't be able to sell them."

As Lyle worked his way into the apple house, through rows of crates stacked four high, he heard the crashing sound of the wagon tipping over and pitching many dozens of apples onto the floor.

"You old coot," Mabel yelled. "I told you so. You'd lose your damn head if it wasn't attached to your shoulders."

"Can I help you?" Lyle offered, taking in the damage.

"I'd be obliged," Otis said. "The woman has a sixth sense for calamity." Mabel threw her hands in the air and escorted Peg and Isaac into the Haskells' home.

"Why don't we get a few paper bags," Otis said. "Anything we pick up, you take home with you. They're probably all bruised by now."

The two men spent twenty minutes cleaning the apple house, Lyle helping Otis make space in the building for more apples. Then they joined the women and Isaac, who were all seated in the kitchen drinking lowballs of golden apple cider.

"I was thinking of taking Isaac up into the orchard," Lyle said.

"You two go ahead," Peg offered, "I'll stay down here."

———

LYLE AND ISAAC PROMISED THEY'D RETURN FOR SNACKS AND conversation, and Lyle drove up to the gated orchard, Isaac climbing down out of the truck and opening the gate so that the old truck could make its way in. Then he shut the gate and ran back to his grandfather. Holding hands, they walked through the orchard, past all the new plantings of Honeycrisp, past the Galas and Zestars, into the very oldest section of the orchard, to where the wild apple trees grew, the trees Otis found over fifty years ago, when the land was just a weekend hideaway from his responsibilities as a professor in Minneapolis.

"I want you to taste an apple," Lyle said. "It's special. So special that Otis and Mabel won't even sell it. It's just for them. And us."

"Why is it special, Grandpa?"

"For three reasons. The first is, this tree doesn't produce much fruit. It's an old, old tree. We're lucky to get a few dozen apples in the best of years. Second, the apples it produces are very fragile; they bruise real easily. So this is a kind of apple that would never sell well in a grocery store—it just can't be transported. Third, well . . . You'll have to taste it."

"Can I choose my own apple, Grandpa?" the boy asked.

Lyle nodded. "Why don't you choose one for yourself, one for your mother, and one for your grandmother. Then we'll pack them away, somewhere safe so they don't get all beaten up before they can even be eaten."

"What do they taste like, Grandpa?"

"You'll find out," Lyle said. And then he paused a moment before saying with some seriousness, "And remember to collect the seeds from your apple. Have your grandmother help you. Maybe dry them out and keep them in a paper envelope somewhere. That way, sometime in the future, why . . . Maybe when your par— when your parents buy a house somewhere, you could plant those seeds and have yourself a special apple tree. And you'd know just where it came from." *You'd have this memory,* Lyle wanted very much to say. *This day. You and me on this beautiful September day in Wisconsin.* But he held back, hoping the day would be enough, the apple would be enough.

But the boy was already shimmying up into the ancient, craggy tree and began steadily passing fruit to Lyle, three round, warty, misshapen apples, their skin pink and green and mottled white in places.

"Good. Now your grandmother wants to make a few apple pies this evening, so we have to pick her a bag or two from the other trees. Will you help me with that?"

And in this way, Lyle and Issac walked back to the truck, picking a few apples from this tree, and a few from that, filling two brown grocery bags, here and there, until Lyle was afraid that the paper bags would burst, spilling their harvest. So they piled back into the pickup truck, briefly visited with Otis and Mabel, and then drove back to Lyle and Peg's house, where Lyle ate a late lunch of chili with grated cheddar cheese, sour cream, green onions, cilantro, and saltines, and then went into their backyard with his favorite Hudson's Bay blanket and, resting in an Adirondack chair, fell asleep.

Which was where Isaac found him as he crunched into the heirloom apple, an unnamed varietal not even cataloged by the great and renowned Department of Horticulture at the University of Minnesota. Isaac stood in his grandparents' humble courtyard and chewed this apple, which somehow tasted of tart raspberries and cream, its inner meat at once crunchy and softly ephemeral, dissolving like a cloud of cotton candy. He could not believe his taste buds and kept biting into the apple for more. Finally, after quickly finishing the apple, he discovered a single seed, lodged in the space between his two front teeth. Extracting the seed with the tips of his fingernails, he laughed quietly and then crept toward his sleeping grandfather, and pulling the blanket aside, paused for a moment, and closed his eyes.

The boy did not understand the "power" his mother and Steven talked about, the power that folks from Coulee Lands Covenant practically worshipped him for. He only knew that he'd first felt it about a year before. His mother had placed him in a day care that he did not like and could tell she didn't much like either. When she dropped him off in the morning, he would often cry and reach out for her, and seeing in her face how it pained her to leave him there, he could not understand why she did so, day after day. The day care was in a small cinder-block building near the highway, the sound of traffic loud and constant. Inside, the carpets were old and smelled of pee. The playground was small and shabby, littered each morning with cigarette butts and fast-food garbage, and the teachers were big women who mostly paid attention to their phones. Some wore earbuds against the crying.

One day, when all the other children were napping, he woke to visit the bathroom. When he reached the door, he heard crying inside. It was one of his teachers. He entered the space so quietly she never noticed until he touched her head, trying to soothe her.

She started as if shocked and he could see in her eyes that she was sad, frightened, and somehow trapped. She reminded him of a wounded animal. And up close, he could see the skin of her arms, her face, and neck; so many ugly bruises—some blue-purple, others old and in faded yellow.

"Are you okay, Miss Amy?" he asked.

She pressed his little body against her and though he couldn't see her face, he felt her crying, felt her body juddering.

"Miss Amy," she said, "doesn't know where to go."

"You could come stay with us," he suggested.

She pulled back from him and managed a small laugh.

"My mom and I would take care of you," he offered, seriously. "Or maybe your mom would help you."

He was not afraid of her feelings because somehow, he intuited that he could make it all go away. It was not that he could erase another person's suffering or sorrow, so much as he could *soothe* them. In his mind, he pictured the shores of a pond, the surface of the water troubled by a violent storm. He could place his hands on that water, and smooth it, like ironing a wrinkled tablecloth. His mother had frequently complimented him on how observant he was, on how empathetic he was.

And so that is what he did. He sat beside his teacher and touched her head, stroking her hair, and with each pass of his hands, he focused on calming her, on gentling her fear and anxiety.

It was maybe two weeks later, when Shiloh picked up Isaac from day care, that this teacher, Miss Amy, pulled Shiloh aside and told her about a dream she'd had in which Isaac told her to move out of her house, to leave "that angry man," and this is what gave her the strength to ask for a divorce, to file for a restraining order, and to move in with her mother.

"Your son," Miss Amy said, "is like my angel."

———

HOLDING THE SEED IN HIS MOUTH, ISAAC THOUGHT OF HIS grandpa, of that afternoon when they had cleaned Peter's headstone, and then he opened his eyes, moved his grandpa's sweater and undershirt aside, and carefully removed the seed from his mouth and placed the wet seed in his grandfather's belly button, and quietly tiptoed backward before running back into the house to the kitchen, where his grandma was working dough into a pie tin, flour on her cheeks and on her forearms, flour on the floor, and the radio singing, *But I'm near the end and I just ain't got the time. And I'm wasted and I can't find my way home.*

In the courtyard, a scant few early autumnal leaves fell, and Lyle slept in the cool shadows of early afternoon, a train in the distance, the sound of a hundred cars, hundreds of wheels, a far-off whistle, warning signals, tree branches shushing past, and the rocking of so much iron weight, side to side, but ever forward. Coal-hopper cars headed for power plants, empty ore jennies bound for Duluth, tank cars full of corn syrup . . .

Lyle awoke slowly from this deep sleep. He could not say why but he was reminded of a Sunday morning so long ago when Shiloh crawled into their bed, and the morning light careening in through the windows, past the gauzy curtains, and the children's books, mounded so heavily on the bed Lyle felt his legs might fall asleep, and how they read together for hours at a time, laughing and tickling, and he felt the desire to dwell in that moment, to collapse time into a pinprick point that might be inhabited forever.

(21)

TRUE TO HIS WORD, HOOT ATTENDED CHURCH EVERY SUNDAY his body allowed him to, dressed in a suit that hung off his shrunken shoulders like a sail on a windless day. But there he was, his red watch cap sitting jauntily atop his head and an aluminum tank of oxygen dragging behind him as Lyle helped him into the car for the drive down to La Crosse.

"Tell you what," Hoot said one Sunday as they drove, "mostly, I think these Bible-thumpers are as full of shit as a Christmas turkey. But," and here he paused dramatically to cough into his fist, "it can't hurt to spend a few Sundays inside a church before I have to walk the plank. I doubt He's watching, but . . . you just never know, now do you?"

Their church attendance had definitely softened Shiloh, who was now more or less back to treating both Peg and Lyle cordially. Lyle supposed it was hard to reconcile that a spawn of Satan would voluntarily and peacefully sit in church for weeks on end, even chipping in the occasional twenty-dollar donation when the offering plates were circulated. Surely it just didn't jibe.

Lyle used the time to study his future son-in-law, and the thing was, Steven wasn't always the upbeat, charismatic messenger-of-Christ that he advertised. Perhaps it was because Lyle really only focused on Steven, but he seemed to notice a correlation between the pastor's mood and the size of the assembled congregation on any given morning. If the Packers were playing a noon game, for example, and more than half the seats were empty, he would launch into a long, angry sermon full of fire and brimstone, Old Testament scripture wrought with rampaging armies and villainous kings and concubines. But when the sanctuary was even two-thirds full, why, Steven put his best face forward. Lately, Lyle noticed him standing close to a beautiful young woman with long white-blond hair and big golden hoop earrings, her skin tanned, her arms and legs hippie skinny. Lyle said not a word, for their interaction was brief, the pastor's arm slung over her shoulder in the familiar way an old college roommate might. But he took note of the young woman, and two Sundays later, when he observed a similar interlude, he peered around for Shiloh, and saw her, arms crossed, in a huddle of other young mothers, staring intently at this woman.

"Is it me," Lyle whispered to Hoot, "or is Pastor Steven enjoying that parishioner's company a little more than your average, you know, member of the flock."

Hoot peered over his coffee cup. "I dated a girl who looked like that before I was married. Her legs were so long she could damn near wrap 'em around me twice. Helluva dancer."

Peg slapped him gently on the arm. "You two. Knock it off. Honestly, we're standing in a house of God."

"Sorry," Hoot said, "but first of all, this is a run-down movie theater. And it doesn't change the fact I had a couple of wild weeks with that chick. I remember, we went camping up by Lake Superior. Had this little tent and—"

"Hoot," Peg said coolly. "I love you, but *please*. Spare me."

"You see who we're talking about though, don't you, Peg?"

"I do," Peg admitted. "But I'm sure it's nothing. He's beloved by this church."

"Want me to spill my coffee on him or something?" Hoot whispered. "Put some Limburger cheese on the engine block of his truck?"

"Hoot!" Peg hissed.

"What's the worst that can happen?" Hoot asked. "He tells me not to come back to his church? What do I care? I've had more churching these past few months than in the prior, what, fifty years? And, I believe, the Lord will be on my side, should the good pastor's actions be . . . ah, less than holy."

———

BUT THE NEXT SUNDAY, WHEN LYLE RANG THE DOORBELL AT Hoot's house, his friend did not answer the door, so Lyle let himself in, saying in a loud voice, "Hoot? Hoot? You decent, buddy?"

An eerie and complete silence answered him, no radio, no whistling, not the shuffle of Hoot's feet. He moved quickly toward Hoot's bedroom and discovered his friend lying on the worn carpeting beside the bed.

"Don't tell Peg you found me like this," he croaked. "I just fell and I—I'm hurtin' pretty bad, amigo."

They drove straightaway to La Crosse where Hoot was admitted to intensive care. The doctors explained that he was once again suffering from pneumonia, and that they were nearing a new stage in his care.

"From here on out," a young doctor told Lyle and Peg, "we need to decide if we're going to continue chemo, continue treating Hoot . . . or whether it's better, more humane, just to treat his pain. To ensure he's as comfortable as possible."

They sat with him all that morning and throughout the afternoon, watching football as he dozed on and off, unable to eat, without even the strength to crack a joke.

That evening, Shiloh, Steven, and Isaac visited Hoot's hospital room, bringing with them several Hallmark cards signed by the church's parishioners along with a bouquet of flowers. Shiloh leaned down to kiss Hoot's cheek. "No beer?" he whispered.

"I'm sorry," she said.

"You're a good woman, Shiloh," Hoot whispered. "You know that, don't you? You've done all right. I've been kinda off to the side the whole time, but I've been watching you.

Watched you grow up. There were times . . ." His voice trailed off.

Shiloh sat down on the bed and took his hand.

"Times I even thought of you as my own daughter. That I wished I had a daughter like you."

She leaned down once more and kissed his forehead.

"You're a good man, Horton Shaw," she said.

———

LYLE HAD DRIFTED OFF INTO A HALF SLEEP, SLUMPED IN ONE OF the room's uncomfortable Naugahyde armchairs, when Shiloh gently squeezed his hand and he opened his eyes to find her crouched down, staring earnestly into his face.

"Dad, Isaac wants to help Hoot."

Lyle was quiet as he absorbed her words. Now he glanced past Shiloh and saw Isaac fidgeting restlessly in front of Peg, her hands massaging his little shoulders, and Steven standing off to the side, holding his Bible. The hospital seemed to breathe quite apart from them: the monitors attached to Hoot, the dry whispers of the heating register, a helicopter departing its landing pad, nurses in the hallway talking softly, laughing.

"Dad," Shiloh said.

"Yes, sweetheart."

"You need to believe now. If you don't believe, then you should leave the room while we pray."

Lyle was tired, but he stood and hugged his daughter. He hugged her for a long time.

"I'm ready," he said.

They stood around Hoot's bed in a tight circle, holding hands, with Isaac positioned close to Hoot's head, to his skinny old shoulders.

For the first time since he'd stood with his cousin Roger beside that summer lake all those years ago, Lyle tried with every fiber of his being to vanquish all his doubts and anger, and to reach out, as he imagined a ghost might, not with his hands, but with his heart and mind—to reach out to this friend of his who was dying. He did not listen to the words that Steven was speaking, no, he knew that doing so would distract him, that, rather than guiding Lyle out, they would sink him deeper into himself. So Lyle focused, he concentrated, and yes, he found himself praying, only, just at the moment when he might've spoken to that God he had more or less foresworn, he felt something snag, felt some sharp spur of doubt, some thought that penetrated those dark calm waters. He opened his eyes.

Isaac's right hand was on Hoot's forehead, and Hoot somehow had a grasp on the boy's wrist. There was no white-blue electricity surging from Isaac into Hoot. The room suddenly much cooler or warmer; and the air did not stir the curtains or the bedsheets or Shiloh's hair. The room was absolutely quiet now and Lyle could not stand there another second, so he gently dropped Peg's and Shiloh's hands and walked noiselessly out into the hallway, closing the door behind him.

SOME TIME LATER, THE DOOR OF HOOT'S ROOM OPENED AND Peg, Shiloh, Steven, and Isaac filed out toward Lyle, who sat near the nurses' station, holding a paper cup of coffee.

"Good night, Dad," Shiloh said, her face drawn with exhaustion and sadness.

"Thanks for coming," Lyle said, nodding at his daughter and Steven.

"I'm sorry about your friend, Grandpa," Isaac said, hugging Lyle tight around his waist.

"Me too, buddy," Lyle said, afraid he might fall apart into a million broken pieces.

ON THE DRIVE BACK HOME PEG ASKED, "WHY DID YOU LEAVE the room?"

Lyle was quiet several beats. "I don't know. Guess I didn't feel that I was really helping him."

A strong west wind kicked up and with it came a sputtering rain and the last leaves of that season were swept off their wet, black branches and across the road, a few of them hitting the windshield and sticking to it, past the reach of the wipers. No other headlights shone through the darkness.

Peg sighed. "I love you, Lyle, and you are one of the most unselfish people I've ever known. But there is something inside you that you think is . . . logical or practical or something, but really, it's just fear. You're afraid to let go, sweetheart. You seem to need to assign significance or blame or success, only life isn't always that way, is it? Maybe life, maybe this whole universe, maybe the whole thing is more than just us. What if there is something greater? Some form of God, or maybe magic? Is it so difficult to imagine that *you* might not have all the answers, and that's okay?"

They drove home in silence. Their house felt cold—the first real chill night of autumn. When Lyle tossed his keys on the counter they made a louder sound than he intended, and he cringed.

"I'm going to bed," Peg said.

"Good night," Lyle said. Then, louder, "I might head on over to Charlie's."

"Suit yourself," she replied.

"Hoot's my friend, you know."

Peg turned and faced him.

"I *do* know, Lyle, yes. And he's my friend, too. Which is why I was willing to try anything, *anything*, to save him. And you know what I did, Lyle? All I did was close my eyes and concentrate. I concentrated on *Hoot*. Not you, not me—*Hoot*. And every good feeling, every good—I don't know—vibration, that I have, I imagined pouring it all into him. And you couldn't even do that. You're too afraid to try and do that."

"Peg—"

"No, go on, Lyle. You go visit Charlie. But promise me something, please, will you?"

Lyle was silent.

"If I'm ever dying, maybe you'll try a little harder than you tried tonight with your friend, okay?"

And with that, Peg walked down the hallway and shut their bedroom door.

———

CHARLIE ANSWERED THE DOOR WITH A WEARY SMILE, AND LYLE was suddenly very grateful to see his friend. A fire crackled in the hearth and Charlie was listening to jazz on his record player, a glass of Scotch in his hand.

"I should have called," Lyle murmured. "Mind if I come in?"

"Sure," Charlie said, brow furrowed. "Everything all right?"

"I don't know," Lyle said, then, "No. Hoot's dying. Peg is . . . upset. Shiloh believes Isaac's a faith healer . . ." He threw his hands up.

"Sit down," Charlie said. "Can I pour you a drink?"

"Sure," Lyle said. "Who're we listening to?"

Charlie poured two fingers of Oban and passed the glass to Lyle.

"Saint John Coltrane. *My Favorite Things.*"

"Saint?"

"Yessir. There's an African Orthodox Church out in San Francisco. The Church of Saint Coltrane."

"Come on."

Charlie shrugged. "Makes sense to me."

They sat in silence a long while, watching the fire, listening to the wind rattle the old windowpanes of the parsonage, the doors in their jambs. Lyle allowed himself to sink into his chair. Outside, a pack of coyotes yipped and howled.

"I love listening to those creatures," Charlie said. "Makes the night feel a little less lonely."

Never having felt much affection for coyotes, Lyle remained silent, took another sip of his Scotch.

"Isaac tried to heal Hoot this evening, over at the hospital," he said at last.

"Is that right?" Charlie muttered.

"I tried, Charlie. I tried to believe. Tried to open myself up, I did . . . But I couldn't. Couldn't do it."

"Why not?"

"I guess I started thinking and it . . . just didn't feel right. I just don't believe the way you do. Maybe I don't believe at all."

"Lyle, part of being a Christian—hell, part of being a good *person*—is caring about everyone, all human life. And I love you, friend, I do. But there are times when I think you feel that a person fails at religion if they're not-always-doing-the-perfect-thing-every-damn-time. The god I believe in has a sense of humor. He was watching you tonight thinking, *That bonehead lets the perfect be the enemy of the good every single time.* You're Lyle Hovde. You're allowed to doubt the world, doubt yourself, doubt religion. But I know you. And you don't have all the answers, either. Otherwise you wouldn't be knocking on my door at ten o'clock at night in the middle of a rainstorm."

"Have you ever seen prayer help a person?" Lyle asked after a moment.

"Sure. Yes, I have."

Lyle sipped his Scotch.

"What happened?"

"Before I moved back, I was the pastor of a little church up in Ely, Minnesota, near the Boundary Waters. This old woman came to me, and she was in so much pain, she was crying. Bad, bad arthritis. Her fingers were all totally crooked, looked like she'd played twelve seasons in the NFL, the NHL, or something.

"So, we prayed over her. Now, I never claimed to be a healer. I didn't claim I had supernatural powers, and in no way did I promise her it would change things, but a group of parishioners and I prayed over her, and guess what? The next Sunday she comes to church and says it worked. She held up her hands and they were still bent like broken tree branches, still totally gnarly, but she *felt* better. So what was I supposed to say? That the prayer hadn't helped? That she still had two grotesque claws for hands? *She felt better.* It worked."

"Huh," Lyle grunted.

"Lyle, let's just say, heaven forbid, that it was you who had cancer. Do you know how the doctors—every doctor in the world—how they'd advise you to beat it?"

"Chemo, diet, exercise, I don't know . . ."

"They'd tell you that you have to *believe* you can beat it. You have to *believe* you can win. Now, you tell me how that's different from prayer. You tell me how that's different from what you were trying to do tonight for Hoot."

"It's false hope though," Lyle said. "It's not the prayer or belief that kills the cancer. It's the chemo. You can't *believe* that you can jump off a cliff and somehow survive. You can't *believe* that you can shoot yourself and live."

"It isn't false hope," Charlie said. "The cliff bottom isn't your body, and neither is the bullet. The cancer *is* your body. *Pain* is your body. Grief and sadness and depression—those afflictions are in your body." Charlie reached over to Lyle and poked him in the bicep with a forefinger. "Don't you think your friend would rather see you there, believing in him, than out by the broom closet, moping around, having an existential crisis? I mean, come on, Lyle."

"You're not exactly making me feel better, Charlie."

"I'm your friend, Lyle. Making you feel better isn't part of my job description. I'm here to give it to you straight."

"Yeah, well, I'm gonna get some more wood for this fire," Lyle grunted.

"Fine," Charlie said. "I'll be right here, listening to Saint John Coltrane."

Outside, the wind lashed Lyle's face as he gathered an armload of dry oak from under the protected cave of the parsonage's porch. The coyotes were close now, yip-yip-yipping, barking, and howling. The hair on the back of Lyle's neck stood on end, and he was happy to step back through the door. He fed the fire two more logs and set the remainder of the pile beside the hearth on Charlie's old wood floors.

When Lyle returned to his chair, his friend's head was pitched backward, eyes closed, and mouth open, offering up the deep snuffling rattle of sleep. Lyle flipped the record and resettled the needle at the outer rim of the vinyl.

"No wonder you live alone," Lyle said. "You snore like a buffalo."

Roused from his brief slumber, Charlie took another sip of Scotch. The two men were quiet for a long time, just listening to the jazz and the gently crackling sizzle of the fire.

"This one day, back in Alaska, about, oh . . . twenty years ago now," Charlie said, "I was working this crab boat. The owner was getting on in years and he, I guess, liked me, because when the weather was rough and he didn't feel up to it, he trusted me with his boat, which is no small deal. The boat was his livelihood, you know. And not just that, it was his retirement, too.

"It was calm when we went out that morning, just me and these two other guys. One was an ex-con on the lam from some banks he robbed down in Oregon, and the other was this real soft kid from Cleveland who was working for a year or two to pay for his studies in the seminary. We teased him relentlessly and the ex-con was always trying to show him porno mags and tell him the dirtiest jokes. At times, I felt a little bad for the kid.

"Anyway, I guess I was a little cocky—hell, I *know* I was a little cocky—because I allowed us to get pushed way off course. The currents are really powerful up there and I was still learning their patterns, and the next thing

I knew, we were totally lost, nowhere near our crab pots out in the Bering Sea. We might've been a thousand yards off the coast, or halfway to Japan—I really couldn't tell you. I didn't trust any of our gauges or charts and I just panicked. I didn't want to radio back home either, because I was embarrassed, so I just pretended everything was fine and pointed us in a direction I felt pretty sure was home.

"The boat was old, and it wasn't unusual that we'd have to troubleshoot a half dozen problems while we were out fishing. We never figured out what happened, whether we struck some shoal or hit an ice floe, but we began sinking, and fast. Sometimes I wonder if the old captain had sent us out there on a suicide mission. You know, sabotaged his own boat for the insurance money . . . Anyway, we got a lifeboat ready and all three of us hopped aboard just in time to watch her go down."

"You've never told me this one before," Lyle said.

"It's not a story I'm very proud to tell," Charlie continued. "And I wouldn't be telling it, except that the seas were so calm. If it had been rough—and usually it's as rough as it gets on the planet—we would have been dead. We didn't have the gear to be out there like that in an open boat.

"But we just drifted through this fog so thick you could almost pack it in your hands like a snowball. And we listened. Listened for buoys. Listened for motors. Listened for anything. For hours we took turns blowing on our life-jacket whistles or screaming out.

"And then, out of nowhere, there was this pod of

humpback whales and they swam all around us, breaching. They were so close that I reached out through the fog and touched one. I saw its eye. We looked at each other, man. For several seconds. That whale was closer to me than you are now. It was *right there*. And the ex-con and the kid touched the whales, too. They swam beside us for several minutes and then were gone. Beautiful phantoms.

"We'd all been working crab boats for several seasons and, I mean, none of us had ever experienced anything like that. Porpoises, sure. And it wasn't uncommon to see a whale breach or blow. But this was different. It was . . . I don't know . . . intimate, you know? Powerful.

"We were out there almost a whole day before the fog finally lifted and we were discovered by another crab boat. They took us aboard and gave us hot coffee, wrapped us in blankets. We'd drifted seventy-five miles from our home port. Another four hours later a serious storm kicked up and we would have been killed, I don't doubt that for a second.

"When we got back to town, the two other guys and I went to a bar downtown for a cheeseburger and some beers. We all had the sense that we'd be going our separate ways. And I remember just sitting around, being real quiet, drinking my beer, and the kid saying to me, 'That was providence that saved us. That was God's work. The odds of us being found . . . The odds of the weather being so calm . . . The only reason we're alive is because He's got a plan for us. And I hope you two recognize that, recognize that we just experienced a miracle.'

"That night in the bar was the last time I ever saw that ex-con. But I remember, I'll always remember, he finished his beer, he took that kid by the shoulder, and he said, 'I never believed in God until we were out there on that water in that little boat. I think I do now. You know what changed me, bub?'

"The kid just blinked up at him and said, 'Getting rescued?'

"And the ex-con looked at us both in the eyes and said, 'The whales.'

"And we never saw him again. He rapped his knuckles on the table, dropped a twenty-dollar bill on his plate, and walked out of the bar. After that, no one would hire me on any crab boat. I was bad luck. The guy who'd sunk a million-dollar boat in still water. So I bummed around. Worked in salmon canneries, stayed with a girl for a while in a commune outside Ketchikan, dropped a lot of acid. And just before I got it in my head to come back here, I decided to buy a kayak and try to paddle that area where we'd seen the whales.

"I camped out in this beautiful cove. Huge Sitka spruce and cedar lining the coast and that cold, clear water. Crystal clear, thirty feet down. I just paddled around every day, fished for my food. Read a lot of Gary Snyder and Jim Harrison. Took photographs. Something was awakening in me and it had to do with those whales and that little boat. One day, I'm sitting beside my campfire on that cove, watching the water, and this huge humpback breaches completely out of the water, then crashes down. Just an epic splash. Like he knew I was there, like he was putting on a show. So I grabbed my camera, and I thought to myself, *What are the odds that the whale will do that again?*

"And it did. Not two minutes later. Breached completely out of the water right in front of me, maybe thirty feet offshore. I stayed at that campsite for another four days and never saw another whale. Then I came back here."

"Isn't that something," Lyle said, clicking his tongue in appreciation. "You still have that photograph?"

"Lyle," Charlie sighed, "I don't need the photograph. I've got the story. I've got the memory, the wonder. Do you understand?"

"No," Lyle admitted, "I guess I don't."

"I don't need proof that God exists, Lyle. I *know* that there's something more. I've felt it. It was in those whales and it's in the coyotes outside this house. It's in that fire and this old single malt." He stood up from his chair and pointed his finger like a knife into Lyle's breastbone. "It's in you, buddy. It's in me. You just need to figure out what your . . . I don't know, where your whales are at. *What* they are. Because I know you see God in the world; I know you feel Him."

Charlie stood up from his chair, sighed deeply, and stretched his back. "But now I'm tired and I'm going to bed. Good night, Lyle."

"Hey, wait a minute, Charlie. You can't just go to bed like that."

"I ain't a missionary, Lyle. I didn't bang on your door tonight, trying to convert you. *You* came to me, remember? Don't you think that's telling? Here you are, in the middle of the night, as lost as I was out on that ocean, and you're searching for something, but every time someone throws you a rope, you wander off in another direction." Charlie threw his hands up in the air.

"Well, help me out then."

"No, you gotta help yourself, buddy. I'm old, I'm tired, and I'm going to sleep. The damn furnace at church is about on its last legs and I gotta figure out how the hell we're gonna pay for a new one. Or find some generous soul to volunteer his time to come resurrect the thing. I'm exhausted. Lock the door on your way out, will you?"

Lyle drank the remainder of the Scotch in a single gulp, patted the armrests of the old leather chair, turned the record player off, and walked back out into the cold, windy night.

(22)

THE APPLE TRUCK WAS OLD, DAMN NEAR AS OLD AS OTIS. ITS rusted bed was made a room by slats of ancient wood that rose up from above the wheel wells, so that standing there, among the loaded boxes of apples, pale early morning light fell in parallel yellow and white lines across the red fruit. Lyle moved about the bed of the truck, adjusting the heavy crates, stacking them up toward the cab before steadily moving his way backward to the tailgate. The morning sun was periodically obscured by low clouds banking in from Minnesota. Lyle felt the shadows chill his back and hands. His breath billowed.

It was shortly after dawn. He was not a man prone to complaint, but this morning was cold. He had stood in his kitchen for a while, holding his mug of coffee and letting the heat of the black liquid transfer through the ceramic into the cells of his callused skin. But not for too long. After last night's spat with Peg, he wanted to leave the house early. He knew that he had violated one of the hackneyed folk rules of marriage, *Don't go to bed angry*. Also, his head was fragile from Charlie's Scotch.

Lyle didn't drive the apple truck very often. No one did. Ordinarily, it sat in the lee of the apple house, collecting leaves in its bed, its tires bulging near the earth, cracked and low on air, as if the truck were too heavy for itself. But that morning, Lyle had been asked to bring a shipment of apples to a grocery store south of Redford, down the Mississippi, toward the Iowa border.

He had packed lunch in a brown paper bag. A salami sandwich with thickly cut cheddar cheese, a leaf of romaine lettuce, and Dijon mustard. A plastic bag of carrot sticks. A chocolate bar. And another plastic bag of pistachios for later, if necessary. He'd chuckled to himself there at the kitchen counter, thinking, *No need to worry about buying an apple*.

Before leaving the orchard, he laid a map on the bench seat of the truck and studied the crinkled paper in the gray light, tracing a finger over the day's route. He knew those serpentine back roads buttressed over by the canopies of ancient trees; he'd taken joyrides all over them as a younger man. In places, the roads followed sandstone gullies and canyons where sparrows nested in the soft rock, forming honeycomb matrices of nests. The roads followed streams and lesser rivers toward the Mississippi, where the sky opened and, along the banks of that wide brown thoroughfare, escarpments and coulees stood against the sky—the tallest things around.

Lyle slid the truck into drive and slowly began to merge onto the road. He did not see the deer until it was almost too late.

The creature stood on the road, big-eyed and blinking, as it went on chewing a mouthful of wet ditch grass, its muscles twitching under the tall crown of antlers framing its head. Lyle slammed his foot on the brake, and the old truck jerked to a violent stop; from the bed came the sound of several crates crashing over, and then a cavalcade of apples plopping down. The deer bounded off across the road and in seconds was long gone. Lyle raised a hand as if in apology. Then he exhaled and, reversing the truck off the road again, sat inside the idling cab and trembled.

He looked at his hands, so thick and dumb. They quaked. He could not remember when they had last looked young or nimble. Lyle was glad it was still so early in the morning; he'd seen no sign of Otis or Mabel, no lights in their windows, no blue glow from the television, the newspaper still peeking out of their mailbox. He would not have wanted them to see him like this, trembling and unnerved. Or their possibly damaged fruit.

Glancing in the driver's-side mirror, he noticed several apples in the gravel behind the truck. He placed the truck in park and stepped out. He commenced picking them up, gathering them in the concave fold of his canvas barn jacket. The apples were dusty. He examined them for bruises. Some he kicked into the tall grasses at the margin of the driveway. Once, in angrily trying to boot an apple, he actually slipped and fell onto the gravel, his back landing hard and flat on the little stones. He lay on the ground some time, the wind knocked out of him; it is always a shock, to lose control of one's body so completely, so unexpectedly, to feel so fragile—and especially so as an adult. It's commonplace enough to watch a toddler teeter over. Comical, even. But a sixty-, seventy-, or eighty-year-old? There is a good chance they might not stand back up, at least not without assistance. He looked at the palms of his hands where the gravel had left indentations, as if bitten by an animal with a mouth full of strange, erratic, and dull teeth. He bent his knees and sat up. All the apples he had collected were on the ground again. *Where they want to be,* he thought.

The diesel exhaust of the old truck hot at his neck and nauseating to breathe, he got to his feet and began collecting the apples again, placing them inside the last crate at the back of the load, and double-checked his cargo for wobbling cairns of fruit or spillage. The day was not brightening, but rather growing more gray. For the first time that year, he felt winter in the wind and examined the heavens for a sign of snow. Then he climbed back into the truck, placing the transmission in drive, and inched forward, and this time he scanned the road four times before moving out onto the lane in a slow and deliberate manner.

"Here we go," he said aloud. "An old man in an old

tank." He rubbed the dashboard in affection. The dials before him were huge and simple. He liked them very much.

Through sleepy towns and unincorporated villages he drove, always ten miles per hour below the posted limit. In the cold, muddy fields cows drowsed, their haunches covered in filth, steam rising off their backs. Down in the ditches, grasses and old flowering weeds heavy with frost lay down until spring, their lines defined in silver and platinum. Only the oaks were too stingy to drop their leaves yet, and there they hung, crisp and umber red.

The truck lumbered on, incapable of great speeds, but taking the corners and meanders of the road with a kind of stable grace that made Lyle almost light-headed, as if he were steering some small, stout ship. He held the wheel in his hands that way, as if he were captain, loosely, attentively, happily. The heater kicked out a dry steady breath of air that warmed his shins and kneecaps.

Lyle studied the geology of the road cuts he passed through, and thought suddenly of a young woman he'd recently met at Coulee Lands Covenant, a woman who'd proselytized to Lyle and Peg about the dangers of teaching evolution in public schools, clearly unaware that Peg had spent her entire career teaching in the area's public schools.

"How old are you?" Lyle had asked, even as Peg lightly swatted at his back with a paper church bulletin.

"Twenty-nine," she answered, already a bit defensive.

"And how old do you think this planet we're on is?" he asked, kindly.

"Seven thousand years," she said firmly. "Give or take." Her eyes were hard, dark.

He nodded and smiled. Then he said, "I'm no expert in evolutionary biology, geology, or anthropology; it's been a long, long time since I've sat in a classroom. But I'm over sixty now. Getting close to seventy. That seems like a good chunk of what you're calling our available history. And I have to tell you something. I hope I keep on evolving right up to the end. But I don't know how it could be that I represent such a vast percentage of history. Wouldn't that mean that my life, about sixty-five years so far, stood for, like, I'm guessing now . . . several dozen feet of bedrock? I don't know the technical terms for these things." He was sincerely interested in her opinion.

She placed her hands loosely on her hips. Several of her children orbited her knees, squawking. "Everything that is here was always here," she said. "God made things just as they are. I don't need to tell you that."

"No," Lyle agreed congenially. "I don't suppose that you do." Then he bent down to her children and shook their little hands. "Good morning," he said to each in turn. They smiled up at him.

He thought of her face then as he drove, this woman who had briefly flashed into his Sunday life. So assured of the world and her place in it. Lyle examined the sandstone walls of the road cut, weeping with spring-fed water, or maybe the heavy dew that must have come down off the hillsides and funneled there. Water weeping out of the pores of the land or perhaps slowly pushed up from somewhere deep inside things. He recalled the trilobite fossil he'd found in a quarry and kept on their bookshelves, one of his favorite mementos. He thought in that moment, *I like buildings made of stone and wood. I like old things.*

Then he thought, and knew, *I am an old thing.* And he smiled to himself despite the gloomy day. *Maybe,* he thought, *Charlie is right. Just let go of things. Try to believe, but ask questions, too. Don't be dumb.*

The apple truck came up out of a valley, and on another, brighter day, the sky and treetops would be lit with the sun's sweet fire. But this day promised relentless gray darkness. On the windshield, drops of rain flattened across the glass and were pushed away by the wind. Lyle found the switch to activate the wipers, but when they whooshed over the windshield unhelpfully, the dry old rubber and metal screeched across the glass. Lyle quit the wipers and stared through the windshield, smeared in places with the remains of insect bodies and the wing dust of moths. The road flattened. On both sides now were fields of harvested corn, stiff, short stalks desiccated to the palest white-yellow.

Lyle squinted at the world. The rain intensified suddenly in a microburst. He rolled the driver's-side window down and with his left arm squeegeed off a parcel of the glass ahead of him. It was useless. The sky and earth seemed to blur together, the air become water. He pulled the apple truck to the gravel shoulder of the road and sat, with the window down, breathing in the cool air, wet and fresh in his lungs. He had not smoked cigarettes since his truncated time in college, but just then, he wanted one. The warmth of it. A tobacco cloud to sit in, time slowing. Across the fields of October corn he saw no movement. The sky full of rags of cloud, as if streaked in soot and ash.

The truck was of a vintage with neither a clock nor a radio. Lyle inspected his Timex. There was no hurry. He glanced back into the bed of the truck. The apples glistened as if waxed, the brightest things in his world. The rain eased back into a drizzle and he turned the ignition on again, watched the hood of the truck steam. He merged back onto the road.

The grocery store was in a river town along the Mississippi at the base of a tall yellow bluff. Motorcyclists favored the town for its scenery and taverns. Lyle found the grocery store and parked the apple truck near the back of the parking lot, out of respect for the store's customers. He had brought no rain jacket or umbrella and walked quickly to the store's entrance through the drizzle. The rain flattened his hair to his head and dampened the sleeves and shoulders of his barn jacket. Inside the store he shook himself like a dog, and walked to the customer service desk. An older woman sat behind the counter watching a talk show on a small television. Lyle waited patiently; the store was warm and well-lit. Only when her program was interrupted by commercials did she turn to regard Lyle. He smiled at her. She raised her chin up as if to ask what he wanted.

"I've got a delivery of apples," Lyle said.

"You need receiving," the woman said flatly. She glanced away from him.

"Well, could you give them a call for me?" Lyle said, his voice soft and pleasant as the rain on the flat roof above them. "On the intercom or whatnot?"

She sighed heavily, pointed toward the rear of the store. "Talk to Getty," she said, turning back to the television.

He walked down an aisle full of the smells of bagged pet food and kitty litter. He regretted not exploring the store properly. Lyle loved grocery shopping. The slow progress of a wobbly cart through a store. The examination of vegetables and fruits. Feeling their specific weights. All the colors of these things, some grown here, some in places Lyle knew he would never visit: Chile, New Zealand, Guatemala. Before Hoot had gotten sick, they'd made the journey north to Eau Claire for the grand opening of a humongous new grocery store. A quarter of a million square feet of groceries. Unfamiliar with the store's layout, and neither of them having brought along cell phones, they wandered the store separated from each other for two hours—lost—before Lyle finally found Hoot in the huge beer cooler.

"Should have known you'd be in here," Lyle chided him.

"My lord," Hoot said dreamily. "Look at these prices. I'm in heaven."

They drove back to Redford that afternoon in Lyle's pickup, Hoot sipping a can of Old Milwaukee and saying,

"That's the reason Redford Appliance went under, you know. Stores like that. The little guy just can't compete."

"Sad, if you ask me," Lyle said.

"That's America though, ain't it," Hoot said. "The invisible hand and all that. Free market. Nobody was ever looking out for the little guy. I think we just got lucky is all. We were insulated from it in our little town. It was only a matter of time before the world found us."

———————

NEAR THE DAIRY SECTION LYLE SPOTTED TWO SWINGING doors. He went that way, pushing through the entrance and immediately saw a loading dock. A young man was standing at an open bay next to an older fellow, smoking cigarettes as they watched the rain fall. Lyle heard the water rushing down toward a drain he could not see. They looked at Lyle then, the young one tossing his cigarette out into the weather and exhaling a stream of smoke over his shoulder, as if caught in the act.

"Oh," said Lyle. "That's all right. I don't mean to interrupt."

"You ain't interrupting no one," said the old man, the butt of his cigarette hanging dry off his lower lip. "What can we do you for?"

"I got a load of apples from the Sourdough Orchard," Lyle said. It was cooler near the open bay door and Lyle shuddered.

The older man said, "Yeah, well, hell if I'm unloading a

truck full of apples in this shit." He drew on the cigarette and it crackled, both his fat hands remaining sunk in his pants pockets. The young man behind him looked down at his feet.

"Are you Getty?" Lyle tried again. "I'm Lyle. Lyle Hovde. I work for Otis and Mabel over at the Sourdough Orchard," Lyle said. "I've got a delivery of Honeycrisp apples and I picked most of them myself. Beautiful apples."

Getty puffed smoke. "Well, Lyle, just pull your rig right up against this bay and we'll get her unpacked. Eventually."

Lyle laughed. "I don't exactly have an eighteen-wheeler. And our old truck is gonna be lower than this loading bay."

Getty shook his head, tapped his cigarette, and wiped his nose with the back of a hand. "Lyle," said Getty, "I don't give a shit if you're Johnny Appleseed. My name is Arnold Getty, and here at Value Foods they pay me eight dollars an hour without any benefits. I been working here since before it was Value and I'll be working here after it gets bought by the next damn group of suits. And so, no disrespect, Lyle, but I ain't going out in that cold-ass rain. I just ain't. That rain's bound to quit at some point. We can wait, or you unload the apples yourself. Your choice. I really don't give a shit."

Lyle looked at his watch. It was ten o clock in the morning. Loading the truck without help had taken him almost two hours earlier in the morning. He knew the apples would not be damaged by the rain and he had no strong inclination to go back out into it. "All right," Lyle said, looking Getty in the eye determinedly, "let's give it an hour."

"Sure," said Getty. "An hour. Though I got to tell you. I'm out of here at five no matter what. So you better hope this passes over. Otherwise you're shit out of luck. These doors get locked at five if those apples are loaded, or not. Them are the rules."

Lyle leaned out of the loading dock and glanced at the sky. He could see no breaks in the gray above, no rifts of lightness. Just an unending shawl of muted darkness.

"If it's all the same to you," Lyle said, "I'm going to pull the truck around where we can keep an eye on it. That way, if it does quit, we can get right to work."

"Right," said Getty. "Sure. Gotta keep an eye on them apples. Never know who's going to come around and steal a truck full of apples. Especially in a rainstorm." He snorted and punched the younger man in the bicep. Getty coughed up phlegm and spit it out the door.

Lyle left the two men and, walking the periphery of the store, was tempted to buy a few fresh doughnuts, then remembered the lunch he'd packed. He jogged across the parking lot to the truck and slung himself into the cab, where it was as dry as a cave. Wishing that he had thought to bring another jacket, or a thick sweater, he turned the truck on and let the heater dry him out. He watched cars come and go, old women with their hair covered in plastic kerchiefs and mothers with little children clinging to their pale wet hands. Lyle ate his lunch slowly, checking his watch more frequently than was normal. The rain continued.

When he had finished eating, Lyle folded the paper bag neatly and placed it into the glove box. He liked to recycle a bag until the fibers of the paper began to deteriorate. Putting the old apple truck into drive, Lyle taxied it around the store to the back, where the loading bay docks were. Then he carefully backed it up against the cement wall of the bay. Still, the truck and its bed of cargo sat three feet below the lip of the bay door. Getty and the younger man were just as Lyle had left them, leaning against the walls of the main bay, smoking and spitting into the incessant rain. Lyle left the cab and moved quickly toward the squat staircase leading up to the loading bays. His boots were thoroughly soaked now and his socks sodden.

Getty looked at Lyle, dripping rain onto the floor of the store's receiving department. "What's your goddamn hurry?" he said, shaking his head.

Lyle shrugged. "I didn't think I was hurrying."

"I mean, it's not like you have another delivery today, do you?" asked Getty.

"You're right," Lyle said. "This is it. The last of the harvest." He looked at the apples with some amount of pride and a small share of sadness, too. He would miss his time in the orchard once winter arrived. He looked again at the sky.

"Well," said Getty, "I think you ought to take a load

off. Sit down. Take a nap if you want. Me and the kid are headed to lunch. You want anything? A milk shake? Burger? Fries?" Getty and the young man were gathering their jackets and baseball caps.

"No thanks," said Lyle. "If things get desperate, I have a truck full of apples."

"Sure," said Getty. "Apples." Getty and the young man left.

Lyle sat on a plastic milk crate and watched the rain unite itself into puddles. He thought of the mercury he and his brothers had once played with as schoolchildren. How their teacher had circulated a beaker of the quicksilver for her pupils to examine in the palms of their hands. Lyle watched the rain find every inequity of the parking lot's asphalt.

A pack of Marlboros sat on top of a wooden desk otherwise buried under sheaves of moldering newspaper sports sections and duplicate invoices. Above the desk, the thin glossy pages of a bikini calendar chuffed gently in the disturbed air. Lyle stood from his milk crate and gently tapped out a cigarette from the soft cellophane pack. He placed the cigarette between his lips. Then he patted the pockets of his pants and jacket in vain, for of course he didn't have any matches or a lighter. Clenching the purloined cigarette between his lips, he rifled through Getty's desk drawers until he found a box of matches. He returned to the milk crate. He was very aware of the cigarette between his lips, aware in a way he suspected only teenagers are when they first leave the safety of their parents and go out into the world, experimenting with everything. He struck a match and considered its small flame.

Lyle thought, *This is probably a stupid thing to do.*

But the cloud of smoke that he made, that he inhaled, was delicious and dry and warmly delirious and his head went light as a balloon. He held the smoke inside his rib cage, as if a secret. Then exhaled, slowly. It was nice to be aware of his breathing. *This must be what yoga is like. Breathing,* Lyle thought. He relaxed his shoulders and legs and stared at the apples. The temperature seemed to be dropping, and he was happy again for the cigarette, for the little fire between his fingers and before his face. How young he felt all of a sudden, how foolish.

He smoked the cigarette down to the filter, then mashed the tip into the heel of his boot and placed the butt into the pocket of his pants and stood, a little haltingly. This was called "fieldstripping" a cigarette, he remembered; someone had told him this one time, some friend back from Vietnam . . . Anyway, he did not like the leftover taste in his mouth. Lyle considered requisitioning an apple to refresh his palate, but then worried someone from the store might accuse him of stealing. So he walked back into the grocery store in search of breath mints. After buying a pack, he detoured through produce, examining the store's inventory of apples. Most were from Washington. A few from New Zealand. He touched the fruit and knew the apples to be past their prime, the meat beneath their skins surely mushy by now and without much taste. He walked back to receiving. Water poured off the eaves, gushed out of the downspouts.

"You want something done right," Lyle said aloud and to himself, "you've got to do it yourself."

Fortified by the cigarette and a mouth full of cinnamon breath mints, Lyle went back out into the rain now and began unloading the truck, standing near the tailgate and placing crate after crate of apples onto the edge of the loading dock. When there was no room for another, he moved back inside and stacked the crates on a pallet he dragged to the center of the room. The rain did not quit, but neither did Lyle. Steadily, the truck was unloaded, the axels groaning with a newfound lightness. Lyle worked quickly; he wanted to stay warm, it was true, but he also wanted the job done before Getty returned from his lunch.

Lyle's garments by now were soaked through and heavy. He wished for a thermos of hot chocolate or hot cider, but there was none and he had already drunk all the coffee from the morning. He wiped water off the crystal of his watch. It was already half past one; Getty and his assistant had been gone almost two hours. And now an eighteen-wheeler was lurching into the back parking lot, its trailer emblazoned with the red-and-white Coca-Cola logo. The driver was a young man who rolled down a window in his cab and yelled, "Where's that fucknut Getty?"

Lyle looked up, rain dripping past his eyebrows, his

eyelids. He held a hand to his brow to deflect the rain and studied this new interloper. "Lunch, I think," said Lyle.

"That fatass," said the driver. "Let me back this rig up and I'll give you a hand."

Lyle was almost done anyway, but he watched the young man expertly back the trailer to the loading bay dock beside the old apple truck. The rear of the trailer kissed the side of the building perfectly—two big things coming together. Then the young man jumped out of his cab and leaped up into the apple truck.

"Let's do a bucket brigade," he suggested to Lyle. "You get inside out of this rain and I pass you the remaining crates."

"Sounds good to me," said Lyle, "but, you know, you don't have to do this."

"Call it karma," said the young man. "My name's James Alan. People call me Jay."

"Jay," said Lyle. "I'm Lyle."

"Well, Lyle," said Jay, "get yourself inside."

Lyle pulled himself up and out of the apple truck and onto the loading bay. The sky was lightening in the west. Lyle grabbed another pallet and began placing the crates upon it while Jay emptied the last of the crates from the truck onto the loading bay and then moved inside to help Lyle. Outside, the rain had lifted. They worked efficiently together. Lyle immediately liked the young man's silence, his brawn, his charity.

Just as the very last crate had been placed on the lip of the loading dock, Getty and his assistant slammed through the plastic doors. "Well, I'll be dipped in shit," Getty said loudly.

Lyle ran down to the truck, grabbed the invoice, and handed it to Getty. "I just need a signature."

"Sure thing. But first, I'm going to have to inspect this delivery," Getty drawled. "You see, normally my assistant here and I unload the truck, but obviously, we had an over-eager driver today." Getty's breath smelled of the tang of beer and greasy food; a yellow smudge of mustard was ingrained on his stubbled chin.

"Go fuck yourself," Jay said, as he reached the loading bay dock. "Sign the man's invoice or I'll talk to the manager right now, you old prick."

"All right, all right," Getty said, drawing a crude X on the invoice and dropping the paper at Lyle's boots. "Anything to get rid of the two of you."

"I don't know how to thank you," Lyle said to Jay. "Would you give me your name and address? A telephone number? I'd like to repay the favor."

"Don't worry about it," Jay said. "Get back in that rig of yours and get warm. This old bastard has been harassing me for years. You just have to know how to threaten him. He doesn't respond to civility."

Lyle extended his hand to Jay, said, "Thank you, son. Thank you for helping an old man out."

"You're welcome," Jay said, shaking Lyle's hand. Then,

breaking into a broad grin, "Now get out of here before Getty changes his mind."

DESPITE THE GLOOM OF THE SHORTENING AFTERNOONS, LYLE felt the day to be brighter, more buoyant as he retraced his morning's route in the ancient International truck. He'd never called a younger man *son* before, and wondered suddenly if he'd overreached, if he'd embarrassed Jay. A wave of emotion washed over him, alone in that dusty cab, and he thought about his lost son, and how, if he'd grown, he might have been about Jay's age now. What paths would he have chosen, what jobs, what women (or men) might he have fallen in love with? He imagined all the days they might have shared, and years: fishing on the Mississippi, deer hunting, baseball games, graduations, marriages, children . . . That abbreviated line of life, of opportunity, that had just disappeared . . .

Suddenly, the truck was struck on its driver's side, near the rear bumper, and Lyle fought with both arms to keep the truck from tipping over and blocking the road. Then the big truck settled all four wheels back down on the asphalt, and Lyle pulled the rig to the shoulder of the road to catch his breath. He glanced in the rearview mirror and saw, to his horror, a compact car, its hood nearly flattened, steam billowing out of the engine, and a driver, a young man, standing out in the rain, flailing his arms.

Lyle left the truck and walked down the side of the wet

road. The young man could not even have been in college yet, just a gangly fellow, all long limbs, floppy fine hair, and the wispiest of mustaches. His glasses were fogged over and streaked with rain.

"Are you all right there?" Lyle asked.

"You *hit* me!" the kid screamed, his voice high-pitched and whiny.

"Are you all right?" Lyle repeated, this time from a distance of five or six feet. He wanted to reach out and console the teenager, but the kid seemed on the brink of a breakdown. "Hey now, calm yourself down!"

"You smashed my fucking sled, man!"

"No," Lyle said evenly. "I did not. Look, you can tell by the tire marks in the road. See?" He pointed to the asphalt where you could see the rubber left by their tires when the collision occurred. "I was in the road, kid. In my lane. You must have been . . ."

He looked up the driveway the kid had come from. It was a long country two track, leading to a humble ranch house. The driveway was at least a quarter-mile long and there were very few trees to impede a view of the road. Lyle looked at the road, in either direction: no traffic—none.

"What the hell were you doing?" Lyle asked. "On your phone? How could you *not* have seen me? I'm driving a one-ton pickup."

"I, uh, well, I mean . . . You didn't see me either," the kid stuttered.

"It's not my job to see you, I was driving *in my lane*," Lyle said. "On the road. Were you playing with the radio? You know what, let's get your parents. They're going to need to know anyway."

"They're not home," the kid said quickly.

"All right then, we need to call the cops."

The teenager lost three inches then, deflated like a sad balloon.

"What's wrong?" Lyle said.

"I, like, *just* got my license," the kid admitted. "A week ago."

"A week ago!" Lyle snorted. He began laughing, hard, bent over at the waist. After all the sadness of Hoot's cancer, Shiloh and Isaac moving out, Isaac's diabetes and all the prayer-healing business, Lyle just let it all go. Laughed as he hadn't laughed in many years. Tears came streaking down his cheeks, and he was glad of the rain, its camouflage. "A week ago!" he repeated, higher pitched this time.

"Very funny," the kid said, "all right, very funny."

Finally, Lyle wiped his face and caught his breath. The kid looked at him expectantly.

"Let me look at my truck real quick and we'll figure out what our next step is," Lyle said. He checked his watch—a little after three—the sun so low in the sky and cloaked behind a cloud range.

The truck, all old American steel and built for the ages,

was basically unscathed, as Lyle thought it might be. The bumper showed a little battle scar of gray paint from the kid's hood, but that was it. The kid's car looked like a plastic go-cart cobbled together after the apocalypse.

Lyle returned to the teenager, now hugging himself against the cold and rain.

"Two options," Lyle said. "We could definitely call the police. You'll get a ticket and your insurance will go through the roof."

"Or?" the kid asked hopefully.

"We call your parents, push your ruined rig back to your house, and we go our separate ways."

"All right," the kid said, "I'll call my ma."

Lyle slipped behind the wheel of the little car, put the car into neutral, and waited for the kid to get off his phone.

"She's done with work in about an hour," the teenager said. "I'm supposed to apologize to you."

Lyle waited.

"Sorry," the kid offered. "I didn't see you coming. I was texting my buddy. It was stupid. I'm sorry." And then he began crying, his narrow shoulders racked. "I saved up for this car, too," he said. "Cost me fifteen hundred bucks."

His face was bright red and his glasses now more fogged over than ever. "Everyone at school is going to laugh their asses off at me."

Lyle set a hand on the kid's shoulder, gave him a grand-fatherly squeeze. Then he gently removed the glasses from the teenager's face and wiped them clean on the soft fabric of his shirt, blowing some steam on the lenses and cleaning them again.

"You should clean your glasses more than once a year," Lyle said kindly. "You might've even seen me coming if these glasses hadn't been so filthy. Come on. Let's push this heap up to your house."

———

IT TOOK THEM FORTY-FIVE MINUTES TO PUSH THE CAR BACK UP the driveway. During that time, not one pickup, car, or milk-hauling truck came down the road. Not a one. The first car they saw was the kid's mom's, her headlights bouncing up the driveway. When she slung out of her vehicle, she simply stood in the driveway, hands squeezed into fists and planted at her hips, and glared at the kid. "A week?" she said, shaking her head.

Later they sat inside the house, around a small, round oak kitchen table, and made polite chitchat. The whole time, Lyle looked out the windows, waiting for another car to flash by, but none did. He checked his watch before he walked back down the driveway. Another half hour had gone by.

———

AFTER LYLE RETURNED THE APPLE TRUCK TO OTIS AND MABEL'S and explained to them why he was late, he drove his own pickup truck home. Peg was waiting for him. She'd made a beef roast with carrots, onions, potatoes, and parsnips.

There was fresh bread and a salad, and she was drinking a glass of red wine. She did not say hello to him, just sat at the kitchen table, reading a novel—Willa Cather's *O, Pioneers!*

"I'm sorry, Peg," Lyle said. "I'm sorry about last night. I'll try harder. I want to try harder. I don't want you to be mad at me. I'm sorry."

She remained in the chair, and licking her finger to turn the page, did not look his way.

He went over to her and dropped to one knee, both of his hands on her right arm. Now she set her book on the table, sighed, and regarded him.

"You're freezing," she said. "Your hands are like death and your face is raw."

"I'm sorry," he repeated.

"I made roast beef."

"I'll try harder with Shiloh. I'll try harder with church. I do think we need to talk to her about Isaac, though, about his diabetes. I'm worried about him."

"Well, you can be stubborn as an ass," she said, "but I do love you."

"I think I'd like to eat something," Lyle said, "and then maybe crawl into bed."

"Let me fix you a plate," Peg said. "Go take a hot shower."

———————

HE ALMOST FELL ASLEEP IN THE SHOWER, THE HOT STEAM FELT so good, the hot water on his cold clammy skin, the smell of his favorite pine-tar soap. After toweling off, he changed into fresh, warm clothes, and simply slunk into their bed.

Peg stood at their bedroom door, now in her nightgown, combing her hair.

"Don't you want your dinner?" she asked.

"I was hit by a car," Lyle murmured.

"What?" Peg said.

"This kid, this teenage kid. He was texting. Ran right into the apple truck."

"Are you okay? Is he?"

"His car is totaled," Lyle said softly. "But it reminded me of old Doc Wagner, you remember him?" Lyle's eyelids felt so heavy, his bedsheets so soft and warm.

"Of course, Doc Wagner. He delivered me. Delivered my mom, too. What about him? Lyle? Is your head okay? Lyle?"

But Lyle was already asleep, and could not repeat the story of the country doctor who, up until his death, had no office to hang his hang hat in, just a beloved forest green Jeep Wagoneer dubbed The Dragon that he drove from house call to house call, armed with an aged leather satchel, musical with the sound of rattling pills, needles, and bottles of syrup. The last of the family practitioners in Redford, a man who accepted as payment eggs, homemade bread, honey, jams, pickles, blankets, pottery, paintings, meat, cheese, milk—anything a patient could offer.

The old doctor who, one day during deer-hunting season, was driving on a back road when a stray bullet fired more than a mile and a half away by a thirteen-year-old hunter passed through the open window of his Wagoneer, striking him on the side of the temple with enough force to apparently trigger an embolism that caused him to die, the lead slug thankfully not entering his head, not even breaking the skin, but simply falling into his lap. The Dragon then slowing to a final stop in a hedgerow of old cedars, where he was found slumped against the wheel.

How is it, Lyle had been thinking all evening, that this boy strikes the very truck I am driving, when, for the next *hour*—and maybe more, who knew?—not a *single* other vehicle passed that way? How did our lines intersect? And how did that bullet, that stray bullet, strike the good doctor in just such a way as to end his life? How, Lyle had been thinking, is it that I am here? That I found Peg? That we found Shiloh? How is it that this isn't some grand dream? How can it all be random, chance, a beautiful cosmic accident? How?

(23)

A FEW DAYS LATER HE DROVE TO LA CROSSE, TO COULEE LANDS
Covenant. The day was bright, clear, and crisp. Down
the flyway came tens of thousands of birds: geese, ducks,
cranes, swans, and multitudes of songbirds in all shapes
and colors. Lyle had called Shiloh a day earlier and offered
to take her out to lunch and she'd seemed excited, even.
Excited to spend time with him. For months he'd been
apologizing, attending her church, trying to atone, trying
to get back in her good graces, and finally it seemed, he'd
broken through, or perhaps just worn her down.

Letting himself into the old theater, Lyle walked toward the church "office," really an old storage room, a
space that in the past had held silver canisters of film, paper cups, great bags of unpopped corn kernels, candy, napkins, and the like. Now, the room was crammed with two

small desks, a copy machine, reams of paper, garbage cans, and office supplies. He heard their fighting immediately.

"Do you love her?" Shiloh shouted.

"How dare you!" Steven said, low and threatening, trying to guide the argument down from its audible heights. "How dare you question me!"

"Everyone sees it! Everyone! You're killing me, you know! We're supposed to be married in the spring and you're . . . you're flirting, you're off . . . what? *Fellowshipping?* With that . . . that piece of trash!"

"I saved you!" he barked now. "Saved you and Isaac. You were lost. Your so-called family, those nonbelievers? We brought you in. Gave you a job. Gave you a path, a meaning. And you question me?"

"Yes, Steven," she responded, "I will question my fiancé."

"No, you won't," he said coldly. "That isn't the *gentle and quiet spirit* that I fell in love with, that the Bible calls for. I'm of half a mind to call the marriage off. You can find another church, another job.

"You'll be right back where you always were, Shiloh. Bouncing around like an old ball. Rolling right back to your parents' house.

"No. I've done nothing wrong, and as the leader of this church, and the leader of *our family*, I won't have you usurping my power. If that's what you want, find another man."

"No!" Shiloh yelled. "No, Steven, *wait!*"

"You give that some thought, woman," he said, menacingly. "You think about what you believe, and where you want to belong. I'm about to get some lunch, and when I come back, I would like to see my fiancée here, that woman that *I know* submits to her *church* and, by God, to her *husband*."

Lyle quickly pressed himself up the narrow stairs that led to the projectionist's room as Steven stormed right by, through the hallway Lyle had just occupied, and blasted through the double doors out front. A moment later, there was the sound of his pickup truck peeling off, and fast.

Lyle waited a few minutes on those broken-down red velvet stairs, sitting there, listening, as his daughter cried softly in the office. Finally, he got up and quietly padded down the stairs, pretending to open and close the front door, and walked up to the office door, giving an innocent knock, knock. The confined space smelled of spilled melted butter.

"Hello," he called out cheerily enough.

"Oh, hey, Dad," Shiloh said, blowing her nose into a tissue.

"Still on for lunch?" he asked.

She sighed. "I'm really not very hungry to be honest." She would not make eye contact with him.

"Darling," Lyle said gently, "is everything all right?"

"Yes," she lied. "Everything is just fine." Then, "Oh, all right, fine. Come on, let's go."

THEY ATE AT A SMALL DINER, SHILOH PUSHING ANEMIC LEAVES of lettuce around her plate, while Lyle felt guilty about the greasy cheeseburger he was enjoying.

"How's Isaac?" Lyle asked. "How's he getting on in school?"

"He's great," Shiloh answered. "You know how smart he is. School will never be a real challenge for him."

"And how about his diabetes?" Lyle continued. It was a direct question, he knew, and a risk that might shut down the remainder of their conversation, but he had to try.

"Fine, Dad. He's fine. He's a happy, healthy little boy." She sipped from a tall glass of cold water.

"How's Hoot?" she asked.

How quickly Shiloh could redirect or distract. It had always been this way, beginning in her teenage years, when she began perfecting her tactics, testing her parents' weaknesses, lobbing artillery and mortar shells at their weakened defenses.

"I don't know," Lyle admitted, looking at his plate. "After I leave you, I'm headed over to the hospital to check in on him." He did not say, *I'm afraid of what I'll find.*

He reached for her hand. "Sweetheart, are you sure you're okay? Is there anything you want to tell me? Anything I can do?"

"Dad!" she said loudly enough to still the dining room. She'd violently drawn her hands away from his touch. "I don't need your *fixing.* I'm fine, okay? We're all just fine. You know what? Could you please just . . . take me back to the church. Steven has some important work for me this afternoon."

He looked down at the table for several moments,

wanted very much to tell her he'd heard their argument, that they'd seen Steven after church with the other young woman, that he was afraid for Isaac, that he loved her more than she'd ever know . . . but glancing up to find their waitress looking at him, concern in her eyes, he simply motioned for the check, left some money on the table, and they walked out of the diner without a word, back into the bright, early afternoon sun.

———————

HE PULLED THE TRUCK TO THE FRONT OF THE OLD THEATER AND Shiloh barely managed a curt *thank-you* before fairly jumping out the passenger side, giving the rusty door a solid swing shut. Steven was waiting just outside the church's door and gave her a hug, keeping his eyes on Lyle the entire time. Then Steven kissed Shiloh on the top of her head and walked slowly toward the truck, opening the passenger-side door.

"You're trying to wedge us apart, Lyle, aren't you?" Steven said evenly.

"I'm trying to watch out for my daughter," Lyle said. "And my grandson, too."

"No. You're sowing discord, is what you're doing. You're planting doubt. But you won't win. I'm stronger than you are."

"You're a goddamn phony," Lyle replied. "I realized it's been a long time since I've had contact with a bona fide confidence man, but that's exactly what you are. You're a two-bit hustler and a goddamn huckster. You're a snake-oil salesman, you son of a bitch. And if you endanger my grandson, I swear to God I will personally kick the shit out of you. And I'll have fun doing it."

With that, he stepped on the gas and the door clapped shut, as if applauding him.

———◆———

HE COULD HEAR HOOT'S LAUGHTER DOWN THE SHINING hallway—that rumbling, sticky-sweet and low-down laughter—long before he reached his friend's room. And when Lyle popped his head past the door, there was Hoot, sitting up in his bed, a pair of nurses and a young doctor surrounding him in a horseshoe of smiles and laughter.

"There's my buddy," Hoot said, his voice stronger than it had sounded in weeks, his eyes clearer, less milky and yellow.

Lyle stood there, dumbfounded. He had half-prepared himself to find his friend, frankly, gone—passed away. He'd prepared himself to sit beside Hoot and say good-bye. But there his friend sat—the old diehard—like a plant that perks right up after a watering.

"He thought I was a goner," Hoot joked to the nurses. "Look at him. You could knock him over with a feather."

"So," Lyle began, a little laugh escaping his lips, "you're feeling better, I take it?"

"I *am* feeling better," Hoot said, though the cough was still there, punctuating his every other utterance.

The doctor and nurses looked at Lyle gamely.

"Well," Lyle began, "that's great."

"Hey, buddy, I'm done with it all," he said solemnly. "I'm done with the cigarettes and beer, Lyle. If they ever let me out of here, I'm telling you, I'm going to find myself a hobby. Something to keep my hands busy. Maybe fix up that other Mustang."

"Crocheting?" a nurse offered. "Needlepoint?"

Hoot snapped his fingers. "Exactly. Genius."

Lyle flopped into a chair. "So the chemo is working?"

Hoot shrugged his shoulders. "Who knows? *Something's* working. I feel good, Lyle. Maybe I've turned a corner on this thing. Maybe I can actually lick it."

"Of course you can," Lyle heard himself say.

"Wanna watch some TV?" Hoot asked, grinning. "*Wheel of Fortune* is on."

———◆———

LATER THAT EVENING AFTER LYLE LEFT HOOT'S HOSPITAL room, the young doctor pulled Lyle aside near the elevators.

"Look," the doctor said, "I didn't want to upset Mr. Shaw earlier this evening, he's obviously having a good day . . ."

"Yeah," Lyle said quietly.

The doctor frowned and rubbed at his forehead. "Your friend's condition isn't actually getting any better. I'm not saying it *won't* get any better or *can't* get any better, but I just looked at an X-ray and . . . the cancer is still very prevalent."

"But you heard him," Lyle said almost pleadingly, "he's feeling better. He's my friend. He's a fighter." Lyle heard a trembling in his own voice. "He might be able to beat this thing."

The doctor laid a hand on Lyle's shoulder.

"I don't doubt you or Mr. Shaw. He's a tough old guy, and we all love him here, I hope you see that. He's a good, good man. But you need to prepare yourself, sir. Your friend might not win this battle. He's going to have days like this. And then there'll be others, bad days. Ups and downs. Do you understand me?"

Lyle nodded his head, might've said, *I was hoping for a miracle.*

WINTER

(24)

AFTER CHURCH ONE SUNDAY, PEG SAID, "I'D LIKE TO DRIVE UP to Lake Superior. Could we do that, Lyle?"

They stood beside their car on a gray late-November day, the wind whipping at their collars, crazing their hair. Hoot was no longer making the trek to Coulee Lands. His health had begun slipping again and he rarely left his house; hospice nurses were visiting twice a day. His sister had somehow heard through the grapevine that Hoot was grievously ill, and that weekend she'd managed to convince him to visit a nearby casino where they could sit for hours, playing nickel slots, chatting, and people watching.

So it was that on that particular Sunday, Lyle and Peg were by themselves after church, without having to shuttle Hoot back home or to the hospital.

"Sounds good to me," said Lyle.

They drove north in contented silence. Lyle hadn't told Peg about his confrontation with Steven, and Lyle suspected Steven hadn't said anything to Shiloh either. A mutual avoidance policy seemed to have taken hold, with either man eschewing the other like an opposing magnet.

The roads were empty. Both the Vikings and the Packers were playing that afternoon, so everyone was gathered in bars and taverns, restaurants and living rooms, hunkered around the TV. Save for the side-sweeping wind, the driving was easy.

Lyle decided to guide them up to Duluth, some three hours away. They'd make the city before sunset, time enough to see the big lake, watch the last of the season's freighters, and then turn right back around. There are days in the American middle west when nothing seems more natural than driving long distances if only to leave your hometown for a handful of hours; a trip that would be unfathomable to most of the world's population might be a recreational way to spend a Sunday: photographing autumnal leaves, tracing the path of the Mississippi or St. Croix rivers, the coastlines of Lake Superior or Lake Michigan (inland oceans, really), hiking a path up to some small waterfall, or perhaps a long foray for something as simple as a slice of pie. When there is nothing to do—drive.

They progressed from farmland and oak savannahs to maple forests and aspen slash. Then the trees were taller, wider—more conifers, and crowded closer to the road. Every so often a deer or two could be seen, racing from one side of the road to the other and then disappearing into the pine forests. Snow began falling, big, slowly sifting-down flakes.

The traffic picked up as they drove into Superior, that old rust-belt town, Duluth's less fortunate and less attractive stepsister. Past sad dive bars, grimy gas stations, and fast-food joints, they continued until being sucked up onto a matrix of high bridges and overpasses, the lake down below them and spread all over the eastern horizon, cold and angry and boiling with huge freshwater waves, a few brave freighters out there, nosing through the onslaught of whitecaps.

They parked near Canal Park, of course, where all the tourists wander around, but it was Peg who led them out onto a long breakwater, waves splashing over the rocky embankments and up onto the concrete path. The wind tore at them and it was difficult even placing one foot ahead of the other. Tears streamed down their faces, the wind was so ferocious.

"You're a crazy woman!" Lyle shouted.

"Just a little farther!" Peg replied.

They turned and looked back at Duluth, the old harbor town so steeply set on its stony hillside, the old brick buildings and the newer more glitzy structures.

"This isn't safe!" Lyle shouted.

"I think you're right!" Peg agreed.

And so they held hands and walked back toward their car, where they blasted the heater and held their faces and hands close to the vents in an effort to thaw out.

At Fitger's Brewhouse, they sat and drank cold dark beer that warmed them from the inside out, first one then two, and then three beers apiece. Finally, their dinner arrived and they ate lustily until they were almost groggy, only to stumble back out into the cold to walk themselves sober.

"Isaac wasn't able to heal Hoot, was he?" Peg asked. "Is that terrible of me to ask?"

"I think," Lyle began, "that we all tried our hardest. Or maybe I should say that you all tried your hardest. And maybe it won't be enough. Maybe the cancer was just too aggressive, too advanced. But at least you tried."

"Do you think he can heal people, Lyle?"

"I don't know," he began. "I really don't. But according to Charlie, I'm supposed to trust my gut, I'm supposed to trust my feelings. It could be that Hoot is just too sick, and maybe Isaac was able to give him a little comfort—I believe that much. Seeing Hoot that one day when he felt great, when he felt like he might beat it . . . Maybe Isaac did that. I don't know, Peg. I've always tried to understand, but maybe that wasn't the right way to go about things . . ."

"I think he might be able to heal people," Peg said, "I honestly do. I *felt* something in that hospital room. I can't explain it."

On the ride home, Peg fell instantly asleep, and Lyle drove through the first blizzard of the season. There were no other tire tracks on the road and driving through the blinding snow felt like drifting through outer space, this new path forward.

(25)

ON THE AFTERNOON OF CHRISTMAS EVE, LYLE FOUND HIMSELF back in Coulee Lands Covenant, the old movie theater drafty and cold, and Peg pressed close to him just to retain some measure of warmth. Lyle noticed that the congregation seemed shrunk by perhaps a quarter, if not a third, far more empty seats than one might expect for such an important day on the church's calendar.

"Where is everyone?" he whispered to Peg.

"Didn't you hear?" she whispered back.

"No one tells me anything, you know that."

Taking a pen from her purse she found an offering envelope and wrote:

Steven was accused of sleeping with a female parishioner

Lyle wrote beneath that:

Didn't we suspect that?

Peg shrugged, scrawled:

Our daughter insists he hasn't

"Uh-huh," Lyle murmured, glancing down the row toward Shiloh, who stared at the band and the makeshift pulpit. For the first time, Lyle felt that the sanctuary, the congregation, all of it, seemed precarious, unstable, close to failure, a charade dangling on the brink of collapse. He took the offering envelope, crumpled it, and slipped it into his pocket.

When Steven stood before the church, no mercurial smile parted his lips. His eyes were without light, and his shoulders slumped. "Let's begin with a prayer," he said solemnly.

The congregation bowed their heads, but Lyle simply looked out, watching the other congregants, as was his custom: a woman twirling a lock of hair around a restless finger, a little girl scratching at her white tights, an old man rubbing at his closely cropped beard to produce a sound like sandpaper. There was a spider's web located almost directly over the pulpit, and for weeks now, Lyle had been silently hoping that one Sunday morning, the spider would descend on a silvery strand of silk and land on Steven's head or shoulders.

Midway through the service, the children's choir took

to the front of the worship area, led by their diminutive director, who summited her wooden crate, raised both hands in the air, and began conducting her charges.

They sang "Silent Night" without an accompaniment, just a dozen or more children, their voices high-pitched but true, their eyes all focused on their leader, this little woman who seemed to draw sound right out of their bodies with her guiding hands, her encouraging face.

Lyle hadn't realized he was leaning forward intently, that he was holding hands with Peg, but he was rapt. There are few things more powerful than a choir, Lyle thought, whether perfectly synchronized or not, young or elderly, supremely talented or entirely humdrum. That a group of brave and generous individuals might decide to collect as one, to raise their voices against silence and attempt to fill an otherwise empty space with art and sound . . . how beautiful it was.

After the song was completed, Lyle gave Isaac a wink and a little wave. The boy smiled back at him, and then leaned toward his friend Sadie, who was not so subtly whispering into his ear, *Merry Christmas, Isaac.*

———

LATER IN THE SERVICE, STEVEN AMBLED AROUND THE PULPIT a few moments, before saying, "I hate to say this to you folks before Christmas and all, but this church is in danger. Our budget is," and here his voice trailed off, "our budget is broken. Busted. At this rate, we can only afford to pay our rent another month or two."

A few gasps erupted from the congregation, mixed with plaintive rumblings and the occasional sob.

"So it's up to you, then," Steven said. "How much do you believe? How much do you care? How much is this church worth to you? How much has this church bestowed upon *you*? What have you taken, and what are you willing to give back?"

He continued pacing the floor near the pulpit, hands in his pockets.

"Many of you," he said flatly, "simply are not tithing. You're not living up to your Christian obligations, the guidelines set down for you *not by me,* you understand, but by the Bible. Your Bible. So, it's up to you. What kind of world do you want to live in? What kind of community do you want for your families? This is *your* church." Steven fell silent now, threw his hands up, as if in defeat. "Let's end with a prayer for scattering."

As Lyle and Peg were departing Coulee Lands, Peg gently took Shiloh's elbow and said, "We'll be going to midnight mass at St. Olaf's. Are you sure you all don't want to come with us? We could have Christmas at our house tomorrow morning . . ."

Shiloh gave Peg a hug and kissed her on the cheek. "I think we'll stay at our own house for Christmas this year, Mom."

"All right, then," Peg said gamely. "We love you, sweetheart. Take care of that little boy."

"I will," she replied.

Back at their house, they wrapped presents, tied bows, and sipped eggnog while listening to an all-day Christmas carol radio station: Bing Crosby and Nat King Cole, Dean Martin and Elvis Presley, everything under the sun, actually, all the way down to Chuck Berry, Run-DMC, and even Wham!

But the day felt very blue, terribly lonely, and eventually Lyle retreated to the living room where he succumbed to a nap in his favorite chair. Christmas simply didn't feel like the same holiday without children, or even young adults. It wasn't until past dinnertime that Peg roused him and they ate a small meal of ham-bone soup and toasted cheese sandwiches.

"I hate this Christmas song," Lyle said at last, turning off the radio.

"You don't like John Lennon?" Peg asked, trying to stifle a small laugh.

"It's just that, only John Lennon could write a Christmas song that made you feel like a fool for ever liking Christmas at all. Paul McCartney would never do that. Or George or Ringo, for that matter."

"Are you okay?" Peg asked.

"I think so," Lyle answered. "Sure. I'm okay."

———————

IT WAS THEIR TRADITION TO ATTEND MIDNIGHT MASS AT ST. Olaf's, and so at ten forty-five they drove to the old church through lightly falling snow and the night was unusually quiet, no trains crazing through town and no whistles. The snow seemed to stymie any sound, and when they pulled into the parking lot, Lyle felt for a moment that he was dwelling inside an old movie, or a black-and-white photograph, the world felt so surreally still. Even the falling snow seemed preternaturally slow, as if each flake were floating in place or languidly flying, rather than traveling down several hundred feet to the earth.

Inside the church the lights were turned down low, and what a pleasant feeling it was, hanging their cold, wet coats on hangers and walking into that long narrow sanctuary, the slate beneath their feet, candles flickering, poinsettias, the smell of pine boughs, the sight of familiar rosy-cheeked faces.

How fragile the world seemed on Christmas Eve, how delicate. As if everyone in the church wobbled on the brink between ecstatic happiness on one side, and the tragic reminder of the departed, on the other; it was a time when ghosts swirled and whispered. It was the one time of year when Lyle felt profoundly vulnerable. And particularly vulnerable to everything that made this evening at St. Olaf's so powerful to him: the extended silences, the sounds of bells big and small, the occasional cough or sneeze, a plastic bag of Cheerios spilling loudly all over the church floor, the flicker of tiny flames, his friend Charlie's voice, Peg's arm wrapped around his, the shuffle of an old man's shoes, the sound of "O Holy Night" or "Silent Night," those songs you ached to sing, even if singing usually filled you with dread. "Silent Night" in a darkened country chapel was, to

Lyle, more powerful than any atomic bomb. He was incapable of singing it without feeling his eyes go misty, without feeling that his voice was but one link in a chain of voices connected over the generations and centuries, that line we sometimes call family. Or memory itself.

AFTER MIDNIGHT MASS, THEY DROVE HOME AND PEG KISSED Lyle on the lips before then crawling into bed. But Lyle could not fall asleep. So he sat in the kitchen, NPR playing quietly on the radio, and simply stared out the window at the slowly accumulating snow. Then, surprising himself, he laced up his boots, donned his heavy red-and-black-plaid Woolrich jacket and his dark green Stormy Kromer hat to walk outside.

The night felt good—soothing. This wasn't the subzero December air that was painful to breathe or slunk through garments and flesh to reside in one's very skull and skeleton. No, this air was wet and almost warm as snowflakes sizzled against Lyle's cheeks and melted in his eyelashes. He walked downhill toward town, through streets so quiet and untraveled, the snow was an immaculate white blanket, unblemished by even the prints of a dog or the tread of a tire. He almost felt as if he were ruining the perfection of it all, though surely a single set of boot prints only lent the whole scene a certain Currier & Ives quality. He walked past the bar—closed—and past the pottery shop and post office and café—all closed.

He paused at the glistening black-silver train tracks. Then, for the first time in many decades, he knelt down and pressed his ear to the rails. He felt and heard nothing, no looming vibration, no quickening or quiver. Just his own heartbeat out there, alone in the night. He stood and walked down to the river.

Such an immensity, and moving as quietly and unremarkably as time. The shores were solidly frozen, as were the waters some hundred feet toward the center of that big, broad channel. But beneath the ice, water bubbled and burbled, rolling and roiling beneath the river's frozen skin.

———

FORTY YEARS EARLIER ON A CHRISTMAS EVE VERY MUCH LIKE this one, he'd begun courting Peg.

A slow, steady snow fell on their shoulders as Lyle and Charlie walked toward the dull sound of the St. Olaf's bell, each toll seemingly loosening more and more snow from the disintegrating sky. They passed a small silver flask of peppermint schnapps between them as they walked, now and then collecting scoops of wet snow to pack into tight balls to toss at the wide tree trunks. Between the two of them they'd drunk a case of Blatz throughout the day as they completed chores around Lyle's family farm.

Lyle's parents had gone to mass earlier that day and, truly, it was not out of piety that Lyle and Charlie chose to attend this service, but rather to rubberneck the out-oftowners, the exiles—easily identifiable in fine, navy blue or camel woolen overcoats, white gloves, colorful scarves, and tall leather boots—come home to throw their aged parents a bone. Lyle and Charlie sat in the back of the church, their breaths positively flammable and the sanctuary slowly spinning around them as if they resided inside a tumbling Fabergé egg; the stained glass windows, the kaleidoscopic light, and the flickering of candles, the tapestries and sculptures of Christ in final ecstasy. And now a young woman sat before them, her hair so long and brown and her earlobes the most exquisite things Lyle thought he'd ever beheld.

"She's beautiful," Lyle said in a loud hiss, hardly even leaning in toward his friend.

"You're practically shouting," Charlie said. "Try whispering."

Lyle studied the girl, inhaled her perfume, wanted so desperately to talk to her, as he might in a bar, but instead he just reached for her hair, as if to pet it, to pass his hands over the top of a field of barley. Charlie swatted his hand away with a slap, and the slap was loud, as if he wielded a wooden ruler.

"I'm in love," Lyle said out loud.

"That's Peg Peterson, I think," Charlie whispered helpfully. "Back from college, maybe?"

Lyle stretched his hand out again and Charlie intercepted it, shook his head, stood and pushed Lyle up out of their pew and out of the church into the silently falling snow.

"Hey, service hasn't even started," Lyle whined. "I didn't walk two miles here to turn around again. Let's at least go back in. Warm up." Though, if anything, his heart was already close to overheating for Peg Peterson.

"Can you behave yourself, sir? Because we're one heavy pet away from being tossed out of church. Pastor Gustafson is eyeballing us. I know it."

Lyle nodded his head. "I promise." He held a hand over his chest as if taking a vow and inhaled deeply the cold Christmas Eve air. It was not quite midnight and the snow was falling more heavily now, no lights for miles around except those filtered through the rainbow windows and slanting onto the white earth in tall rhombuses. No headlights on the roads. The world asleep. They heard the old organ groan and Charlie ushered Lyle back into the sanctuary.

They filed back into their pew to find a small slip of paper torn from the night's bulletin waiting for them. *You're drunk*, it read. Lyle snatched it away from Charlie, grabbed a hymnal and balanced it precariously over his knees—an unsteady tablet.

"Writing utensil!" he whispered loudly, and Charlie seized a miniature, blunt pencil from the back of Peg's pew, stabbing its dull point into the backside of Lyle's hand. The friends exchanged a protracted stare, Lyle stone-faced even as Charlie's smile started spilling over to show his white teeth. Then Charlie turned the pencil over to Lyle, who began scribbling out a message that he rapidly crumpled into a ball and then, leaning forward, balanced the paper sphere on her shoulder where it sat for a long second before his index finger nudged it to plunge out of their sight.

They watched as Peg's parents noticed the note bounce into her lap, and then turned their critical eyes toward the drunk young men who now held a single hymnal between them, its pages opened to any old random hymn, and their voices suddenly jumping in volume as they recognized the organ farting out the familiar notes to "O Little Town of Bethlehem."

During any other service, they would have been quickly fingered as frauds, but now, they raised their downcast eyes from the hymnal (then opened to "Now All Vault of Heaven Resounds") and smiled broadly at Peg's parents, though careful not to make eye contact with Pastor Gustafson, then standing at the center of the church's altar, singing, his eyes aimed directly at the only two inebriated parishioners St. Olaf's had seen in a long, long time, perhaps ever.

At the end of the hymn the two young men sat heavily in their pew, before the pastor had even announced to the congregation, "Please be seated." Just ahead of them, Lyle thought he detected the sniffle of a suppressed giggle from Peg. He closed his eyes gently and relished the fuzzy frequency of blood in his toes and fingers, the sensation of schnapps infiltrating his bloodstream, and the opulence of the building's old radiator warmth, those ancient pipes clinking, trembling, and puffing off steam. He was about to loll off into sleep when he felt something roll off his lap and land in the dirty puddle of melted snow between his boots. He reached down for it, but not before Charlie scooped it up, read the message, and then tossed it at Lyle's chest, scoffing. Lyle peered at the paper, the bubbly cursive: *Coffee at the Coulee Café? The day after tomorrow? Come sober.*

Once again he stole the hymnal roughly from the back of her pew, then ripped another scrap of paper from the bulletin and began scribbling, *I think I'm in love. Mary Christmas.*

He never did say anything to Peg that night, just sat behind her, almost as close as any two humans could sit without actually touching, and he studied her shoulders beneath the silver gray wool sweater she wore. He studied the veins of her neck, the curves and fine folds of her ears so like some beautiful seashell. Her hair, the smell of her bath soap, and the faint fragrance of her perfume, *sprayed where exactly?* How he wanted to explore every line of her topography, each rise of her every rib, the oft-ignored skin behind her knees, the small of her back, the fine soft hair of her thighs, the nape of her neck.

He rose in reaction to the pews ahead of him, where parishioners were already beginning to shake hands and well-wish one another. The bell of the church began to toll lazily, though not too loudly, as it was just past midnight. Lyle and Charlie pushed out of their pew and toward the narthex and the oversized front doors, then raced out of the church and headed toward Lyle's home, Charlie now lighting a cigarette, but Lyle hovering, flying over the earth, snowflakes melting on his hot face, new wings carrying him over the fields and draws and coulees he knew so well.

———◆———

THE RIVER FLOWED ON, SILENTLY. LYLE STEPPED OUT ONTO the ice, scuffling toward the main channel, alert for groans and shudders beneath his boots. Some fifty feet from shore he stopped and listened to the otherworldly noise of new ice forming, one of his very favorite sounds.

It is, he thought, *a miracle, all of it. It is a dream, a miraculous dream, surely, to have been alive at all.*

He walked back toward his house, stepping in his own boot prints, and back inside, removing his coat, he was overcome with exhaustion and considered simply falling asleep in the living room, bathed in the light of their cheerfully glowing Christmas tree, but decided instead to fall asleep in his own bed, as he listened to the snow melt as it met his windows.

(26)

IN THE MORNING, AFTER COFFEE AND BOWLS OF OATMEAL
with blueberries and brown sugar, they drove to La Crosse,
to Shiloh's apartment, where they unloaded a scandalously
large cardboard box filled with presents mostly for Isaac,
but not a few presents for Shiloh as well, and, for Steven,
a copy of Marilynne Robinson's *Gilead*, a book Lyle hoped
might cause the young pastor a moment of pause or even
grace.

As soon as they entered the apartment, Lyle noticed that
the space seemed to judder with some unseen malice that
Lyle could not pinpoint. The thin beige walls thrummed
with a latent menace; Lyle had never before noticed the ab-
sence of decorations, of color, of furniture or books or art,
all of which made the space as bare as a prison cell, only
all the more so when it was chosen, when the family living

there was doing so of their own volition. The Christmas tree, a lone outpost of color or decoration, looked chintzy with its sad tangles of silver tinsel, a few strands of lights, and so few ornaments that Lyle might have held all of them in his hands like a juggler. Shiloh was uncommonly quiet. No—she was compliant, even resignedly vacuous. And in the space her voice once occupied, her warmth or touch, Steven seemed to have further imposed himself, grown larger, more verbose.

"You open many presents this morning?" Peg asked brightly.

Isaac turned to look at his mother, who smiled back wanly.

"We spent this morning in prayer," Steven said. "A group of us. A dear member of our church is in a good deal of pain, and it was all hands on deck."

"Well," Peg said, hanging her coat in the small cold closet near the front door, and vigorously rubbing at her arms, "we're so happy to be here with you all. Would you like to open some of our gifts, Isaac?"

———

THEY STAYED ON FOR ABOUT THREE HOURS. SHILOH NEVER once offered them coffee or even tea. No hot chocolate, no plate of cookies or steaming apple pie awaited them on the kitchen table. The windows were laced with frost, and even inside, Lyle found himself hugging his own shoulders for warmth. The thermostat read sixty degrees but felt closer to fifty. Watching his grandson leaf through a new book, Lyle noticed that the boy looked sickly, his skin and lips the bluish tone of skim milk.

When they stood to leave, Isaac threw his arms around Peg and asked Shiloh if he could stay with them for the night, but Shiloh just seemed to study the threadbare, thin carpeting before Steven said sternly, "It's Christmas, Isaac. You belong here, at home."

It was the first time the boy had ever cried when Lyle and Peg left, the first time Lyle could remember ever seeing him truly upset—not overtired or hungry or exhausted but *upset*, sad.

Lyle lifted the boy into his arms and hugging him fiercely said, "Merry Christmas, Isaac. We love you so much. You know that, don't you? You know how much we love you?"

"Then why can't I come with you? Please, Grandpa? I'm tired of praying. I'm tired of church."

"Isaac!" Shiloh and Steven shouted in unison.

Lyle squeezed him tighter.

"That's up to your mother," Lyle said. "I love you so much, buddy."

———

AND THEN THEY WERE OUTSIDE AS AN OLD PICKUP DOWN THE street revved its engine, putting out a steady cloud of gray-brown exhaust. Another neighbor carried two plastic bags to the curb, one all filled with bottles and jangling loudly, and the other fat with Christmas wrapping paper and discarded boxes and packaging, some of it poking out of the black plastic.

Lyle and Peg drove home in silence, Peg wiping tears off her cheeks.

———◆———

IT WAS A WEEK LATER THAT THE PHONE CALL CAME FROM A number Lyle didn't recognize.

"Hello?" he asked, politely.

"Lyle Hovde?" a small, tremulous voice asked.

"This is Lyle Hovde. Who may I say is calling?"

"Your grandson is in danger," the voice said simply.

"Who is this?" Lyle asked, switching the phone from one hand to the other. "What danger?"

"Can we meet somewhere?" the voice asked. "In Eau Claire, maybe? Eau Claire would be safe, I think . . ."

Lyle concentrated. The voice sounded familiar to him. It was a woman's voice, yes, but distinctive. Precise in its enunciation, and powerful, though not loud.

"Should I go to him now?" Lyle asked. "Is he okay? Should I call the police? I'm calling the police."

"No!" the voice nearly shouted. "You do that and you won't see him again. I can almost promise you that. Meet me in three hours. Randy's Family Restaurant. You know it? Off the highway. Near the soccer fields."

"I'm bringing my wife," Lyle said.

"Good," said the voice. "See you both soon."

"Wait," Lyle said, "how will I recognize you?"

"Oh," the voice almost laughed, "you'll know me."

———

AT NINE IN THE EVENING, FOUR FULL HOURS AFTER THE DIN-ner rush of cotton-topped, blue-haired geezers had filled up on liver and onions or roast beef and mashed potatoes, Lyle and Peg sat listlessly in a vinyl booth, ignoring their mugs of decaf and confounding the kindly waitress, who seemed befuddled by their lack of interest in the pie carousel, dinner menu, or breakfast-served-all-day.

When the children's choir director from Coulee Lands Covenant, this woman who could not have stood even five feet tall, tottered slowly toward their booth, both Lyle and Peg stood up to greet her, this unlikely messenger.

"Sit down, please," the choir director said. "There's so much we need to talk about, and, well, quickly."

The waitress brought them a pot of fresh decaf and after insistent prodding, three plates of pie: apple for Lyle, strawberry-rhubarb for Peg, and lemon meringue for the choir director.

"Sylvie North. I know we've met at Coulee Lands, but I don't know that I've ever properly introduced myself. I'm Isaac's choir director. Talented young man. In so many ways." She shook her head wistfully.

"Well, um, Sylvie, I guess we need to thank you for

calling us," Peg began. "We've suspected at times that we weren't always getting the full truth of things, but we couldn't guess that Isaac was in any real kind of trouble."

Sylvie sipped her coffee, nodding. "Look, I apologize for the cloak and dagger, but the thing is, if Steven finds out that I've contacted you, I'm pretty sure he'll just move them somewhere else. He thinks he's got the golden goose."

"Excuse me," Lyle said, "the golden goose?"

"Yessir. He finds the right community, one desperate enough maybe, they'll give all they have to him. He could set up a church and in six months be a millionaire. I believe that. If Isaac really has this gift, this touch, he'll make Steven a mint.

"But I think he's ill," she continued. "He doesn't have any energy. No energy at all. He falls asleep when he shouldn't. Just passes out. And . . ."

"And what?" Lyle asked.

"I don't know if it was a coma, but the boy was in bad shape not long after Christmas and there was a call that went out for a laying-on of hands. I went to their apartment. We all prayed over him. And he came back. But they blame you two." She pointed gingerly at Lyle.

"Especially you."

"Isaac is diabetic," Peg said. "That isn't Lyle's *fault*."

"Well," Sylvie said, "explain that to them." Then, setting her coffee mug down, she continued, "We're well beyond logic and reason now, you understand that, right?

This is a whole separate ball of wax. This is more about group dynamics, mob mentality.

"Steven is losing control and he knows it. The church divided against him because half of the membership was, uh, how shall I put it? *Aghast,* that he was using Isaac to allegedly heal people. So they left. The other half suspects that he's got something of a wandering eye, that maybe he's been . . ."

"Unfaithful?" Lyle offered.

"Correct," Sylvie said. "I guarantee he's already looking for a new place to set up shop."

"How do you know so much about him?" Lyle said. "Who are you?"

Sylvie sighed. "I'm one of the founding members of Coulee Lands. I helped hire Steven. Saw some of his sermons on YouTube and thought he'd be a great leader." She glanced down at the table. "I'm ashamed, but I was taken in by his looks, by his charisma. I was smitten, I guess. But now I guess I can see him, I can see who he really is, and I want to help."

"You've been following him," Lyle said. "Steven."

She nodded, glanced around the warmly lit kitschy dining room. "That's right. I tried telling the local cops. They even visited the apartment—did you know that? But that's one of the illusions that people like Steven are so good at producing. To the cops, it looks like a clean Christian home. A tight-knit family. They see that and it doesn't really compare to the other horrific stuff they see, some trailer where a bunch of vampires are cooking meth or a day-old baby is already addicted to cocaine. So they dismissed it.

"I talked to some of his old churches. Same thing happened, with young female parishioners. He has two children in other cities. Bet you didn't know that either?

"That's why we need you. We need you to step forward at the right time and do what's right. We need you to be ready, and sooner rather than later. We need you to save Isaac. If we can catch them praying over Isaac rather than taking him to the hospital, as the law requires, we might be able to bring this down on Steven. And stop it."

Beneath the table, Lyle and Peg joined hands.

(27)

FOR DAYS AT A TIME IT SEEMED, LYLE HELD HIS BREATH. HE LAY in bed at nights, hands on his chest, staring at a crack in the ceiling's plaster. Or gazing outside the window, watching the night sky slowly rotate. Never a fast reader, he tore through a book a day. The only thing there was to do was to live, to persevere until the moment when the telephone rang and he sprang into action. Though he didn't know what precisely he would do, only that he'd respond.

Some days he visited Hoot, and that did seem to help. No longer drinking his beloved beer, Hoot had switched to chamomile tea with honey. They sat together in Hoot's kitchen playing cribbage or maybe flipping through the channels on Hoot's TV; Hoot preferred old reruns of *Star Trek*.

"You want to go for a ride?" Lyle asked one afternoon.

"No," Hoot said, "thank you. I'm comfortable right here."

"Want to go out into the garage? Futz with that other car, see if we can fix it up any?"

"I never thought I'd get to ride in either of those cars again," Hoot said. "That was one of my best days. Hearing that old car rumble and then that dinner."

"Is there anything I can do for you?" Lyle said.

"No. Just sit here with me, please. You don't have to say anything. I'm just happy for your company."

———

WHENEVER POSSIBLE, PEG FOUND WAYS TO INSINUATE HER-self into Isaac's life: shuttling him to sporting events, pick-ing him up from school, babysitting . . . Even the long hours of driving were precious to her, chores she'd never have given up, for any *second* Isaac was in her company was a second that he wasn't left around Steven. Shiloh had once again barred Lyle from seeing his grandson, that dag-ger she seemed to hold in the small of his back, stabbing deeply as she saw fit.

Lyle, for his part, found himself missing that old country doctor who might've paid a house call on Isaac and monitored his diabetes, maybe would've even called in favors to big-city physicians in La Crosse, Eau Claire, or even Rochester. But it is tricky ground to occupy as a grandparent when your grandchild is in danger, almost every option untenable and, more than likely, unpalatable. There is no source of hope greater than that which is held by a parent for their children—to lose hope in a child is to lose hope in the world—and Lyle, even now, was unwilling to quit on Shiloh.

(28)

WHEN SHE WAS SIXTEEN, SHILOH RECEIVED A LETTER IN THE mail from her birth mother. Peg had been the one to find it in the mailbox, and she later told Lyle that she'd thought long and hard about burning it. Not because she carried some grudge against Shiloh's birth mother; she didn't. In a nearly infinite number of ways, the woman who had given birth to Shiloh had saved Peg's life, given her meaning, answered her prayers.

But sixteen was a volatile year for Shiloh. Peg and Lyle suspected she was experimenting with marijuana (they'd found a strange glass pipe in her bedroom) and the kids she was hanging out with liked to loiter near an abandoned train bridge where in the fall they spray-painted graffiti on the old steel girders and during the summer and spring leaped off the highest beams, knifing down into the river below. She wore flannel all the time now, every day, and took the new non-flannel clothing Peg bought her to the St. Vincent de Paul store, as donations. Everything she wore needed to look frayed, torn, secondhand, dirty. For years it felt that Shiloh was this sullen ghost, sulking through their house, subsisting on junk food while she eschewed Peg's cooking, communicating through pained grunts and cries of, "You don't understand!" or "You're so old!" or, simply, "God!"

Oh, Lyle was patient. He coped with Shiloh's insolence in the only way he really knew how—with small doses of humor and affection. This was his daughter, after all, though perhaps it was easier for him to remain cool under fire when Peg was the target of so much of Shiloh's anger. But at every opportunity, Lyle enveloped Shiloh in a hug, even as, most of the time, she no more than suffered his affection, with a stiffened backbone and two arms held as rigidly as a soldier awaiting uniform inspection.

"I want to go visit my mother," Shiloh announced one Monday evening at dinner. "And if you won't take me, one of my friends will drive me. Or I can take a bus. I don't care. But I'm going. I have to see her."

Lyle and Peg wiped their mouths with cloth napkins and sat back in their chairs.

"I think that's probably a very good idea," Peg said.

"When do you want to go?" asked Lyle.

———

SARAH HILL LIVED OUTSIDE INDIANAPOLIS IN A NEWER SUBDI-
vision of three- and four-bedroom two-level homes, each
wrapped in some shade of beige or brown vinyl siding,
each with a three-car garage, most with a basketball hoop
standing vigil beside a wide blacktop driveway.

When Shiloh, Peg, and Lyle were welcomed into the
entryway, Lyle recalled how golden the light was in the
house, how warm it seemed. The air smelled of potpourri
and scented candles, the thick carpeting was immaculately
vacuumed. Soft music was playing, trickling out of an unseen speaker.

Sarah greeted them at the door and the first thing she said
was, "Oh, praise Jesus. Praise Christ Jesus, you're *here*. Look at
you. Look at you. A miracle." Her hands were trembling as she
held one of Shiloh's forearms. Then she touched Shiloh's head,
running her fingers through the hair that only two weeks ago
Shiloh had dyed obsidian black with streaks of purple.

Sarah's husband, Lance, came to the door then, a
strapping man with a perfectly angular jaw and the sort
of closely cropped crew cut that spoke of years in the mili-
tary. Lyle saw not a single whisker on his face or neck,
nor were there any razor burns or cuts; even his ears and
nose were scrupulously free of those pesky wires so many
middle-aged men battled at the bathroom mirror. Three
boys, all much younger than Shiloh, greeted them wearing matching light blue collared button-up shirts tucked
into freshly ironed khakis. Lyle stared down at his own
somewhat battered pair of Wranglers. They weren't his

worst pair, the pair he used to change the oil on his truck or to cut wood, but they were worn at the pockets and knees, worn along the cuffs . . . worn. His plaid flannel shirt, he noticed, was missing a button at the breast pocket. And his boots looked out of place there in that brightly curated entryway.

The Hill boys orbited Shiloh like some kind of strange grunge oracle, peering at her clothing as if she'd just walked out of the wilderness after years of wandering. And Lance watched from off to the side as Sarah held Shiloh's hands and occasionally broke down into tears of what appeared to be relief or happiness.

"I can't believe you wanted to meet me," Sarah kept saying.

"Of course," Shiloh said. "You're my mother."

Lyle held Peg's hand even as he could hear her heart breaking, the way a cracked mirror falls in sharp shards, not all at once, but in that slow avalanche of fractures, some pieces clinging to the frame even as the center has fallen away, given up.

———◆———

OVER THE NEXT YEAR, SARAH WOULD CALL THE HOVDE HOUSE every Sunday evening, and she and Shiloh would talk for at least an hour, and Lyle, washing dishes in the kitchen, or perhaps reading a book in the living room, would catch Shiloh's all-too-rare laugh, only then to hear her voice drop in volume as if she were confiding something to Sarah, and then again—the laughter, or giggles, like something Lyle and Peg had worried she'd lost forever or, worse yet, cast into the deepest, darkest, swiftest-moving part of the river.

Then, during her freshman year of college, a couple of weeks before Christmas, Shiloh called home sobbing. Sarah Hill had died of a brain aneurysm.

"I'm going to Indiana for my Christmas break," Shiloh told her parents. "I want to be with Lance and the boys. I want to help out however I can."

"Of course," Peg said. "We understand. Do you need anything? Some money for your travel? We're happy to mail your gifts to you . . ." Her voice trailed off.

"No," Shiloh said. "That's okay."

Lyle had always wondered what happened during that Christmas break, because Shiloh stopped mentioning Indiana, her half brothers, Lance Hill, that warm house in the suburbs—even Sarah. It was almost as if they had never been in her life at all. And then, a few years later, as Lyle lay on a piece of cardboard beneath Shiloh's perennially broken Dodge Neon, he casually asked her, "Hey, kiddo, whatever happened that one time you went to Indiana, after Sarah passed away? You've always been kind of cagey about that."

He felt, in that moment, that it was the safest opportunity he might ever have to ask her about that time, his voice somewhat diffuse as it rattled around in the guts of that jalopy, his boots out in the sunlight, oil streaks on his cheeks and forehead, Shiloh occasionally passing him a wrench. He heard her sigh.

"One night," she began, "I woke up and Lance was in the bedroom where I was sleeping. He was just standing there, watching me. But he was . . . he was just wearing a towel around his waist, like he'd just come from the shower . . ."

Lyle pushed out from under the car. "Did he?"

"No," Shiloh said bitterly, shaking her head. "But he tried."

"I'm so sorry, Shiloh."

"It's okay, Dad," she said, smiling at him. "I defended myself."

"You did?"

"I think he thought I was going to kiss him. Of course he did. He was that kind of sleaze. You know? Like, how could a woman *possibly* resist him? So he really didn't anticipate my kneecap crushing his nuts."

Lyle gave her a big, solid high five.

"You want me to go down there to Indiana?" Lyle asked. "Go down there and kick his ass for you?"

"I told you," she said with a smile, "I took care of it already."

They were quiet for some time. Lyle wiping oil and grease from his hands onto an old rag. Shiloh tying her hair behind her head.

"I'm proud of you, daughter," Lyle said. "You know that, don't you?"

She kissed him on the forehead.

"He kicked me out of the house that night, Lance did. It was below zero. I thought he would've come to his senses and apologized or something. Blamed it all on the grief of losing his wife. That he was, I don't know, confused—anything. But after he recovered he just grabbed all my things and threw them out into the snow. Threw my keys and purse out into the snow, all my clothes, even my hair dryer—all of it. And I remember standing out on their driveway and he called me a fraud. Said my real father had raped Sarah, that was how she became pregnant so young.

"Then he slammed the door in my face. I could see those boys looking out at me from their bedroom windows. I could see their little hands waving at me.

"And then I drove home. All through the night. About ten hours, I think. When I got here, you guys were so happy to see me. You made me chocolate waffles with freshly whipped cream and good hot coffee and you and Mom were just, like, so excited to see me."

"You're the best thing that ever happened to your mom and me," Lyle said. "And your mother loves you more than anything. *Anything.*"

"Sometimes that's a hard weight to bear," Shiloh said. "That kind of love."

Lyle moved a loose strand of her hair behind an ear, which he then tugged softly.

"Part of being a parent is loving your child more than they'll ever love you," he said.

"Dad . . ."

"It's true. You'll see someday. You'll see."

(29)

IT WAS MARCH, MONTH OF WET BACKBREAKING SNOWS WHEN old men and women die not digging their own graves, but simply shoveling their own driveways, their hearts exploding beneath sweaty layers of clothing. Great leaders, great businessmen, men who fought in Korea or Vietnam, women who birthed ten children in their own bathtub, those workaday heroes keel over, clutching their chests, waiting for some younger face to peer down at them and call an ambulance that might rush to their aid, blue and red lights flashing, siren wailing, and perhaps one last drive along the long blue-brown river before departing ahead of the springtime thaws and the farmers again planting their crops.

Already, seven inches of snow had fallen, and Lyle was at Hoot's, walking behind an antiquated snowblower, cleaning out his friend's driveway. They'd had the most innocent of pushing matches there, beside the snowblower, when Lyle had first seen Hoot trying to start the old machine, yanking on its cord to turn the motor over. Two old men still too proud to ask or pay for someone else to move the snow off their driveway.

"Get away from that contraption and rest," Lyle had squawked at Hoot. "I don't need you dying on me."

"Fat chance, you old fart," Hoot had shot back, somewhat out of breath.

It was something of a miracle that Hoot was still alive. But it seemed that the chemo had helped some, that the cancer was no longer progressing so quickly. And maybe Hoot had something to do with it all, too, because he'd given up on cigarettes and beer and was eating healthier than he'd ever eaten before. On days when his energy was high, he'd walk circuits around his house, or greet neighbors from his garage, where he'd sit in the shadows, waving.

"I need you to make it at least until Shiloh's wedding day," Lyle said, checking the oil on the snowblower. "Or if you're feeling up to it, maybe we can mail Steven to Afghanistan. Antarctica. What do you think?"

"I think I've always loved a good December snow, even a January blizzard. But these March snows are for the birds," Hoot said, leaning against the rear bumper of one of the Mustangs, slightly winded. "I'm ready for spring."

Forty minutes later, Lyle had cleared both the driveway and Hoot's sidewalks of snow, but by now, another inch had fallen. Lyle was drenched in sweat, and wet with melting snow when he sat on a folding chair, steam rising off his Stormy Kromer.

"There are moments, you know, when I question why I live here," Lyle said aloud. "Not often. But there are moments."

"Nah," Hoot said, "living here toughens a person up. You move down to Florida or Arizona, what's the challenge, you know? What do you have to fight against? Scorpions, I guess. Goddamn Burmese pythons."

"Look at it coming down," Lyle said, motioning to the blizzard.

"Supposed to be almost another foot before dawn," Hoot said. "Wanna come inside, dry off? I got some almonds. We could play a game or two of cribbage . . ."

"Almonds. My, my."

"Well, sometimes I sprinkle a little salt on 'em. That ain't gonna kill me, is it?"

How nice it was, in Hoot's kitchen—that his friend was still alive, still around, that this time was possible. They sat easily at the little table, in no hurry, Hoot shuffling a battered deck of Bicycle cards, Lyle eating almonds by the handful as he peered out the window, snow crazing the night.

"*Blizzard* is a good word," Hoot said.

Lyle smiled. "Look at you. There's a poet inside you."

"You know what other word I like?"

"I can't imagine."

"Boobs. Looks just like what it is. Sounds like it, too."

"Never mind what I told you about that poetry business. You are who I thought you were. Besides, when was the last time you saw a real pair of boobs?"

Hoot looked off into the middle distance and gritted his teeth.

"Christ," he whistled. "Almost two decades now. I mean, the stuff they show on TV these days doesn't leave much to the old imagination, but . . ."

The phone rang, even as Lyle shook his head.

"Hello," Hoot said, answering. Then, his voice gone serious, "It's Peg, for you." He passed the phone toward Lyle.

Less than a minute later Lyle was charging out back into the blizzard, with Hoot peering at him from the kitchen window as the truck spun its tires for a moment before racing toward Charlie's house.

———

THEY DROVE THROUGH THE NIGHT ON ROADS THEY HAD NO business traveling down, through snow no headlights had shone upon, where no plows had made the way easier, and through which tall snowdrifts broke like waves, shrinking their passage in places to little more than a single lane.

"When a person imagines a crack rescue squad," Charlie said, peering into the gloom, "I don't expect they envision us."

"She said he was barely holding on," Lyle said, "and no one was so much as lifting a finger to help him."

"Yeah, well, I really think we should call the cops,"

Charlie said. "For one thing, Isaac might need an ambulance right away."

"She tried before, but they didn't take it seriously. And on a night like this, with this weather, we'll make it there just about as fast as any ambulance."

"Still, I don't like it. Charging in there like we're the law."

"I'm his grandfather," Lyle growled.

"Okay, *okay.*"

"If for some reason we can't get Isaac, that's the next step," Lyle continued. "But we're going to get Isaac, take him to the hospital, and *then* call the cops. That's the order of operation. I don't want him out of my protection anymore. I don't like the idea of Shiloh refusing care, or anyone barring me from the hospital."

"And what's my role, exactly?"

Lyle glanced over at his old friend, his long hair wet with snow, his glasses a bit foggy with all the excitement, grimacing against the cold and darkness.

"My dad always told me, before you pick a fight, scream real loud at the other guy."

"Why?"

"Because he might be more scared than you are."

"So we go in a hollerin'."

"That's right. And we get my grandson."

"I've always had a big voice," Charlie offered.

LYLE LEFT THE TRUCK RUNNING OUT ON THE CUL-DE-SAC; THE driveway of Shiloh's duplex was packed three deep with cars, as the two old men strode toward the front door. Lyle felt younger than he had in many years, like gasoline was running through his veins. The front door to the unit was unlocked, and they walked right in, easy as you please. A half dozen women stood in the kitchen cleaning dishes or restocking a hardscrabble potluck banquet laid out on the kitchen counters. Lyle recognized all of the faces from Coulee Lands.

"Where's my grandson?" Lyle boomed.

No one budged until finally, a teenage girl pointed toward Isaac's bedroom. Lyle marched that way, seizing the doorknob with a huge hand. It was locked. He pounded his fists on the door.

"Go away, Dad!" Shiloh shrieked from behind the door. *"Please!"*

"I'm not asking again!" Lyle said.

He kicked at the knob only twice before the cheap, hollow-core door gave way and burst open. The room was dark and stank of perspiration and urine. Candles flickered in the corners of the room. A few church elders sat around Isaac, and two younger men and Shiloh stood beside Steven, who held a Bible, open on his lap.

"I'm right behind you, partner," Charlie shouted. "Give 'em hell."

Lyle inhaled before bellowing at the top of his lungs, "Out of my way—I'm taking that boy to the damn hospital."

Steven stepped in front of Isaac just long enough for Lyle to deliver the best punch of his life—a right-hand haymaker that sent the young pastor down on his stomach before he turned onto his ass where he sat, holding his jaw with both hands while his tongue, which he seemed to have bitten almost in two, bled all over the front of his shirt.

"You drive, Charlie," Lyle said, bending down to scoop up Isaac. Then, "Oh, Jesus, he's hot. We've gotta race, buddy."

"Dad!" Shiloh screamed. "Daddy, wait!"

But Lyle did not turn back, moving through the apartment, past the outstretched fingers and hands of people he'd sat with on Sundays at Coulee Lands, through the front door, out into the blizzard, and into the truck, where he held Isaac, closing the passenger door behind him. Then Charlie dropped the hammer in that old Ford pickup and they tore through the blizzard as if all those inches of snow were nothing more than confetti, a ticker-tape parade for this unlikeliest ambulance.

———————

LYLE CARRIED THE LITTLE BOY'S BODY DIRECTLY INTO THE HOSpital and the nurses wasted no time, waving them into the ER, where a young female doctor started peppering Lyle with rapid-fire questions.

"He's diabetic," Lyle spat. "The kid's diabetic and his parents haven't been treating it. He's been admitted here before. He's probably badly dehydrated."

"This boy is . . ." The doctor glanced at Lyle. "Look, we'll do all we can to save him."

Until those words, Lyle had never really considered that Isaac might be in mortal danger, no. That he might die. But as the ER nurses pushed him back to the admitting desk, back toward the paperwork Lyle knew would only complicate the situation more, he feared that he might be about to lose another boy, and that was when he collapsed on the cold tiled floor, dirty snowmelt pooled near his hot cheek, and the last thing he remembered was Charlie's voice, Charlie saying, "Get somebody over here, for chrissakes!"

SPRING

(30)

THE HEAVIEST THING IN THE WORLD IS THE COFFIN THAT CAR- ries the weight of a little child, for no adult who has ever borne that burden will ever forget it. To bury a child is a tragedy many parents never overcome. It blots the sun, steals every color, snuffs out any music—it dissolves marriages like acid, bleeds out happiness and leaves in its wake nothing but gray despair.

No one knew this better than Lyle and Peg, who would always recall with perfect clarity the parade of mourners from St. Olaf's to that church's cemetery a short distance away, watching two of Lyle's old uncles carrying the coffin of their son. The funeral had been held on a cold, gray, rainy May morning when the air felt more like winter than spring. The wind had been gusty, and several in the procession lost their grips on gust-stolen umbrellas and off the parasols went, twirling and dancing down the road, chubby old women giving clumsy chase as the umbrellas raced on ahead of the procession, until a few parents sent their children to do the retrieving, and then the parade was no longer together at all, but groups of children, laughing and chasing those umbrellas as they blew through brown vernal puddles like huge black petals, and the old people whose wet-handed, palsied grips had failed them, how they turned their sad, defeated faces to Lyle with doleful, apologetic eyes and cheeks now streaked with rain.

But there are even worse things in this world than a child's coffin.

Since that March blizzard, Isaac had not left the intensive care unit in La Crosse where he lay in a bed, attached to any number of life-support machines. More than a month had passed, and the doctors could do nothing but wait. The boy was in a coma.

The world had more or less fallen apart: Steven had already left town by the time the police arrived that night, a wide gauze bandage holding his broken jaw in place. A search of his apartment later produced evidence that he'd been stealing from his church, and weeks later a young woman discovered she was pregnant with what could only have been his child. And like that, Coulee Lands Covenant collapsed like a house of cards. Shiloh broke her lease and was now living at the hospital; every night she slept in a chair beside Isaac's bed.

Lyle, for his part, was barred from visiting his grandson. Peg was allowed into the room, mostly, Lyle thought, because Shiloh wasn't stupid—she needed food and water, needed fresh clothes, toothpaste, and the occasional shoulder to cry on. And Shiloh wasn't blaming Peg for anything. It was Lyle who was responsible. Lyle who had destroyed her life.

———

BEFORE SHE MOVED AWAY FROM LA CROSSE, LYLE MET WITH Sylvie North once more. This time, there was no need for cloak and dagger; she drove out to Redford and he welcomed her into his house. They sat in Lyle's kitchen, drinking tea, and after some time she suddenly apologized, and then burst into tears.

"If I'd called you two hours earlier," she cried. "Two hours! He might have been fine. I'm so sorry, Lyle. I'm just so, so sorry."

Lyle fidgeted in his chair for a moment until he couldn't stand it anymore and drew down to the floor, to his knees, so that he might rest a heavy arm on her tiny, heaving back.

"Hey now," he said quietly, handing her his handkerchief. "I don't blame you. How could I blame you?"

But she continued weeping.

"Look, none of this is your fault, Sylvie. You're the only one who told us the truth. You did your best. Without you, I don't know that Isaac would even be alive today, and that's the truth. You saved his life."

She was such a small thing that it killed Lyle to see her suffer such sadness.

"How's Peg?" Sylvie asked, wiping at her cheeks with the handkerchief.

"Oh, she's angry," Lyle said. "Angry with Shiloh, angry with Steven, angry at the church . . ." He neatly omitted the fact that Peg lay some blame, too, at Sylvie's feet. "Peg and I lost a son before he ever reached his first birthday. I don't think she can even begin to cope with losing Isaac."

"And you?" Sylvie asked. "How are *you* doing, Lyle?"

"I'm . . . ," Lyle began. But there was nothing more he could say, and he found himself standing from the floor and walking into the living room where he looked out their big picture window and downhill, toward Main Street, where a train was just now passing through town.

"Lyle?" Sylvie called. "Are you okay?"

But he was afraid that when he opened his mouth, nothing would come out but a horrible wailing sound, all the sadness pouring out of him like a tragic siren. "Thank you, Sylvie," he managed to say, "truly. But you should go now. I know we'll stay in touch."

"I'll be praying for Isaac," she said as she held the door open to leave.

"Good," Lyle said, looking down at his feet. "Thank you for that."

Lyle watched Sylvie drive away in her little Ford Fiesta, hardly bigger than a golf cart, then set his frame down on their front stoop to take in the late-morning light.

It had been an abnormally hot spring, with temperatures in the seventies and eighties all through April, and the trees in Lyle's neighborhood were leafing out a full month ahead of schedule. The river rode high between its banks, and on weekends the townspeople picnicked as close to the water as possible to watch the last remaining rafts of ice float downstream on its muddy brown current.

Sitting around the house did him no good, and Otis wasn't quite ready to begin work in the orchard, so Lyle was left in a crippling kind of limbo. He decided to walk the three miles to Charlie's house.

Hot spring weather always had the effect of unnerving Lyle. He imagined too-skinny polar bears exhaustively swimming the North Sea in search of ice floes to hunt on, or glaciers calving into steadily warmer ocean waters as tourists oohed and ahhed from the decks of luxury cruise ships. Lyle preferred to live in a colder world rather than a warmer one—no one, in his experience, behaved very rationally once the thermometer tipped beyond ninety degrees.

Lyle began sweating almost as soon as he left the house. His head felt congested with stress and sadness, and the warm April air did nothing to tamp those feelings down. News of the dissolution of Coulee Lands and of Isaac's condition had hit the La Crosse media, such as it was, and Lyle had heard insinuating rumbles that perhaps Shiloh would be charged with the reckless endangerment of a child. Lyle wasn't sure what sort of justice that served. All that he cared about now was Isaac recovering.

By the time Lyle reached Charlie's his shirt was soaked with perspiration and he was overwhelmingly thirsty. Charlie was sitting out on his front porch talking to Lyle's cousin Roger, both men sipping what looked to be iced tea with lemon slices. They smiled broadly as Lyle walked up the porch steps.

"Roger," Lyle said, extending his hand in greeting, "I didn't know you were back in town."

"Let me give you a hug," Roger said. "I'm sorry to hear about Isaac, Lyle, I truly am. I'm going to visit him in the hospital tomorrow."

The two men hugged clumsily.

"You didn't have to hug me," Lyle said. "I probably smell like hell and I'm about as lathered as a racehorse."

"Listen, I've been living in Africa," Roger said. "I don't think there's been a day in the last twenty years I haven't either been sweaty myself or given a sweaty person a hug."

"Anyway, thank you," Lyle said. "Hey, Charlie, any chance I could get some of that iced tea?"

Charlie poured him a glass. "Any news from the hospital?"

Lyle shook his head. "The same." Then, changing the subject, "How long are you back for, Roger?"

His cousin sighed. "I think for good."

"Really?" Lyle said, a little stunned. "But this has been your whole life, being a missionary, being in Africa. Where will you go?"

"Maybe back here," Roger said. "I don't know yet. I'm

not sure how to explain it, Lyle. I guess I don't feel called to do that work anymore. Maybe the Lord has another plan for me." He shrugged. "And maybe not."

"Huh," Lyle said.

Charlie and Roger regarded Lyle.

"You okay, Lyle?" Roger asked.

"It's just that . . . I don't know. Honestly, Roger, I never understood your calling, or even what the point of being a missionary was. But it was, I don't know, comforting for me to know that you were out there, trying. What can I say? I'm happy for you, though. Happy to see you're back."

"Thank you," Roger said.

Lyle sat on the front steps of Charlie's bungalow drinking his tea, wiping his brow.

"Would you like to pray, Lyle?" Roger asked. "It might make you feel a little better."

All three men were very quiet. Just the sound of songbirds zipping through the trees and the creaking of the porch's floorboards under their feet.

Lyle turned to face Roger.

"Yes," Lyle said, "I think I would like that."

And so the three men got up, standing in an awkward sort of huddle, their arms resting on each other's shoulders, and on that bright spring afternoon, Lyle closed his eyes and instead of scrutinizing each word that left Roger's mouth, he let the words drift over him like musical notes or curls of smoke, and he thought of his grandson back in that cool, antiseptic hospital room, and he prayed that they would have another day together in the orchard, that Lyle could look up from his work and there would be his beautiful, beautiful grandson, running through the grasses and climbing through the trees and singing his favorite songs and living in the world the way a butterfly does, or a hummingbird. And he clenched his eyes shut and prayed with all his being that this vision he imagined might yet become true.

When Roger said *amen*, Lyle did not want to open his eyes, no. He preferred to remain in his vision, with Isaac, in that orchard, where everything was safe, and not there, on Charlie's porch, the air already so warm, his body sore and sweaty. So he remained just as he was, and Roger and Charlie stood with him, their arms around him, supporting him.

(31)

DURING THE FIRST WEEK OF MAY, MANY OF THE APPLE TREES IN the Sourdough Orchard began blooming, those frail, ephemeral bursts of pink on white. Nearly every bough was decorated in this way. But the year's helter-skelter weather continued, and so it was that Lyle found himself in Otis and Mabel's kitchen looking at a five-day weather forecast that showed temperatures descending into the teens, with freezing rain predicted for the following day.

"Those temperatures," Otis began, "we've had low temperatures like that before. That doesn't scare me. We'll lose some of the blossoms, but not all. It's that freezing rain I worry about, that'll wipe out the whole harvest. It'll bust the trees, be too much for the limbs. I don't know what we can do."

"It's a pity," Mabel said, "to think of a year without

apples. Neither of us has many seasons left." She laughed bitterly. "Well, what can you do? We're old. Maybe this summer we can take a vacation. Visit the Grand Canyon."

"That wouldn't be all bad," Otis admitted.

"Is there anything I can do?" Lyle said. "Anything I can do for the trees?"

Otis shook his head. "We've got forty acres of apples, Lyle, you know that. What are you going to do? There's nothing you can do. It's life. You get bumper crops and then you get years like this. The worst-case scenario is that it's that kind of freezing rain that builds up on the branches until they bust off. Then we'll really be in a bind."

"All right," Lyle said, "I'll sit tight and await further instructions."

"These meteorologists don't know their asses from a hole in the ground anyway," Otis said. "I worked in academia over half a century. Meteorologists had to be some of the least respected scientists on campus. At the end of the day, they look at their fancy radars, they punch in their projections on a computer, shake some chicken bones on a table, light a black candle, and say a hundred Hail Marys. Somebody could sneeze in Seattle and disrupt their forecast. This could be a whole lot of nothing. Go home and wish for warm weather."

The next three days, the cold never quite crept in. The ground was unusually warm from an early spring and night temperatures stayed just over freezing. In the mornings,

Lyle would drive out to the orchard and inspect the trees in fog that was so thick it seemed to cling to Lyle's clothing like tufts of cotton. And yet, the blossoms were safe. He leaned down and smelled them, and what a feeling that was—closing his eyes, inhaling deeply, and breathing in that clean, natural, tender perfume.

From his pants pocket, he produced a pair of garden shears and carefully snipped a short bough from the tree, all laden with blossoms.

That night, after Peg had fallen asleep, he drove down to the hospital in La Crosse. The huge building was quiet, and peering into Isaac's room, he saw that Shiloh was asleep on a mat on the floor, a thin blanket pulled over her. He moved into the room as lightly as if hovering.

Lyle bent down and kissed Isaac on the forehead and touched his little-boy ears and his hands. The child looked as if he were merely sleeping. Lyle held the apple-tree bough near the boy's nose for a moment, then found a glass of water to place the little bough in, leaning it against the wall for support, and once more kissed his grandson good night, though he had a dreadful sense that it might be a longer good-bye.

He left the room without saying a word, without making a sound, and in the hallways he encountered no one, and on the roads he saw no other cars, so that entering his house and slipping into his bed, he allowed himself for a moment to believe that everything, the entirety of the last year, all of it was a grand illusion, none of it real, and tomorrow he would wake up and everything would be perfectly in its place.

———◆———

BUT ON THE MORNING OF THE FOURTH DAY, DARK CLOUDS moved quickly across the sky and the rain came cold and fast.

Peg had already showered, made coffee, and was moving about their house with determination.

"Good morning," Lyle said.

"I'm headed to the hospital," Peg said.

"How is he?"

She shook her head. "The same, I'm afraid, the same."

"And Shiloh?"

"I don't know, Lyle. I think she might be . . . she might have had a breakdown or something. She's not really talking either. I sit in that room . . . I sit in that room and it's almost like I'm with two ghosts. I don't know what I'll do . . ."

Lyle went to her and hugged her tightly and she began to beat her fists against his chest.

"It's not fair!" she cried. "He didn't do anything wrong. And we left him there in that apartment, with those people, those monsters! All they had to do was get him insulin. Bring him water. Take him to a doctor. And they wouldn't do it! They would've let him die. That little boy. Our grandson!"

She just stood there now, leaning against him and weeping, as he rubbed her back and looked out the window into the backyard where freezing rain was already bowing their lilac bushes down, slowly bending those staunch old plants to the ground.

"There are moments," Peg said, "when I'd like to slap her for what she's done."

Lyle understood what she meant, but said, "We have to be there for her now. We're all that's left."

"She's such a smart woman," Peg continued, "to be duped like this. It's so, so dumb."

"I prayed for him," Lyle whispered. "I prayed with Charlie and Roger."

She edged back from him and stared at his face, as if he were a stranger come to their house bearing a mysterious message. "You did?"

Lyle nodded.

"Why did you pray?" she asked.

"It felt right," he confessed. "And I guess I didn't have anywhere else to turn."

"Do you feel better?"

"Maybe," he allowed.

She hugged him again. "I'm going to tell him that today." She wiped her eyes. "What else should I tell him? What are you going to do with yourself today?"

The stoic, rock-solid Peg was back now, ready to be the resilient face her daughter and grandson needed. Lyle often thought that the world, so loudly and violently governed by men, was in fact held together by women like Peg, women who suffered quietly, loved immeasurably, and at the end of each day, put all the pieces back together after everyone's face was clean, their bellies full, and their fears assuaged and disappeared. And then, in the morning, they did it all over again, without the least bit of fanfare—360,000 babies born each day to mothers who feed them, sleep with them, and answer their cries in the middle of the night.

"I'd like to find a way to save the orchard," Lyle said, struggling to master his own sense of defeat. "Any bright ideas?"

Now Peg was buttoning her winter jacket, fumbling for her keys and purse, a warm hat. She looked at him with one hand on the doorknob.

"I know that in Italy they burn straw in the vineyards to warm the air temperature."

"What?"

"That's what I read somewhere."

"Straw?"

"Straw and diesel, I think? They want a lot of smoke, I guess."

"I love you," Lyle said. Then, "How did you know that?"

"What can I say? I like to drink Italian wines. I google things. Good luck," Peg said, leaving the house.

———

LYLE DRESSED IN WARM CLOTHES: THICK SOCKS, FLANNEL-lined canvas pants, a cotton T-shirt, and a warm sweatshirt. In a duffel bag he packed: more thick socks, another pair of pants, two more T-shirts, a sweater, a fleece jacket, gloves, several sandwiches, snacks, bottles of water, and his thermos of coffee. Then he drove to Charlie's house.

"Crappy day out there, huh?" Charlie said. "Want to come in? Me and Roger are planning a day of watching spaghetti westerns. We'll pop corn, maybe make a pot of chili, drink some beers . . ."

"Charlie," Lyle said. "I need your help."

"Well, then, come on in, it's cold out—"

"Charlie," Lyle said, "I'm serious. Get Roger, too, will you? I need you to go over to Willy's place. Buy as many hay bales as you can from him. And get about ten gallons of diesel from the Kwik Trip, too. Bring it all out to the orchard. I'm going to get some wood."

"Lyle!" Charlie hollered out into the rain.

But Lyle was already retreating back to the warmth of his Ford, in the bed of which was over a cord of dry, seasoned oak and a mess of good kindling.

HE KNOCKED ON OTIS AND MABEL'S FRONT DOOR BEFORE LET-ting himself in. At the breakfast table, he told them his plan.

"Lyle," Mabel said, "the die is cast. There's nothing you can do now. Either those trees will survive, or they won't. It won't be the end of us or the orchard. Hell, we'll plant new trees. We've done it before. It's job security."

"She's right, I hate to say," Otis put in. "You can't save all those trees."

"I'd like to at least try," Lyle said with some firmness in his voice. "There's nothing else for me to do but try."

Otis glanced at Mabel, and they both shrugged.

"Well, we were going to visit Isaac today," Otis said. "Mabel was going to bake a dozen cookies. We know he's . . . that he's in a coma and all, but we thought he might at least appreciate the smell."

"You're both very good people," he said at last. "Tell him his old grandpa says hello."

LYLE BEGAN IN THE BACK CORNER OF THE ORCHARD, NEAR the old wild apple tree he'd shown Isaac. He began with a base of balled-up newspaper, then pinecones and birch bark, and finally, a teepee of larger oak logs. Then he knelt down and with a Zippo his father once owned, he lit the fire.

The rain and wind blew incessantly, and Lyle could already feel his face reddening with the cold and wet, but he stood in such a way that the young fire had time to catch and grow, and when he was satisfied it was healthy enough, laid on a few more pieces of wood before moving on to another spot in the orchard.

In this way, Lyle worked his way down through the orchard, building and lighting fire after fire and always in the space between four trees and in those vacant aisles of grass where in summer and fall, Otis and he would either mow or park their tool-laden truck as they pruned the little trees. Steadily, the orchard filled with smoke and light.

Lyle moved slowly down each aisle of grass, building a fire, nurturing its flames, and then moving on to the next one, always glancing back to that first fire, and when he noticed its flames diminishing, running an armload of wood back to the fire and feeding it yet again. Sweat was pouring down Lyle's chapped face as he knelt in the cold grass and watched his countless fires roar. Looking between the trees now he saw equally spaced fires illuminating the slick undersides of the boughs and blossoms. The orchard was very gradually growing illuminated, with orange, red, and yellow flames of light.

It was just before noon when Lyle heard a horn honking and turned to see Charlie in the cab of a pickup, waving at him. Behind the pickup was a wagon laden with rectangular bales of straw.

Lyle walked briskly down the hill to open the gate. "Thought you boys weren't coming!" he called happily.

"I brought the cavalry." Charlie smiled, and from the passenger seat Roger waved brightly.

"Long ways from Africa, aren't you?" Lyle said.

"Wouldn't want to be anywhere else," his cousin said, offering him a firm handshake.

Charlie parked the truck, and then he and Roger leaped out into the rain.

"Now what are you doing here, Lyle?" Charlie asked,

taking in the scene. "This feels like some Don Quixote–type foolishness."

"We're saving the orchard," Lyle said.

"All right," Charlie nodded, "we're going to save an orchard. There are crazier things in the world than saving trees, I guess."

Lyle walked the two men up to his line of fires, showed them how to build the fires in the center of four trees, then clapped his hands like a coach sending his team back out onto the pitch. Charlie and Roger began carrying bales of hay into the grassy aisles between the rows of trees. The rain continued to pound them, now and again turning to sleet, or even hail. The men were soon enough thoroughly soaked, but they moved about the orchard with loads of logs stacked in their arms or cans of diesel, lighting fires here, or adding wood to a dying fire there.

By five in the evening, the orchard was filled with a dense, smudgy smoke lit by the erratic dance of a hundred or more fires, and the three men sat on the tailgate of Lyle's truck, eating sandwiches, drinking hot coffee, and sharing that particular silence that settles over those who have labored all day long without rest or complaint.

"Thank you," Lyle said, "for helping me. I'm just so tired of losing . . . I didn't know what else to do."

Charlie kissed the top of his friend's head with a mustache wet with perspiration, wet with frozen breath, frozen snot.

"You've got a little Saint Jude in you," Roger said. "My favorite patron saint."

The temperature continued to fall. In the forests around the orchard, great big old oak limbs and branches so burdened by the ice crashed to the forest floor, as loud as buildings falling, and the men would whirl, startled by the distant din. In the clouds overhead, arthritic fingers of bright blue lightning moved through the sky, and the thunder boomed out deafeningly.

"Strange days," Roger said, joining Lyle by a roaring fire.

"Sunset isn't even for a couple more hours and already it feels as dark as night," Lyle said.

"You tired?" Roger asked.

"A little bit."

"Go on and take a nap," Roger said. "Change out of your wet clothes. I'm not telling you to go home, because I know you won't. Just sit in your truck and warm up. Charlie and I have things here under control. For a while at least."

Lyle nodded, scratched at his face. "I'm going to take you up on that."

He walked slowly back to his truck and sat heavily behind the wheel. He started the motor and leaned back in the driver's seat and enjoyed the heater blasting warm air at his cold feet and hands. He was very tired, indeed, and it wasn't long after that he closed his eyes, and fell into a deep sleep.

He could not say how long he slept, but he awoke to the

sound of rain thumping heavily on the roof of the truck, a deep thrumming, and outside the fires were flickering, failing. Lyle changed into dry clothes, then headed back out into the storm. Now the sound of branches breaking was more frequent, and from within the orchard, too. He found Charlie kneeling beside a struggling fire.

"It's raining too hard, buddy," Charlie said, his words bending around a cigarette between his lips. "We can't keep them all going, I'm afraid."

There was ice in Charlie's mustache and on the chin of his beard, but his eyes were bright in the firelight.

"I'm thinking about taking Roger back to my house," Charlie said. "The poor guy just gets back to Wisconsin from Africa and we've got him out here, in this horseshit, trying to save a bunch of apple trees. I'm worried his tropical constitution can't handle this weather."

Lyle nodded. "Go on. It was always a lost cause, I guess—I'll just stick around and focus on a few fires, maybe."

Charlie stood, hugged his friend. "I'll be back. If not tonight, then tomorrow morning for sure."

Lyle watched Charlie and Roger load up into Charlie's truck. Both men waved at him, and then the headlights of the truck flashed over the orchard, turned, and pointed out of the gate. Lyle walked to the entrance of the orchard and secured the gate shut.

Now he was alone. He looked back at the orchard from its lowest point. The hillside still glowed with dozens of pale fires. But the rain beat down. Lightning flashed and popped in the heavens like a pinball game. He began walking back up the hill, stoking fires and adding logs or bales of hay as he went. His supply was dwindling. It would be impossible to save all the trees. Even as he walked between the rows of trees, he could see major branches broken off clean back to the trunks, blossoms battered to the ground like so much trampled confetti.

Down in the valley, a train split the night with its horn, long and low and lonesome.

The air was filled with smoke and steam as Lyle piled the remaining hay bales and diesel in the back of his truck and drove to that very oldest corner of the orchard. There, the fires still burned brightly, buffeted somewhat by the neighboring forests. Nor was the damage nearly as terrible up here; there must have been something in these old trees that made their wood stronger, hardier.

Lyle stoked these first four of his many fires, then sat in the truck, running the heater and watching the lightning spark and shimmer in the clouds, like the sky cracking and shattering.

His old cell phone rang.

"Lyle," Peg said, "are you okay?"

"I'm all right," Lyle reported back. "How is he? How are things at the hospital?"

She sighed. "No change. I read him *Paddle-to-the-Sea*. Shiloh used to like that one."

Lyle was quiet, simply staring out at the fires.

"Otis and Mabel told me you're still out trying to save the orchard."

"Trying," Lyle said, "I don't know if I'm much succeeding."

"I told Isaac you prayed for him," Peg said.

"I'm glad," Lyle said. "God . . . ," he began, "I wish he'd just wake up. I wish he'd just wake up and come home with you. We could eat pancakes tomorrow morning and go down to the river."

Outside the smoke drifted diagonally through the diminutive treetops before moving out into the forest. Lyle had very little wood left in the bed of his truck.

Inside his head, a great congestion, a throbbing pressure expanded and pounded, and Lyle knew this was fear and sadness, and something like grief, too.

"Will you be home tonight?" Peg asked.

"No," he said quietly, "I think I'll stay here. Do what I can."

"He would've wanted to be with you," Peg said, "he would've liked that. Tending to those fires. He would've wanted you to make s'mores. It would have been an adventure to him."

Lyle almost smiled. "I suppose you're right."

Peg sighed. "Anyway, I'm going to take Shiloh back to our house. Poor woman needs a shower and a good night's sleep in a bed. I finally convinced her."

"Good," Lyle said.

"Hey, Lyle?"

"Yes."

"Did you bring an apple bough here, to the hospital?"

"Yes."

"It's beautiful. I love you."

"I love you, too."

And with that, he put the phone down, sitting inside the warm, dry cab of his old truck and surveying his last little stand against the storm, felt his courage waning. He had cried enough in the last year and he didn't care to cry now, even as the hurt and sadness built inside him like a boiler about to explode.

Down at the bottom of the orchard, two headlights eased toward the gate. Lyle suspected it was Otis, who, to his surprise, had yet to visit the fires, and Lyle suddenly had misgivings about this whole idea. The orchard was now a mess. *If* they'd managed to save any trees at all, they'd now need to clean up these fires, plant new grass, and clean up what branches had come down with the freezing rain. Maybe all he'd done was make a mess in an orchard that did not even belong to him. He drove his truck to the gate.

"Well, what took you so long?" said Otis from the cab of the apple truck. "Charlie called me and told me you might need a hand so I threw a load of wood in the back here, and I thought I'd come out and save the day. Even brought you some more hot coffee."

"Good to see you, Otis. All right then, let's keep these fires burning."

They drove back up the hill, and stoked up eight more

fires. The rain seemed to have slowed, but a deeper cold now threatened the trees.

"This weather is gone by noon tomorrow," Otis said. "After that, the sun is supposed to pop out and temperatures will be back in the fifties."

The rain had turned to snow, huge, slow-falling snow-flakes. The night was still loud with the sound of tree limbs groaning, then cracking, and falling to the ground, but the snow did something to muffle those sounds as it accumulated quickly.

"Thanks for visiting Isaac," Lyle said quietly. He forced the words out quickly, afraid that if he spoke slowly he might fall apart.

"It was good to see him," Otis said. "He's a strong boy, Lyle. He's got grit. All he's been through."

Otis looked into the flames. His old face was etched with sadness and concern and Lyle could plainly see he was struggling to stay warm.

"Oh, you can smell those apple blossoms, can't you?" Otis said. "Even through the smoke and ash. Come on, let's stoke these fires up one more time."

Otis stood and offered his hand to Lyle.

"You think it's worth it?" Lyle asked.

"I've owned this orchard for decades, Lyle," Otis said. "And in that whole time, it was never about the money. It was always about this. About these trees. That fruit, this smell. It was about having something to do. So help me unload this wood. I don't know if I can take this kind of cold for long. It gets into my bones, and takes me days to warm back up."

Lyle climbed into the bed of the apple truck and began throwing out the logs of wood into pyramid-shaped piles. Then the two men shook hands once more.

"I'll let myself out and shut the gate," Otis said. "And, Lyle."

"Yes?"

"I'm sorry about your little boy."

Lyle nodded and waved through the smoke and gloom.

———

HE MOVED MORE SLOWLY NOW, CARRYING THREE OR FOUR logs at a time, stoking what fires yet burned. The orchard groaned under the weight of all that heavy ice. The snow continued to fall. It was after midnight now, and Lyle's woodpile would not last until dawn. All the hay bales were burned, all the diesel expended. Lyle dragged fallen branches to the healthier fires, taxing work indeed. His eyes burned from the smoke.

Just after one, he crawled into the cab of the truck and slept.

———

HE AWOKE AN HOUR BEFORE DAWN. ALL THE STARS SHONE, every one, and the orchard was a crystal sculpture garden—rows upon rows of little trees, some still bearing their delicate blossoms, all encased in a layer of ice so thick they seemed shellacked. Between the trees, the remains of the bonfires smoldered, only a few of them still flaming brightly. The trees shimmered and glittered like glass in the starlight and the light of the fires, the world so serene, so quiet, Lyle was aware of the sound of his own breathing.

The night was perfectly still, and the moon hung over the horizon like a searchlight. Lyle walked between the trees, the astral glow, the moonlight making strange shadows, and the smoke drifting over everything. Could it even be? Many, perhaps even most, of the blossoms were intact. And the air was warming.

Returning to his favorite apple tree, Lyle slumped to the ground. He lay on his back, in the deep, soft, yielding snow, and felt his heart flutter and skip, lightning pain shooting through his arms and fingers until a numbness replaced the throbbing. He could see the light of sunrise down the valley, over the river, and on the western hills. Golden light in the ice-covered trees. Apple blossoms fell and drifted onto his face, into his open mouth. He closed his eyes and fell asleep.

———

WHEN HE AWOKE, CHARLIE WAS CROUCHED BESIDE HIM, LOOK-ing down at him with obvious concern.

"Lyle? Are you okay?"

He pushed himself up on his elbows but the pain was searing.

"No—stay still," Charlie said, "I'll call an ambulance right now."

Lyle shook his head and reached for Charlie's arm, then his hands.

"I saw him here, Charlie, I saw Isaac."

Charlie shook his head. "Lyle, that's impossible, Isaac's still in the hospital."

"No," Lyle said, tears rolling down his cheeks, "no he was here, and we were going to plant a tree together, right here, his tree. And we lay down together in the snow and then I felt this . . . this little explosion . . . like a hand un-clenching, and this tree grew up out of my stomach, and the roots were inside me and I could watch it grow, watch the branches expand, and the leaves grow, and blossoms bloom and change into apples and we were together and we were holding hands.

"He was singing to me, Charlie. He was singing and playing and I was just lying here, watching and listening."

He wiped his face and Charlie sat down beside him.

"Oh my God, it was beautiful, Charlie. And he was right *here,* right beside me."

"You were dreaming, Lyle."

"Was I?"

Charlie nodded.

"I didn't want it to be a dream, though, I wanted to stay there, with him."

"I know," Charlie said.

"Help me get up?" Lyle said.

"Okay, but we're gonna need to get you to a doctor," Charlie said, raising his old friend up from the ground.

"No, no—please," Lyle said, "let's just stay here a little while longer."

So they stood there looking out over the orchard, down the slope of the hill, smoke drifting between the trees, and hanging in the branches, the white and pink blossoms shining brightly on their boughs, or as they slowly fell into the already melting snow. The western hills brighter and brighter and the sun now above the eastern tree line, the sky immaculately blue, a single contrail swiped across the sky behind a faraway airplane. And from every tree, the sound of water dripping and gathering and running downhill to join greater water.

Now the river shone, a long silver path in the new morning light.

And it shall come to pass in the last days, saith God, I will pour out of my Spirit upon all flesh: and your sons and your daughters shall prophesy, and your young men shall see visions, and your old men shall dream dreams.

ACTS 2:17

AUTHOR'S NOTE

ON MARCH 23, 2008, MADELINE KARA NEUMANN DIED IN Weston, Wisconsin, from complications of undiagnosed juvenile diabetes. The eleven-year-old had complained to her parents for days of exhaustion, and when she slipped into something like a coma, rather than take her to a hospital or call an ambulance, her family prayed for her recovery.

It is thought that hundreds, perhaps thousands of children die each year in America because of preventable health problems, even as their parents and guardians pray for their recoveries rather than utilize medicine or science.

The author would like to acknowledge the clergypeople who have helped in the writing of this book: Pastor Peter Bredlau, Pastor Kurt Jacobsen, and in particular, Pastor Bill Swan.

ACKNOWLEDGMENTS

THANKS TO: TIM BRUDNICKI, MARCUS BURKE, ALEX AND CYN-thia Butler, Jim Carter, Nick Cave and Warren Ellis, Mark Connor, the Chippewa Valley Book Festival, Julian Emerson, Brady and Jeanne Foust, Jason Gerace, Peter Geye, Nick Gulig, Kaitlen and Reidar Gullicksrud, Bill Hogseth, BJ Hollars, Tracy Hruska, Betsy and Sheridan Johnson, Mildred Larson, Sara and Chris Meeks, Nick Meyer and Volume One, Van Morrison, Nik Novak, Ben Percy, Drew Perry, L.E. Phillips Public Library, Brett Rawson, Jeff Rochon, Aaron Rodgers, RZA, SHIFT Cyclery & Coffee Bar, Charmaine and Josh Swan, Mike Tiboris, Hilary and Mike Walters, Steve Winwood.

Infinite gratitude to: Rob McQuilkin—consigliere and maestro, both. Everyone at Massie & McQuilkin. Megan Lynch. Sonya Cheuse. Daniel Halpern. Emma Dries.

Miriam Parker. All my foreign publishers, editors, and translators. All the independent bookstores, booksellers, libraries, and librarians who have supported my career. This book would not have been possible without the support of Bette Butler and Jim and Lynn Gullicksrud. The author would also like to acknowledge the family of Dave Flam, in particular Jill and Derek Pulvermacher, Kevin Flam, and Betty and Jerry Harper.

Love, love, love to: Henry and Nora and of course, Regina—Queen of the North.